Badlands

by Deirdre Chapman

Vagabond Voices
Glasgow

© Deirdre Chapman 2025

First published on the 6th of October 2025 by
Vagabond Voices Publishing Ltd.,
Glasgow,
Scotland.

ISBN 978-1-913212-40-7

The author's right to be identified as author of this book under the Copyright, Designs and Patents Act 1988 has been asserted.

Printed and bound in Poland

Cover design by Mark Mechan

Typeset by Raspberry Creative Type

For further information on Vagabond Voices, see the website,
www.vagabondvoices.co.uk

For Christopher and Jane, Lucien and Jillian, Dorian and Tara, Jules and El, Christian and Fergus, Helena, Louisa, Corinne and Ariana.

Badlands

Chapter One

Cold. Too cold for April. April?
Looking at this he loses his grip and falls a long way, then . . .
Cold. Too cold. For April?
Two things here.
COLD. He concentrates. An iceberg drifts towards him, polar bear on top. Cute bear, not doing much though, so APRIL. April is letters, green letters, vertically stretched, hanging behind those other things that keep the light out, eyelids. He opens his eyes.
The light is coming through curtains, thin, green, shiny and closed. He never closes curtains. Fact. His eyelids snap shut on the fact while he tries to digest it.
Too slim to digest on its own it sets up a craving for other facts, nothing picky, cricket scores, inflation rate, prime minister's name, song titles, anything will do, plenitude is the object . . . *was* the object, but that is shifting now, plenitude not enough, particularity is the thing, singularity, the vital fact, the answer. In search of the answer he will stop at nothing, in search of the answer he will . . . sit up.
He is upright, eyes open, on a bed. He swings his legs off the bed and plants his feet on the floor, feeling it through the soles of his shoes, wood floor, uneven boards, under a rug. He is wearing shoes, black shoes, the laces tied, on a bed in a room where someone has closed the curtains.
SOMEONE. This is it, the essence. His eyes close again as he reaches inside to flush out the person responsible. There's no one there, no one at all.
He opens his eyes. He stands. He is standing facing the window whose green curtains have been closed by a person

or persons unknown. There is a window, there must be a door.

The door opens silently onto a corridor, artificially lit, stretching left and right, right channelling a distinctive and not unpleasant catering smell, left leading to a door marked FIRE EXIT. Right runs towards a T-junction. He takes a step in that direction and the door closes behind him.

The corridor has dark resonant boards muffled down the centre by a strip of green carpet. On the walls are prints. Bare-legged men are heaping shot stags onto ponies, pheasants accumulate in soft mounds, a mountain without trees rises in the background hiding a view of nothing much happening behind it. No doubt about where, then. But when and why? April.

The smell has a name, roast beef, it hides in the walls and, towards the T-junction, hangs in the air. The right crossbar of the T is more corridor but the left leads to a brilliant space like a clearing in a forest, a gallery of golden light, magnanimous in its proportions, opening to a staircase that descends, pauses, is joined by its twin and broadens into a single shallow drop carpeted in something deep and golden that levels to a foyer just as deeply carpeted in one of the yellow tartans.

On the point of descending he stops to consider. There will be people. To be with people he will need a self. To make a self he will need more facts. He touches his chin. Clean-shaven though perhaps not obsessively, he last shaved… yesterday? The framed prints are centred below his eye level so six-two, six-three. And nothing is telling him he needs a cigarette.

His right foot is already on its way, the carpet sighing as its pile relaxes, when he hauls it back and aligns it with the other black Oxford, laced and polished beneath a charcoal trouser leg, knife-edge creased. Faultlessly turned out then but for what? What does he *look* like? Who *is* he?

He is wearing a jacket. It matches the trousers. It has pockets. The pockets are empty. He takes his left hand from its empty pocket and looks for his watch. A watch-shaped patch of paler skin confirms that until recently he had one.

A draught comes from somewhere and there are voices. They intensify as a heavy door closes. People have come in from somewhere chilly bringing the chill with them along with a convivial hum and a whiff of waxed jacket. They are not of his tribe nor, more to the point, is he of theirs though he has history there. He knows this. But he doesn't know himself.

Another door opens releasing the sharp and finite scent of whisky. His senses are on overdrive compensating for the space where an identity should be. Below in an alcove is a dark polished sideboard with an arrangement of roses in an antique vase. Some of the petals have fallen onto the polished surface where their curled margins would, if he were down there, be reflected in the lacquer as in a still life. Next to the roses is a telephone directory. When the waxed jacket people have gone in to dinner he will go down and look at that. He can't now. He doesn't know if he is thirty or fifty, blue-eyed or brown, pleasing to look at or with a face that makes people turn away.

He retraces his steps along the corridor and stops at the door opposite the picture of the wildlife eradication squad where a tarnished 12 in antique bevelled digits says that the style is traditional and the door probably not self-locking.

The handle turns. He steps inside. His right hand reaches for the light switch. On a trestle table is a weekend bag, open. On a rug a muddy footprint and a single damp leaf. On the bed a woman in a green satin dress, very still, very cold.

He closes the door behind him.

Throughout the journey she has kept her mood more or less in balance, but now with that last disc growling to a close and his hand reaching for another she totally snaps.

"Who *is* this?"

It comes out as a bark, but she's cracking up here. He brakes for a sheep on the road and looks at her, the CD still in his hand.

"Because I don't actually care for Tom Waits. Can't stand him actually."

The long, long tunnels of the glens and the light at the end that is only ever the start of another, there's only so much a thinking person can take. The sheep is still there, broadside on, waiting for a change in the status quo.

"It's Leonard Cohen, actually."

She shifts position and turns to look at him, Lomond, Lamont, she didn't really catch his name. He looks injured. He has cause. He's in the driving seat and she has barely acknowledged him since he picked her up but, well, tough. She goes on watching the sheep which is rewarding in close-up, studded all over with plant samples of the Arctic tundra, geography on the hoof you could say, history too, its ancestors famously influential in the politics of these parts. She looks at her watch. An hour to the appointment. He starts to edge round the sheep.

"What *would* you like?"

Echoes from the other world, Charlotte thinks, the one that got capitalism and the industrial revolution. Wider options in her personal life, like not having to accept lifts from boring people with crap taste in music.

"We could try silence for a bit."

He drops the CD on the fascia and she goes back to looking out of the side window. The sky was just clearing when he picked her up outside the bus station, the first car to slow. The night journey from London was endless and sleepless, the stopover for coffee too short and too featureless and the long stretch to Inverness lost in sleep. He had been her saviour; she should show some gratitude. The letter, though, had spooked her.

Rerunning it now she may have over-reacted. The urgency in it that set her hurtling north may have come from somewhere rooted in the scrappy set-pieces of her memory and not in the formal but cordial sentences of a Highland solicitor.

The sky up ahead has worked itself into a semblance of brightness, a sort of bright beige. The grass here is still last year's, blown and bent into clumps like the rotting sheaves of a blighted community of Little People. Miles of it, miles more still to go, kyles and lochs and bealachs, and that unearthly light that tells you that the land up ahead is running out. But before that happens she has to deal with another extinction, the final curtain for Saskia, curtains for the whole family, herself excepted.

She flips back the hair that has been protecting her right profile and takes a fresh look at him. "What *have* you got?"

"Look in the glove compartment."

He is seriously offended; she should be nicer.

She pulls out some discs, heavy metal, Bruce Springsteen, The Lion King, someone called Mary-Kate McMurtry fronting an accordion and two fiddles, more music to slit your wrists to. Although – she needs to pull herself together here – it might help fix her in the here and now. She slots in Mary-Kate and sits back to listen, but her mind is now taken up with the contemplation of gloves. Of *a* glove rather, a glove worn on a hand attached to an impossibly glamorous arm. The arm is Saskia's, as is the death that is bringing her north though these things seem in conflict.

Saskia, eternally glamorous great-aunt, lives in Vienna, or did until one day last week when, still in Vienna it seems, she died. She was old, very old, impossibly old now that she thinks of her as mortal, but until yesterday she was the sophisticated society girl of a city and an age where you dressed for dinner and the music never stopped.

The arm is long and the glove which is elbow length feels very soft when it reaches down to touch her face, soft and pale, not silk or satin, a glove made from an animal. Kid. She is sitting on the floor and the hand reaches down to stroke her cheek. There is perfume and a lot of hair which falls across her when the person with the gloved hand bends further to kiss her forehead. She is engulfed in hair and perfume but necessarily wary for the other hand is holding a cigarette, a long, lit, and therefore dangerous cigarette that comes close enough to her face for her to feel the heat of the fire on its tip and make her wonder again why people smoke. The hand without the cigarette is taking from her own hands something she has been playing with. It's the blue velvet case she loves, not the opera glasses. The cigarette is stubbed out in an ashtray. Not a long cigarette, she thinks now, a cigarette in a long holder. The holder is put in a beaded purse along with the glasses in their velvet case. Her aunt is off to the opera. An overture drowns the soft voice and two fiddles.

April is the coolest month. Is it? No way. If only because of the lilacs. Lilacs?

He surfaces with a jolt. Awake is better. Awake, cold and in a chair.

Something is burrowing in his sinuses and a phone is ringing. He swivels towards the sound of the phone but half way to standing reconsiders and slumps back. He is in the armchair by the window, the curtains are open, there is daylight and somewhere in the vicinity a fucking air freshener sending fumes of synthetic blossom into his airways. The phone stops ringing.

He reaches out to touch the radiator. It's cold. He sneezes and starts feeling around for a pocket. He has many pockets, five in the parka he found in the wardrobe, three in the suit jacket and two in the trousers where he finds a single Kleenex. Where did that come from? The box in the shower room. He stands and flexes a few muscles. The sky is white and the daylight reaching into the room squares up to the orange light from a desk lamp. He turns it off and reviews himself in the mirror, a man affirmatively six-three. He is wearing a blue cashmere sweater over a white shirt and the charcoal trousers. Had he been in a position to choose, this is how he would have looked. His hair is black and his eyes are blue. He thought that might be the case but last night chose not to look. Amongst other things he was afraid to find himself blonde. It wouldn't fit.

He moves back to the window and turns on the radiator. Only then is he ready to look towards the bed. She is still there, still justifying last night's decision to turn it off despite his low cold tolerance threshold. He couldn't release the duvet without moving her.

He is hungry. The two shortbread fingers he ate last night along with the tea he made from the kit on the night stand and the chocolate from the mini-bar were enough to let him get to sleep, but torture by kippers and bacon can't be far off. He didn't touch the drinks in the mini-bar. His head may be empty but at least it's clear.

He fills a glass with ice-cold water from the tap in the en-suite and drinks it slowly. He would like to clean his teeth. The under-floor heating in here has kicked in now and the water in the shower is piping hot. He showers and shampoos using the miniatures on the rack which contain Extracts of Genuine Highland Heather and have a wisp of that plant affixed to silence doubters. Dressed again he fills the kettle, keeping his eyes below mirror level. Getting to know himself should not be over-indulged. He makes coffee using the last sachet of creamer, sits in the armchair and lets the view from the window fill his gaze. And now he is ready to glance back at the bed. She is, alas, still there and still dead. He settles back into the chair by the window to address his morning reading, the tariff of the Achindarnoch House Hotel and the Highlands and Islands phone book.

The solicitor closes his folder. He is done with her now, and she . . . she is totally done with him. With his office, its carpet, its kettle, its teacups and shortbread crumbs. Some remembered shred of the etiquette expected of her family keeps her expression pleasant and in listening mode but in her head she's out of here. She won't process any of this until she's in some space that doesn't threaten her identity. But as she's getting to her feet he pulls out another box file.

"Ah" – he reaches into it – "there is also this!"

She remains standing, observing the sandy neon-lit crown of his head. He is tugging at something that has jammed inside the file, something that seems crazy to have filed in the first place.

Behind his stooped shoulders, the window back-lit by a weak sun, there are gold letters on the glass spelling out in mirror writing GRAHAM MACMILLAN AND SONS SOLICITORS. Above the letters a slab-sided mountain looms uncomfortably close to the village. Now he is slapping the box file, smiling up at her to keep her engaged while his fingers crawl along the desk to find a paper knife with an enamelled crest on the handle, crossed golf clubs on a green background. With the paper knife he winkles out a crumpled chocolate box with a gilt edge.

"Well now."

He tilts the box lid towards her. It is shamelessly exotic in this setting, pink and white blossoms, cherry or almond, framing a street scene where amongst the elegant women stalking past, one has turned to make eye contact with the person holding the paint brush and ultimately the chocolate box. The air is scented with violet and vanilla and something winged and charged with recall flashes past as he opens the box and the face on the lid drops out of sight.

"Letters," says Graham MacMillan. "Her note says," he consults a postcard with a sepia cityscape on the reverse, "for Charlotte if the bastards get me."

Charlotte grips the chair back to steady herself. She heard the words not in the voice of a Highland solicitor.

"Poignant," he says, "in the circumstances." He looks again at the card. "If puzzling."

"The date? What's the date of that?"

He studies her, surprised by the abruptness of her tone. "She didn't date it. I could ask my secretary to look through my old appointment diaries if it's important." He is returning the card to his own file. "It was some time ago."

"Appointments diary? She was here, then? She came here?"

"Certainly."

"Could I *have* that?"

He looks at the card in his hand, apparently reluctant to hand it over. She could just reach out and grab it. She must have it. She knows that view.

"Of course."

He swivels his desk chair and brings out a large padded envelope, drops the card and the chocolate box into it, and coming round the desk, removing the protective strip, calls "Kirsty!" A girl comes in wearing a white blouse with a Peter Pan collar and black bondage pants. She has ice-white skin and striking titian hair which is clearly natural.

"Ah, Kirsty. Could you bring the appointment diaries for the past, let's say, three years."

"No need." She can't stay a minute longer. "It doesn't matter."

"In that case, Kirsty would you be so good as to show Miss Ross . . ."

"Kaufmann"

"Miss Kaufmann . . . out?"

"No probs."

Graham MacMillan, the elder MacMillan Charlotte supposes, hands over the envelope, pauses for another weighing-up moment, shakes her hand warmly and steers her to the door.

On the landing Kirsty calls up the creaking cage elevator, leans round her exuding scents of musk and fresh cotton, and indicates the G button.

"Have a good one, eh?" she says as the cage shuts.

The hotel sits under a mountain. It rises abruptly from the far side of the car park and fills the view in that direction. A sketchy torrent hurtles down, turns briefly into a waterfall then drops out of sight behind a clump of trees.

None of the half-dozen cars parked there can be his for the simple reason that he has no car keys. The pockets, all ten of them – he still can't see them as *his* pockets – were empty. There were no keys on the desk where he first looked, no car key, house key or room key, ditto the nightstand, the weekend bag and the floor. The wallet, which *was* on the floor, held two cards, a credit card in the name of Charles C Merchant and a business card devoid of contact details which read SYNCHRONISED SOLUTIONS. There was no driving licence, no pass card, no bank notes in any currency. There was £6.75 in loose change. The change was on the desk. The pockets were devoid of dross, receipts, ticket stubs, crumbs, scraps of paper with scribbled phone numbers, notably devoid of a phone. There is no diary, no pen. Though he believes himself to be fairly fastidious as well as cyber-literate he can't relate to pockets purged of paper.

He is hungry. In the past half hour, ravenous. The dining room, he imagines, will have a view of the waterfall, the lounge more of an indoor feel. Were it not for her he would be down there in search of breakfast and his identity. Not for the first time he notes the primacy of his unknown self and contrasts it with the response she evokes.

What he does know, that he is not a medic. There was nothing practised or notably compassionate about the way he searched for a pulse or the vestige of a breath against his cheek. He may have shortcomings in the compassion department except that his wish to have no dealings with this girl feels specific to her type. The dress is too shiny, the green too synthetic, the skin too pale – he's still having trouble with the personal pronoun – the hair too bleached, the breasts too large and too encased, the heels too high. Her necklace is too juvenile and tacky. He believes her to be a plant. Perhaps that excuses the lack of compassion. He has spun this out of something complex that leaves him marginally culpable or at least not entirely innocent. Something that will play him like a fish until he can think his way out into open water.

And then she's outside, doing up her coat as a flurry of sleet sweeps down the High Street from the mountain end and off into whatever wasteland lies beyond. She stands gathering her thoughts. Her exit, that was rather hasty. If she'd asked they'd have told her how the hell you get out of here. When she faces left sleet settles on her eyelashes and accumulates around her cheekbone. In the other direction the High Street stretches away with a dispiriting absence of people.

Kirsty would have known about taxis, always supposing they have taxis here. She is weighing up a return to the office against the chance of hitching a southbound lift in a street with no traffic when she spots a man hurrying away from her in the infinity direction and hurries after him. He seems to be speeding up, but when she calls after him he stops and turns. He looks at her intently as she puts her question.

"Tocksi? Tocksi?" He shakes his head.

"Bus then."

"Bus?"

He smiles, shifts his weight back onto his heels and raises an arm in the direction of the blown sleet. His face has lit up and his eyes when he turns to face her are very bright and a strange colour. Ginger. She looks where he is pointing and sees nothing but grey air and a turbulent blank where the buildings stop. She waits, wondering if he is gathering himself to recite the entire bus timetable from one place she has never heard of to another.

"Warmorial," he says, and vanishes.

The door as it swings behind him funnels voices and beer. When it closes the street seems emptier than before. A short walk back takes her to a butcher's shop with no one behind the counter, a bank that is closed and an undertaker's premises she has no wish to enter. She turns again and hurries back to where the voices came from. The door when she pushes it is very resistant. Above it a warrior holding a round shield brandishes what may be a claymore. A plastic supermarket bag has snagged on the blade and flaps in the gusts. The door, a massive studded thing built to withstand a battering ram has a sign that says PUBLIC BAR Someone has written RE before the PUBLIC and AN after it and someone else has tried to wipe it off. She puts her shoulder to it and is catapulted into a small dark room. She senses a communal reaction before the door swings shut.

There is a cluster in the gloom, all men, she thinks. They don't look up. The barman finishes his conversation and comes to the end of the bar with an expression that says he knows she isn't here to order a drink, so now she has to. She leans an elbow on the bar and feels it stick, stops herself from looking down and says, "I'll have a . . ." but the sound of her voice has silenced the customers who are waiting to pass judgement on what she says next. "Whisky," she says. The barman looks mildly interested but makes no move. When sufficient seconds have passed he half-turns towards the grim ranks of up-ended spirits behind the bar. "Give me a Glen . . . oh I don't know." The barman side-steps infinitesimally to widen her view of enough Glens to slice the country in half. All conversation has stopped. "Lagavulin."

He brings it and fills a jug with fresh chilled water. Is it too soon to put the bus question? Reading the room it's much too soon. She pays, thanks him and carries her glass to the table furthest from the door and takes the seat facing it.

She places the glass slightly to her right where it sits like an ornament. She has no impulse to pick it up, let alone drink from it. The solicitor's envelope she places in front of her. Over-stuffed, out of place, it sits there challenging her. In it the undead are talking. It may be the key to secrets, mysteries, anomalies she has long since sworn not to take an interest in. This is no place to open it. She opens it. She leans an elbow on the table and feels the cashmere stick where it mopped up the beer stain from the counter. Saskia's coat, Nepalese cashmere, vintage Dior. She pulls out the chocolate box and its crumpled gold edge flashes a warning.

It assumes an approximation of the surroundings it came from. It will also assume some understanding of family history. She picks up her glass and takes a sip of the Lagavulin. It is smooth and smoky, redolent of something equally out of place. Her father. She puts him on hold along with the bus timetable and the chocolate box and sits back to rerun the past thirty or so hours.

The letter that came from Graham MacMillan was dropped off at the café by Trish who had a proper address and let her use it for formal purposes. On headed paper it asked her to phone him, so she stepped out for a smoke and did that. She is not a smoker but uses a fictional habit to get out of the café when business is slack. She kept her back to the windows dangling an unlit cigarette, and heard a girl's voice answer. She said, "hang on a seccy," and a man's voice said, "Good morning. Do I have the pleasure of addressing Miss Charlotte Ross?" She took the phone from her ear and looked at it, decided not to quibble and said, "That's me." The voice introduced itself as Graham MacMillan. He seemed to know a lot about her and disarmed her into listening properly and answering seriously which she was seldom inclined to do with people in any sort of authority. There were questions to confirm her identity. With that sorted Graham MacMillan explained that he was her great-aunt Saskia's solicitor and that it was his painful duty to inform her that Saskia had passed away. He had had a call from the family solicitor in Vienna informing him of her death and asking him to impart the sad news as he had no contact details for her, and indeed he himself had had some difficult finding an address for her. Since he, not the Vienna solicitor, was responsible for Saskia's estate this would entail her visiting him in his office. At her convenience he said with an acknowledgement in his voice that for a person presently in London such a visit would never be convenient. Where was his office Charlotte had asked, abandoning the pretence of smoking and pushing the cigarette into her pocket. "Sutherland," he said, and was beginning to elaborate when there was a rap on the café window, Jessica signing to get herself back inside, "I do know where Sutherland is," she said. "Of course," said the voice. "Will you be travelling by car?"

"Just give me the address," she said. "No, of course, I have that on your letter." They said their goodbyes and taking the Marlborough out of her pocket she stubbed it automatically under the fake bay tree and went back to work. For the rest of the day Graham MacMillan's words played in her head and at five o'clock she called him to say she would be there tomorrow.

She picks up her glass and takes another sip. The peaty scent once again evokes her father but his side is peripheral in this context. Her mother's wraith flits into the bar, shudders, and leaves. The identity she has put together for herself comes from that side of her family and right now it is challenging her to engage with its improbable cast, frayed but fashionable Habsburg hangers-on, totally out of place in this setting. She reaches for the chocolate box and draws out a letter.

Vienna
Tuesday

Darling Cec,
It's all rape and pillage here at the moment so I thought I should be grown up and Take Steps. You know whereof I speak. Wish you were here. For my sake, not yours.

Kisses,
Sass

Her hand goes to her glass and finding it chunky and square, turns a sip into a slug. Cecilia and Saskia, glamorous grandmother and uber-glamorous great-aunt, to be addressed only by their Christian names. Charlotte embraced by Saskia as a reprise of herself without the vulgarity of producing descendants of her own, Cecilia, enervated and possibly always slightly drunk from the effort of warding off the daughter she did have, Charlotte's mother Julia. Cecilia returned to Britain after her marriage in Vienna during the war to an officer in Field Security broke down, Saskia remained unattached and in

Vienna. Julia at the age of twelve removed herself to a boarding school. Charlotte, the sole product of her many relationships, spent her time between her grandmother and her great-aunt. Summers were spent in Vienna, sometimes dropped there by Julia to stay on her own with Saskia. In Saskia's company she had enjoyed the peace of being with a similarly self-contained person who spoke only to inform or to amuse. After Julia's death in a road accident she and Saskia exchanged Christmas cards but the visits stopped. She must have been very old, Saskia, she had never given it that much thought. Cecilia, two or three years older, died in a care home leaving Saskia and Charlotte sole remnants, or so Charlotte has always believed, of a once distinguished but now totally fucked up family. Each to her own and better that way she thought, she in London and Saskia in Vienna, which city, Charlotte believed until this morning, she had never left. She reaches for a second letter.

Vienna
Wednesday

Dear Cec,
Sporadic bulletins for now until Colin comes and carries these off to the post. You remember Colin? Third cousin once removed, something like that, very much removed in fact, beatific in countenance, absent in manner, ambitions for the clergy but meanwhile in Military Intelligence (he's based, would you believe, in the barracks at Schönbrunn!) and in pretty deep I think. He's promised to pass on our mail to whomsoever is due home leave, so if I break off suddenly it is not the bullet, or only the bullet if also the bloodstain.
    Yesterday I started digging in the cellar. With cutlery, we have some very adequate cutlery. The floor tiles down there were loose, asking to be pulled up really, and the layer beneath was damp and crumbly. The joy of slicing through the dirt with a monogrammed silver carving knife and prising up the bricks with the matching fork . . . I just can't tell you. The very carving

knife FJ would use when he insisted on carving the roast.

It became rather urgent when Colin brought some stuff. Sensitive stuff, stuff that has to vanish for now, he said. Possibly forever, depends how the show ends, he said, no one else he can trust. Our friends in the attic he especially doesn't trust.

Needless to say Mother never goes down here, has possibly never gone down, will die without having gone down. She's well. In the evenings we sew or sing, light source permitting. Who would have thought it would come to this?

Sass

Friday

No Colin yet, but Excavation Complete!!

For wrapping I've used the monogrammed pillowcases, possibly the most pointless of essays into self-advertisement in the house, as if you might need reminding of who you were when you waken, although perhaps a useful aide-memoire to the occasional partner. Anyway it's all in there, the silver and the sparklers as a topping to Colin's layer. Not a moment too soon really. As you know when they carved up Vienna we were lucky enough to find ourselves in the British sector. But lately our erstwhile allies from the east have resisted the constraints of their own sector and gone on the rampage, the victors entitled to enjoy the spoils of the vanquished. We are of course still British in our heads and our speech as well as our history. Last night was the worst since Kristallnacht. The Russians of course suffered terribly but is this the way to avenge their wrongs, dragging young women and mere girls from their homes and the streets into the parks. Their officers seem powerless to prevent it. You remember the Schröders two doors along? Last night for the third time they buried little Bettina in the coal cellar in case they came looking. When I have to go to the door I take one of father's hunting rifles. They don't stay to argue.

Mother did ask for her emeralds but she'd forgotten by teatime. I'll try to find out what people generally use to stick down tiles. Perhaps Colin will know.

Sass

The Cellar
Monday

Still no Colin.

Rather anxious but increasingly resourceful. I've been asked to Help Out. Couldn't be happier.

Am also rather handy with the tiling. There's some useful stuff down here in the cellar, cement powder, main ingredient of, I believe, concrete. It doesn't have to secure the tiles, just fill in the gaps. In my next incarnation I shall be an odd-job man, or, if not odd-job, a man tout seul.

Pray Colin comes soon. Ma keeps asking.

Sass

Tuesday

Darling Cec,

Colin is missing. His friend Hugh came to tell us. He says someone will get these to you in the next week or so.

How can this happen now? This is the aftermath. What used to be called Peacetime.

Pray he's OK.

Sass

This is the last of the letters on hand-cut grey paper, each in an envelope that had been opened with a paper knife and is addressed to Cecilia in London but with no postmark, censor's stamp or other indication that it has passed through a postal system, and indeed from the text it is clear that they were to be picked up and carried in person to the UK.

Sitting back, refocussing, failing at that, she reaches for her glass and finds it empty. The sounds of the pub are far away, the voices in her head clear and concise, talking the talk of adults, going on about the shortages, shortages of bread, butter, candles, cooking fat, heating fuel, soap, problems of another time, problems she had no time for. Their past was indeed another country.

The next batch of letters is on airmail paper, and addressed to Saskia, with all the marks of passing through a complex postal service. She unfolds one. It is from Cecilia in London and drones on about British wartime shortages, the necessity of having friends who farm and can bring one fresh eggs and the occasional chicken. The will to read on dies in Cecilia's self-regarding prose. She lays down the letter and lets the house in the inner city of Vienna swim back into her memory.

She is seeing it in her great-grandmother's painting, gilt-framed, hanging on a wall that is papered in something silky. If silky then surely silk, no compromises were entertained. Then there were the post-war photographs, black and white, of the bomb-damaged city, their house miraculously spared. No miracle there, says a sardonic voice, just good friends in Bomber Command. Hence the payback, someone else says. Payback? The lodgers. Ah, the lodgers.

Then she sees it through her own eyes. Her mother has turned from paying the taxi driver and as she turns with her they see the immensity of the building with a door already opening. And then it's all about people.

A blast of cold air slices through to her table and ruffles the letters. A man using undue force has been projected through the door as she was. He stands there looking windblown and surprised. A stranger, she guesses. His dark matt parka looks new and urban and he has not come here to mingle. He approaches the counter much as she did triggering the barman's delayed response, though this time with eye contact. The newcomer's eyes, recognisably blue from this distance because they tone with the sweater which shows beneath the parka, glance around the room, generally sussing out. Then he turns to the barman and orders. He carries a half pint of something to the table next to hers and she puts the letter back in the box, the box in the envelope and the envelope in her bag. Time to ask about the bus.

Will there be a bus? The barman shakes his head. No bus till tomorrow, 10.36 at the war memorial. And the taxi is currently taking some gentlemen to catch a train at Inverness where it's scheduled to pick up some other passengers and will not return for some hours. He is certainly up on the detail, perhaps he owns the taxi. Perhaps he owns the bar. Why had she given so little thought to her return journey? Because she left on impulse, a dash up the road and down again, nothing that could get on top of her.

So now she's probably looking at an overnight. More outlay, more scenery, more than she can handle right now with her head stuck in Middle Europe. And whatever Saskia's legacy turns out to be it has not so far included ready cash.

"Is there a hotel here?" she asks. The barman, proprietor, whoever, raises his head from polishing a glass and tilts it towards the ceiling which has not been painted since the introduction of the smoking ban. "*This* is a hotel," he says. "The Claymore."

He is waiting for a reaction but all she can imagine happening upstairs is a flophouse for over-the-limit drinkers and a breakfast of fried things, black pudding, bacon, bread, token tomato slice. If he owns the taxi and the bar he will also own the hotel.

"Is there somewhere . . . quieter?" she says into the silence. It might get noisy at night, most pubs do.

"Achindarnoch House Hotel." The voice comes from somewhere along the bar. She picks out the bright ginger eyes of her bus informant, breaking ranks. The barman/proprietor shoots him a look. She aims a smile in his direction.

"Is that in walking distance? Can you give me an idea of what it's like?"

"Upscale traditional," says a voice from behind her. It's the newcomer in the flash parka. He picks up his glass and brings it to the bar. "Picturesque situation. Ensuite facilities, tea and coffee kit, internet connection, dinner inclusive deals. A little draughty."

"You're staying there? Could you direct me?"

"I can *take* you," he says, and setting a three-quarter-full glass on the bar counter he nods to the company and ushers her decisively through the dodgy door.

Outside sleet is still falling. She pauses on the pavement to fasten her coat and to suss out what she's getting herself into. He is looking away, avoiding her gaze.

"Are you on holiday?" she asks as they set off. Nothing about that seems probable.

"I shouldn't think so." He is facing ahead as he says this so she can't see his expression. They pass the butcher, the bank and the undertaker walking in silence and as they approach the doorway of MacMillan Partners he takes her elbow to steer her across the empty street. They pass a newsagent – he glances at a billboard outside it – then a school with an empty playground. She tags all these as landmarks in case the village up ahead erupts into urban sprawl. But the pavement is narrowing here and seems likely to run out here at the mountain end of the village. The road forks and they are clear of buildings so, she thinks, a country house hotel. "You see," he says breaking a long silence but without breaking his stride, "I've lost my memory."

She slows – better not to stop – and turns up her coat collar, glancing back at the solicitors' office, wondering if she should make a dash for it. This feels, after an hour spent among glamorous ghosts, all too real. His silence was calculated, his voice is serious.

The High Street, now that she's leaving it, seems a place of charm. She has slowed the pace further, half-turning from time to time as if she might be weighing up her options, country hotel versus high street, but his hand comes up to cup her shoulder and turn her towards a right fork like a date he's steered into his choice of bar.

"And I'm counting on you to help me get it back."

It's quite a hike to the Achindarnoch House Hotel and he is using the time to sell the primacy of his predicament over whatever boring back story she might have. Distant traffic sounds reach them from the A road she saw signposted but now they are walking along an erratically surfaced road with trees closing in on either side and something is drawing her onwards more urgently than he is steering her. The place is beginning to talk to her, drowning out most of what he is saying. Once this tiresome escort duty is over and before she returns to her travel options she will explore these surroundings. But as they arrive at a pair of handsome gateposts leading to a tree-lined drive a thought strikes her.

"Why me?"

He stops and looks at her as if she is being deliberately obtuse. "You're a stranger here. You can't be involved. Can you?"

Involved in what? As they start up the drive, crunching along a carpet of mulched tree debris it's the 'can you?' that she's hearing, a bleat of self-doubt in an otherwise unvarying and uninteresting account of the hotel layout and his exit from it. For the first time he is wondering about her. Like, who is she?

Who indeed? By-product of nineteenth century economic migration, refugee from light opera in far too many acts. Bit of a hybrid, bit of an orphan if she was inclined to see things that way which she is not.

The question, though, must have been rhetorical because he hasn't waited for an answer. He is telling her in some detail of his escape from the hotel. He watched from his bedroom window as the hotel proprietor who was wearing a kilt saw off two groups of guests from the car park. Once they had gone the hotel proprietor had glanced round furtively then moved into a small clump of trees where he took from his sporran a pipe and tobacco, a pipe-smoker in denial, giving him the chance to escape the building unseen and find his way out of the grounds to the high street and the sanctuary of the pub.

The building coming into sight puts an end to what's left of her attention. It's a converted shooting lodge, she guesses, set in a huge wild garden, protected by a stand of trees she recognises, can even put names to. Beyond the hotel is the end-of-the-village mountain. All this – the building, its grounds, its trees, the scent that is pine resin, the other that is wood smoke, the non-metropolitan bird that shrieks and gets an answer – is familiar.

She is still walking but he has stopped. She turns to find that he is waiting for a response to something and only now does the essential oddity of his story start to hit her. "Why didn't you just" – he has turned away and she waits till he resumes eye contact – "I don't know, just go to the reception desk and tell someone?" He's been holding out on her. Or she hasn't been listening. Now he has all her attention.

"There's someone in my room." His voice is calm and rational. "A woman. She's dead."

He holds her gaze in a manner that, as the implications sink in, is clearly intended to reassure. She keeps her eyes on his and in doing so turns this into a two-way transaction in which she will take the lead.

"A *young* woman?"

"I'd say so. Late teens, early twenties."

"Natural causes?" She diverts her gaze to the beech tree behind him.

"I would think not."

"Did you . . . do you think you might have killed her?"

"Then wouldn't I be feeling something? Loathing? Or guilt?" He notices the self-validating inversion and wonders if she does.

"I don't know." She faces him again. "I've never killed anyone. Have you?"

"I shouldn't think so. But then . . ."

"Did you feel *anything*?"

"Distaste. Surprise and distaste."

"OK. Putting myself in your situation . . ." she pauses to let that idea self-destruct ". . . I don't think I would be returning to the scene. Why are you?"

This is not helpful. Questions are not what he needs from her, actions are. Before he frames the answer he will have to run it past himself. For a while now he's been getting messages from the person he thinks he is, and this person's need to know is off the scale, way ahead of his anxiety to save his skin. His patient sifting of the meagre facts strikes him as meticulous, well-honed, even enjoyable. And that makes him wonder.

She is still meeting his eye. If he has scared her she is still in control. He smiles and shrugs, watches himself doing that. "I have to find out who I am."

The lobby of the hotel is empty. She calls Sean. It goes to voicemail.

"Look," she says quickly, "I'm in Scotland. *North* Scotland, OK? That means an overnight, so I would like you to be, well, *mindful* of, you know, the passage of time? Call me if you get this." Which it's odds-on he won't.

She ends the call as a man in a kilt emerges from a door marked Office. Proprietor she decides. Not manager.

"Good afternoon," he says, then signals an apology as the desk phone rings.

She steps away as he answers and uses the time to take in her surroundings, an expansive wood-panelled hall, obviously a survival from its hunting lodge origins, with a log fire burning in a capacious fireplace and more logs stacked in a sort of heraldic wrought-iron tumbrel. There are animals on the walls, armchairs and a low table with magazines at ground level and, deep into the space, a broad and handsome staircase designed for sweeping down but utilised now, she supposes, for wedding photographs.

"Now, how may I help you?"

"I'm looking for a single room. Just for one night."

"Ah, let me see." He consults a screen then glances up, anticipating her scepticism. "We have a conference this evening. Some of the participants are staying with us. But yes, I believe you're in luck."

All of this spoken in the voice of an actor. An actor, Sandy by name, of not too fond memory, her mother's beau, her preferred term for the relationship. That sort of actor with that sort of voice and delivery.

The desk phone rings again, leaving Sandy to solidify in her memory. Rep revival hero, seen a bit of action, friends in high places. So typecast that when the type died out he lingered briefly then went with it. To her lasting relief. All of which makes the man behind the desk her natural enemy. He finishes the call and looks ready to find her amusing.

"May I ask what brings you to these parts?"

"Business."

He turns the register towards her and passes her a pen, following her upside-down writing with a practised eye.

"A long journey." Meaning that he heard no car engine, she has no baggage, he doesn't believe she lives in Belgravia and she has pink hair.

"Train to Glasgow and a lift from there."

"Ah."

"I didn't expect to have to stay overnight." Bloody Sandy. His ghost has returned to make her over-explain.

"And how did you find us, may I ask?"

"You were recommended." He waits for elucidation which it pleases her to withhold though she has in mind the man with the ginger eyes, not the one currently skulking outside.

He turns to a board and unhooks a heavy brass key but takes his time passing it to her, weighing the hair against her voice and the coat. The key has a plate with the number 24.

"I'm giving you the garden view," he says, "better, I think, for you than the mountain." She is set to argue, but he anticipates that. "The mountain side has the wind. They say it may snow tonight."

"It's April," she says belligerently.

"I know."

He asks if she needs help with her luggage which is plainly provocative. She shoulders her bag and the padded envelope drops out. She retrieves it as he makes a move to come through the door in the desk to help her. As she heads for the staircase he returns to his office.

She pauses on the landing to take stock. It's rather lovely, filled with cold light that is warmed by the gold of the carpet. There are paintings. Someone has painted a man watching a girl chase a hen. She looks up at a glass cupola where damp snowflakes are beginning to turn the daylight grey. Why is she here? Because she is presently in an alternative reality to be waited out, not understood. Because the bus that is coming from somewhere unimaginable to carry her south will not do that until tomorrow. Picking her up, she understands, from the war memorial which is slowly taking shape, towering above her on a day like this with wind and the threat of snow. A kilted soldier stands on a rock-cut plinth with names cut into it, names she is standing on tip-toe to read until her mother pulls her away leaving the soldier to gaze out into the deadlands as she has pictured the place beyond the end of the high street.

There are voices somewhere in the building. The man waiting for her outside will hide from the voices. She should find her room then do as he asked. She has options of course but she is inclined to trust him. A person without a name or a past has a lot going for him. Filled in, he might be less interesting or, depending how the dice fall, more. But not boring. Which inclines her to overlook one dead body.

Never get involved with someone who lacks the capacity to be boring. Who said that? She just did. She does this – invents platitudes, proverbs, cautionary stuff, probably because no one *in loco parentis* ever bothered to. And since these platitudes are her creation she hardly ever goes against them.

I'm safe, she thinks. Not from him, maybe, but from myself. And deploying the massive key she unlocks the door of room 24.

Chapter Two

The dining-room lies to the right of the hotel entrance, close to the car park and the waterfall. It has bay windows, two of them, facing this way. A quick glance has told him there are people in there as he strolls past, off the gravel and across the lawn, stepping round a clump of yellow crocuses, making small adjustments to his demeanour. Slow down, he tells himself, think Wordsworth, notice the crocuses. No, don't look back, that's overcooking it, act normal. Normal? In fact he does seem to know what's normal for him and it isn't tiptoeing around bloody crocuses. The lightweight high-end goose down parka he found in the wardrobe is keeping off the wind which is noticeably freshening, bringing snowflakes now, so closer to freezing than freshening. Perhaps the jacket is really his. He bought it. Sound choice. A sunbeam fingers the back of his neck as a gap opens in the clouds. Is this crazy fluctuating weather normal for April? A distinctively accented voice is saying, "We also have plans to fix the weather." He has heard that recently. If he heard the voice again he would recognise it. The smell of wood smoke pulls him back from the place that was real but not normal and the feel of the grass under his feet keeps him in the present. To ground himself he half turns towards the hotel reasoning that if someone in there, a guest or a waiter, were to raise a friendly hand his troubles would be over, he could make a start on the new normal. New normal? It's the old he's trying to reach. Someone who exchanged a word with him as he spooned cereal from the breakfast buffet. Alone or accompanied.

He averts a stumble and pursues the thought. The bed is a double. But if accompanied it would not have been by her, or if by her and if the bed then not the breakfast. Clear about that and pleased by his honesty he brisks up his pace and glances casually towards the window and sees the head of man seated at the window table turn his way showing a face he recognises and is starting to respond to when the man's arm comes up, points his way, takes aim and fires. He hits the ground. Time passes and when nothing has happened he gets to his feet. The man is still there, laughing now. When he finds who he is he will kill him, meanwhile he turns away and walks back across the grass to the parking area and with his sleeve wipes the grass from his face.

One car has left the parking lot. Three more have arrived. Did he really know the guy? He did. There were two of them at the table, when she gets back he'll have her check the hotel register. Two single rooms or perhaps a twin. That is if they're staying. And while she's there she can check out a Charles C Merchant.

What can be keeping her? She only had to find her room and his and maybe fluff up her hair or whatever she does to make herself feel good. Unless . . . unless right now she is telling the whole story to the hotel owner. Of course she's doing that, she'd be crazy not to, why the colossal assumption that he had her on his side? Because he is accustomed to having women on his side. That would explain his unexamined trust in her.

At the sound of footsteps crunching on gravel he drops behind a white van keeping below window level. The footsteps stop close by and her voice says "Hullo?" and he stands up feeling foolish. She is amused and he lets her see that he can laugh at himself which hides the satisfaction of finding that he is right to trust his judgement. She has put on some lipstick and ditched that envelope. But as he lets his approval show in his face she walks past him and starts to climb the stile over the fence at the far side off the car park. Fence climbed she looks back at him. Taking charge. Well, he can play along with that. "Let's walk," she says. "Let's have a look at that waterfall." And so they do.

For a short waterfall it is surprisingly noisy and too close to the car park for him to risk shouting over it so they stand there in silence observing it. Obviously she wants to and he finds that he can tolerate the distraction, using the time to check her out. Posh punk he thinks, hard to see which is dominant. Frayed denim skirt and black leggings under a very classy cashmere coat. She trawled a high-end branch of Oxfam or she's genuinely indigent with a good source of hand-me-downs. Whichever, she has a near-perfect profile and pink hair. The waterfall is the colour of sherry, on the Oloroso side of Amontillado, and the pool it falls into is ringed with skeletal dog roses studded with orange hips among frills of orange and grey-brown bracken with the tips of green shoots just showing, all of it screened by a spreading rowan recognisable from those of last year's berries not yet eaten by the local wildlife. So he's in the drinks industry, fashion, or perhaps he runs a garden centre. None of these sets his pulse racing.

There is a cultivated patch to one side where someone has planted non-native shrubs and a fingerpost points to a path that leads onwards and upwards, curling round the small bare mountain which rises dramatically but to no great height, so not a Munro or one of those others with a two-syllable name, he knows these things or would know them in his everyday identity. The sort of mountain that could stand in for something higher in a brief sequence with a cast of unfit narcissists. A rustic sign says unnecessarily FOOTPATH.

"I've been here!" She is staring raptly at the sign, something he thinks one could stick in any bit of ground not tarmacked or featured on a road map.

She turns to him, her eyes shining, expecting a response. None comes to mind. This seems to annoy her.

"I *remember* it!"

"You're supposed to remember things."

"But I don't. Didn't. I've never been here. Except that I clearly have. I must have been very young."

"On holiday, do you think?" Patronising bastard absolutely not the way to go. "Look, I don't even know where you're from. Or your name even." Cue to offer a handshake and introduce himself, but he can't see himself as Charles Merchant and of course she knows all this.

"I'm Charlotte. Charlotte Kaufmann."

"Really?" His smile is spontaneous now. "So am I!"

God that scared her. She steps away from the edge of the pool.

"I mean I'm Charles. Charles Merchant. Same name." It *is* odd. And now he has to embrace it. They start to walk up the footpath.

"Do they ever call you Charlie?" Her voice sounds different, quite gauche and girlie.

"I shouldn't think so. But of course I have no idea."

"Oh yes. I forgot."

"You?"

"At school. Not now."

"Where was school?"

"Here and there."

"So . . . where do you live now?"

"London. I suppose there's no point in my returning the question."

"I don't think I'm Scottish."

"You don't sound it. I don't think I am either but I am. A bit."

"How big a bit?"

"Half."

"That is quite a big bit. Mother then?"

"Father."

"Really? And where does Clan Kaufmann have its seat?"

"I changed my name. My mother said it was simpler."

"Than what?"

"Ross."

"Yes that is very difficult. I'm surprised the whole clan doesn't follow your example."

She turns away abruptly and so does he, confused. His plan was to disarm and debrief her, outline some things he would like her to do. This is *badinage*. He knows the term but not his own name which he is pretty sure is not Merchant.

"They lived in Vienna."

"Ah, the Habsburg Rosses."

"Actually my mother was Scots too. Half at least. Maybe more. Quite likely more."

He is losing patience. "Look . . ."

"OK. I went to room twelve."

"And?"

"It was unlocked."

"Well?"

"She wasn't there."

Shit, she's just playing along, she didn't go there, didn't believe him. If the body had been found the whole hotel would have been in an uproar which it was not. Then why had she come back? She has not, he realises, told him what she's doing in these parts, probably because he hasn't asked. Might it be relevant?

"Is there a chance . . . might you have been looking in the wrong room?"

"I'm not dyslexic. I can read 12."

"Sorry. I'm just confused."

"There was a bag in there. On that trestle thing. One of the cups had been used. There were crumbs on the tray."

He is seeing satin, the green satin that was everywhere in that chilly gloom, curtains, her dress, the bedspread, cold, glassy and slippery. A thought strikes him . . . could it be that with the passage of time and a tightening of ligaments causing some shifting in the centre of gravity . . .

"Could she have fallen off?"

"Spontaneously you mean?"

"Did you look?"

"I didn't go inside. You said not to. A fallen body was not in my brief. Why did you want me to look in there anyway?"

To see if the door was still unlocked, the room untouched. Perhaps to see if she had started to decompose, giving him a time reference. Really just to know if they knew. Why had he left the bag? Because he was making a getaway. And he doubted it was his.

"There was no one on the floor." Sounding a little sulky now. "I would have seen from the door. The bedspread was wrinkled. Crushed in fact."

"OK." If he voices this he can move on. "Then someone must have taken her away."

She walks over to the edge of the path and looks down at the slopes below. A thread of smoke is rising from a clump of trees.

"The chambermaid I expect. She's some sort of Slav. They'll be barbecuing her down there in that clearing in the forest." She rejoins him and they walk on in silence.

They have rounded the shoulder of the mountain which has a gentler slope on the other side falling away to a broad valley. Glen. He had hoped for a sight of a main road or a town. The glen has a lake – loch – in it and not much else. Quite a small loch. Beyond it the rise of the next hill has been planted with conifers, already tall and dense, and its outline signals the start of a range of higher purple hills, mountains even, with peaks picking up a low gleam of sunlight which seeps from the low cloud cover. No road of any sort, no buildings. Insofar as he has thought about it he has seen himself walking along a distant road in a different sort of glen, one with a better climate perhaps. And where news is slow to travel. It will lead in time to a centre of civilisation where he will be listened to and believed. Not this way it won't.

Something subsides that was helping to hold him up. He sits down on the grass by the track. She considers him.

"I don't think you're dressed for that." She means the suit.

"I don't think I expected to come on a walking holiday."

It's quite pleasant sitting here. The grass is soft and cool. He could just let things take their course. But she's standing over him, reaching out a hand.

"Come on."

He takes the hand and gets up. Surrendering something small but intrinsic to their short relationship. The sleet is starting again and now it's snowing, big soft flakes which a wind from the empty side is whipping up around them. They turn simultaneously and start back towards the waterfall, but as it comes into earshot and the hotel into view he realises he has made no decisions.

As they reach the car park a sports car draws up, a Porsche. The driver lowers his window.

"Greetings Charles."

He was so sure he wasn't Charles. A more flexible identity has been dangling just out of reach and he caught a flash of it just before the guy spoke. For which reason he will only allow himself to see this as a temporary setback. From the corner of his eye he sees Charlotte walk on towards the hotel entrance.

"I might have known you would be here first," says the driver of the Porsche nodding in her direction. "And accompanied."

In the ensuite, shaving, able now to look at himself in the mirror, he is marshalling his thinking. He has had something short of twenty-four hours to inhabit an identity, an identity he doubts, whereas the average guy has put in a lifetime working on his. How will this affect his performance?

There were people in the foyer, some wearing lapel badges, and on a table a pile of leaflets. A conference. Is he a delegate?

Right now he can't get enough of his face, the blue eyes, the black hair. What does that make him? Easily recognisable.

The guy with the Porsche is Ben. They walked together into the foyer and as he headed for the stairs the guy stopped at the desk to check in. He didn't catch the second name.

The radio has speakers in the shower room – surely there was no radio before, he would certainly have used it – and it's forecasting snow but now that the radiator is flinging out heat it's not his problem. Someone has been in to tidy up and straighten but not change the sheets. There are no bloodstains. He checked. He has a razor after all and the heathery accoutrements now extend to aftershave. He has a clean shirt and with any luck a bunch of mates somewhere in the building clued up on his identity and awaiting his fragrant presence. Ben signalled that Charlotte was *de trop* yet there were women in the foyer. So is he to meet him separately?

The news headlines have a new planet and an extinct marsupial. There is a long item on trust. A poll of millennials suggests that their reliance on social media as a news source is waning but has not yet been replaced by a return to the traditional news media. There has been a Russian-American spy swap at Vienna International Airport. A post mortem on the homeless man found dead in a London street is said to have found traces of a recently identified designer drug thought to be of Eastern European origin. The man was a regular rough sleeper and attempts to trace his recent contacts have so far been unsuccessful. Environmental activists protesting at a super highway through ancient woodland who felled a tree to halt the road works and to demonstrate at ground level the size and magnificence of the endangered trees have been told that they may have cut down the oldest oak in England.

What sort of people would confer this far north? It's safe to rule out industry. He can't see himself in industry unless at a stretch PR. Arts organisations? Faith groups? Environmentalists? Indeterminate inter-disciplinary experts with five or more syllables to their specialty? Big Pharma? Wee Pharma? The thought triggers a snort of laughter. That word takes the teeth out of anything it touches. It has probably screwed up this country's identity more than any gory defeat on the battlefield. This country! Scotland. Not his country. Big Pharma though, any sort of Pharma would surely require an ease with the human body, dead or alive, in which he has found himself to be lacking.

The continuity announcer is trailing a programme on fake news which will look at the effect the undermining of the previously consensual acceptance of facts is having on identities, familial, local, ultimately perhaps even national. Misinformation until recently was associated with war games, the tricks that Nazi Germany and the Allies played on each other, a guy is saying. "The BBC Home Service and the Light Programme and the national and local press were the only sources of news. Political as well as popular opinion was based on these sources. Today we see a very different story."

He turns off the radio wondering how current his own informed self will seem in conversation. Perhaps not current at all. His friends will have to fill him in. If he is expected to contribute to a conference, though, his input will be zilch.

He ties his tie, puts on his jacket, takes it off again, puts on the cashmere sweater and replaces the jacket. It isn't that warm. If it's a casual meet-up in the bar he'll ditch the jacket. He looks for the room key - it's still missing - and is on his way out when the things he has been avoiding stop him in his tracks. Since this morning his room is down a body and up a shirt and a razor. Why? Someone is still on his case, someone who is still around.

He turns off the light and, turning back to check he hasn't forgotten anything, is struck by a pinpoint of light coming from the wall opposite the bed. He turns on the light. The pinpoint vanishes, but the place it was coming from is the painting on the wall opposite the foot of the bed. It's The Stag At Bay, any stag at bay, he's not that familiar with the original. He runs his fingers over the canvas. There is a rough spot in one eye of the stag where the canvas has been pierced. He tries to lift it off the wall but it has been secured somehow though it will allow him to swivel it to one side which releases a chunk of packing material and the sound of men's voices coming from the next room. Two voices, sporadically distinct. There is more packing in the space. They are laughing and he hears the clink of a glass on a hard surface. Words come in snatches, expletives, jargon words, something that sounds like 'Arkadi's hit list' is dropped in so lightly it could be a reference to the Russian charts. "Then there's the big one,"

one of them says. A silence follows this as if they have scared themselves into remembering protocol. Then more jargon words, Cybersoliciting, a reference to Marco Polo which brings a shout of laughter, Tribalism, Narcissism and Exceptionalism. One of the men has moved away, to the ensuite it turns out for there are sounds of peeing, flushing and hand washing, then his voice moves again to somewhere close to the door into the corridor. "In fact you may be about to see an essay into Celtic Exceptionalism." The second more derisive voice says "What does Theo know about Celtic anything?" There is the sound of their door opening and Charles moves across to his own door to hear from the corridor the first man say "Nothing. But he knows everything there is to know about the manipulation of exceptionalism."

"You mean that lot downstairs, the conference delegates?" They are still in the corridor, finishing their thread. "What do they want?"

The first man replies, "Theo hasn't decided yet."

He lets the sound of their footsteps die away then gives it another few minutes before he checks himself again in the mirror and heads downstairs to mingle and to forage for food.

All these people milling about, who are they? Charlotte, combed, re-lipsticked and with teeth cleaned thanks to the kit the nice lady in housekeeping brought her has come downstairs to find herself one of a throng. Of course. The conference. There's a placard over by the desk. She'll have a look at that once she's found something to eat.

Someone has set up a tea and scone welcome extravaganza in a glass-partitioned area of the foyer. It's self service, so no problem there. She hasn't eaten since early morning except for the Kit-Kat Lomond or Lamont shared with her and the peanuts that came with the Lagavulin. A girl sitting behind a desk decked out with identity discs asks her name.

"Kaufmann? Kaufmann? I'm sorry I don't seem to have . . ."

"Ross then." The girl in a scratchy looking hand-knit gives her a long look. It's a look that takes in her hair colour and the attempt to pass herself off as someone else.

"You're press? Press are not invited."

"Oh no, not at all. My name is Kaufmann-Ross. I tend to shorten it."

This seems to make sense and the girl reaches for a disc. "Ross, yes. Here we are, S.J. Ross."

"That's me."

She pins on the lapel badge and heads for the buffet which has three types of scone helpfully halved and half a dozen varieties of jam, each in a ceramic bowl with a botanical illustration of its fruit. She is shovelling gooseberry onto a plate stacked with wholemeal scones when through the glass partition she sees Charles coming down the stairs. He looks trim and sorted. The conference, then, may have triggered his memory and he is set to join his colleagues, ill-matched though they seem.

At the drinks table there are six sorts of tea, similarly identified. She goes for Mountain Tea which has a not too helpful picture of a mountain and is filling her cup from a giant samovar when a man alongside her whips out his phone, slamming his elbow into her cup. Mountain Tea everywhere, fortunately not much infused. He turns to apologise but isn't really seeing her, his gaze fixed on Charles who has paused to get his bearings. "Foyer," he says. "Now." Through the glass she sees two men move across to where Charles is approaching the desk with the IDs. They stop when they see that the desk girl already has him in her sights and is giving him a full-on welcome into my life smile. The tea-spiller who had been moving towards the door pauses and hangs back. She carries her tea and scones past him into the lobby.

"Merchant? Merchant? the girl is saying. "I'm sorry . . ."

"Don't worry about it." His back is to her but she can tell from the girl's face he is making eye contact. "I didn't expect to make it but my final meeting was cancelled and I caught the last flight. Give me one of these and I'll do my own." She obliges and passes him her pen.

He is writing Charles Merchant on the disc when she touches his arm and he turns smoothly without a shift in his expression "Charlotte!" He leans across and kisses her cheek but picks up her sense of urgency, only returning the pen before he lets Charlotte lead him away from the desk.

"So glad you made it Charles. How was LA?"

"Humid. Glad to get to DC."

"OK," she draws him towards the tea room, "Don't turn round. There are two guys lurking at the foot of the stairs. They were closing in on you when you decided to get ID-ed."

"Really? Are there more of these?" He takes a scone half from her plate and downs it more or less in one.

"In here." The tearoom now is nearly empty.

"Can you point them out?" He is loading his own plate, apparently unconcerned, but taking care not to turn.

"Not now, they're still watching." But as they see her look their way they turn and drop back out of sight. The tea-spiller is nowhere to be seen.

"It's OK. They've gone." She looks at him. "So . . . it didn't come back? Your memory?"

"I should have thought that was obvious."

"On that showing you're a career con man or a spook. A spook with the wrong briefing. Did that come out of your memory bank?"

"I don't have a memory bank."

"The frequent flyer routine."

"I fly. Most people do."

"To John o' Groats? I don't think so. Not without a private jet. Is that a possibility?"

"Absolutely not."

"Because if that's a sample of your lifestyle I'd say you're in the enemy camp here."

"You've lost me."

"Look around you. Your colleagues? I don't think so."

It's true. The wired, tailored or constructively de-tailored set he would have expected Ben to be part of would not have dealings with this lot. The people who were here, people he was too preoccupied to notice, have filed through a door on the far side of the lobby. He sees the back view of a man with a stick and a girl with weight problems. The ID girl is beckoning him and Charlotte. Still holding their plates, they go with the flow.

"Sorry sir, you can't take that in there." A girl in a navy suit is glaring at Charles who is still wearing that unhinged smile. He responds by taking the last scone and handing her his plate, brushing her with the smile before he turns away. Charlotte cashes in with her own plate and Charles waves her ahead. She follows the people filing along the rows, trying and failing to place them, environmentalists, neighbourhood action group, market research cross-section with anyone sexy scissored out. Charles is hanging back. He walks halfway down the side aisle looking pleasant and approachable. No one approaches him.

"Did you gather what this is about?"

There is an empty seat next to Charlotte's with a leaflet on it which he picks up as he sits. She shakes her head and returns to her copy. In fact there are many empty seats. He nods companionably to the man on his other side and looks at the leaflet. The front page has a stylised map of the British Isles with the northern half of Scotland enlarged and across the central belt a banner headline, WHITHER SCOTLAND? The question mark is a shepherd's crook.

The utter unhelpfulness of this to a man in search of precision brings on a shout of laughter. A man in the row in front turns to show his disapproval. It is not on the whole a merry seeming company.

On the podium a man in a kilt is demanding a listening silence. Since everything he sees and hears may be instructive he gives him his full attention. Thinning reddish hair, sparse beard, rimless glasses, pale eyes bulging with import, tweed jacket, silver lapel badge, shirt in some sandy coloured fabric engineered to resist ironing. Permacrumple. He snorts aloud at his own joke and wonders if this is a habit. The sporran that presumably keeps the guy's car keys and loose change is fashioned from some small fractious creature whose beady eyes dangling at crotch level seem to be sussing him out. There are hairy socks with one of those dagger things tucked into one, red garters with tassels perhaps compensating for slack knitting and over-polished brown brogues. The others on the platform seem equally averse to synthetics. There is a young man of poetic appearance in something that might be a shepherd's smock, a girl in unstructured cheesecloth with a tartan bandeau round her forehead and an older woman in a black cape wearing a heavy pendant in the form of a Celtic cross. *In extremis*, a weapon to match the sock knife. These are people, he decides, who would not risk their fragile egos on anything that is likely to succeed. And this is familiar. He has sat in the uncomfortable chair, heard the motivational speaker fire up the ill-assorted audience, seen them re-assemble time and time again, inspired and bound more tightly by their successive failures. Heard this, seen this, always with detachment. Never involved.

Glancing along the rows he sees a senior citizen with leather elbow patches, a ponytailed fifty-something with a canvas satchel and a skinny sixty-plus with skimpy statement stubble wearing an over-washed Fair Isle tank top. The people that time forgot. Many of the women are in tartan skirts and again he finds himself arranging them into types, superficially but expediently, out of need for a definition. The older women are fierce, he wouldn't care to tangle with them, while the younger ones share a facial expression that eludes him until he borrows a context. Devout. These people are here to be manipulated. What do they want? Theo hasn't decided yet. The man sitting next to him defies the trend. He is trim and centred and his jacket is acrylic. When he catches Charles looking at him he turns away. Ben is not here. Ben will be in the bar.

The speaker concludes some routine matter of dates and time then prepares to engage. "Friends, Compatriots. Observers too." This with a nod, Charles thinks, in their direction. He unfolds his leaflet to avoid eye contact. "Welcome and thank you for the journey you have made today through space, through time, and through history, a history, we know now, that has been written by others for their own ends." There is a mutter of agreement and a foot is stamped.

"We have come here to the haunted places of our ancestors echoing still in their absence with the wrongs that were done to them" – ah, that will be the Highland Clearances – "and the call to right these wrongs. We will journey together today to a time when these glens were full of our people and their livestock, adapted, man and beast, to our pasture and to our climate which fluctuated only within the bounds of the season. A time when one man spoke out against the evils that were coming from people who had no regard for land and the natural world. One day, he said, these people would reap the rewards of their blindness. The south would be consumed by the sun and the sea and the crops would fail and people would turn again to the north, which had kept its integrity and the purity of its air and its water and the wisdom of its people. One man stood up. One man spoke out . . ."

"A question, sir?"

"Yes."

It's Charles's neighbour in the acrylic jacket. "The purity of its people? I ask you to consider, sir, how the Highlands today would fare without the many people from England who have chosen to relocate here and in their hundreds are running post offices, village stores, craft outlets and in the process in many cases have become spokespersons for their communities." He knows that voice. It's one of the guys he heard through the bedroom wall.

"I take your point, sir, I will be happy to address this later. But if you will allow me . . ."

Charlotte is tugging at his sleeve, pointing to something in the leaflet, he sees the words HECTOR OF FARR, SEER OF SUTHERLAND. He opens his own leaflet and scans it for short cuts to the tedious whole, something he feels he has done often. Then a charged silence makes him look up. This time the speaker is definitely looking his way.

"So welcome, Sir." No special welcome for Charlotte. That will be the hair. "You will not regret your decision to join us."

Pretending to look at the leaflet again he reruns what has happened since he came downstairs. In his efforts to be recognised by someone who could vouch for him he has drawn a blank along with a whole heap of unsettling attention. For a man who wakened with a dead woman in his bed his behaviour has been wilfully deviant. He is now the focus of a roomful of strangers.

The man is saying something about a book. Glancing up again he sees that he is brandishing something book-shaped and there is a pile of books on the desk in front of him. So just a book-launch? The book-launch at the end of the universe. The speaker lays down the book in his hand and turning to a heavily ornate box reaches into it and draws out a smaller book which he holds up for the attention and, it appears, the reverence of the room before beckoning the identity tag girl. He says something to her and now she is heading his way bearing the book on outstretched hands. Everyone is watching. At the end of his row she smiles across at him and hands it over to be passed along. He smiles back at her and takes it from the man next to him whom he has tagged as unobtrusive and relatively normal. The book is small and slim. Tactile, disagreeably so, bound in animal skin, perhaps the left-overs from the creature of the sporran.

The man on the platform is watching him, waiting for a response. He looks down again, turns it over. Reverently, that seems the way to go. Someone has put a lot of work into it. Something coloured is etched into the front cover, a hazy representation of a scholar in scholarly robes. Plus an animal. A unicorn?

Time to take back control. He switches his expression to neutral, fights down an attack of flippancy, prepares a diplomatic response and is saved by the bell. A fire alarm, startling and deafening, somewhere close. The girl who brought the book claps her hands over her ears, the kilted man shouts a plea for calm and the girl in the navy blue suit throws open the door and shouts, "Everybody out!"

The sound is all sweetness. Angel trumpets, clanging cymbals, the grand finale to Act 1. He's out of here, out of everything that brought him here, whatever it may have been, and though he will file out in an orderly fashion he won't stop until he reaches the real world.

Charlotte is saying something in his ear. "Odd reaction." She's right. Harried by the girl in the suit everyone but the platform party is leaving. The platform party is sitting demonstrably tight, looking consummately validated and unsurprised. It's a lot to put into a look but they're doing it. As they rise slowly to their feet they are magnificent.

"Well now," says the speaker.

"*Quelle surprise*," says the lady in the cape.

"I think," says the speaker, "we can draw our own conclusions. We shall foregather shortly."

The man in the next seat has also been slow to leave. Synthetic jacket and jeans, synthetic laptop case. Aware of being noticed he heads for the door and Charles and Charlotte follow.

Outside the snow is thickening. They hang back under the canopy over the front door and as the platform party emerge the lady in the cape looks sharply at Charlotte then meaningfully at Charles. "À *bientôt*," she says. He ignores her as pointedly as politeness will allow but notes the assumption – that he, Charles, or perhaps Oliver, Tristam, Zachary, one of those – is essentially like-minded while Charlotte in her hair colour is transgressive and to be avoided. In fact she has become part of a girly group, hotel staff, presumably drawn to her on those grounds. The entire vista, trees, the car park and the mountain are polka dotted with fat snowflakes, falling so slowly you can track a single flake as it soars in over the silhouettes of the trees then hovers, losing conviction, to become one of a crowd. Behind the snowflakes people are gathered like figures in a Dutch painting. Scarves are unwound and draped over heads, hands tucked into sleeves. They shift and turn like hooded members of a secret order. The car park has seven more cars and a mini-bus. One of the cars has, in place of the jaguar, a creature with a single horn. A unicorn.

He moves away from the building towards the trees that mark the boundary but as he turns back he finds someone is approaching him. The speaker in the kilt and behind him the lady in the black cape. Her Celtic cross swings as she moves, its heavy shine pulsing through the snowflakes. They are after him, those two. He feels the familiar drag of being wanted and not wanting, of being the answer to someone's present need.

He starts to walk away from them round the back of the building, looking for the bar exit where Ben will surely be, sharply outlined, black against the white, perhaps with a cluster of friends. He sees only a lanky boy in a chef's apron leaning against the wall and talking to two plump girls in overalls.

The caped lady and the speaker are now in a huddle with others of the platform party, their backs to him. He edges further away skirting a bed of daffodils and arrives in the clump of trees which arc away to where the hotel grounds meet the mountain on the far side of the car park. The huddle breaks up and re-forms as a posse. The posse moves in his direction.

He climbs over the boundary fence, catching his left trouser leg on barbed wire, feeling it tear. It's sheltered here where the near bank of the waterfall broadens into a shallow slope and flattens out towards the level ground. The trees this side of the fence are interspersed with scrubby bushes which screen him from the hotel grounds. The hotel staff will be doing the rounds, checking the rooms. When they give the all-clear he'll let them get back inside then he'll go to reception and ask for Ben. If Ben is not forthcoming he will check out the cars for accessibility and if he finds one bountifully unlocked, and with a key, drive south.

The snowflakes floating hypnotically close to his eyes, skimming his lashes, bunch suddenly then swoop off horizontally, making as they go an amplified swooshing sound as he drops unaccountably to the ground.

He sits up spitting snow, his hearing strangely muffled. He struggles to his feet and turns back to the hotel to see if he can make sense of what just happened. As he watches, a flame leaps from a window to the left of the door, the window, surely, of the room they've just left. And now it's all not OK, the fresh shirt, the aftershave, the now you see her, now you don't status of dead girl, the Charlotte meeting, the Ben encounter, the oddball assembly and their interest in him. The man in the dining room window and the men Charlotte spotted in the foyer, that's where his focus should have been.

His head spins the facts but his feet are already carrying him towards the unknown side of the mountain, the side that does not face the hotel and does not have a waterfall and dog roses and a sign-posted footpath. The snow is already obscuring what's underfoot, solid clumps of bracken root, brambles, rabbit holes, mole hills, but then, also, his tracks. Briars like mantraps clamp his ankles while snow slides into his sock tops. He falls often and before he can stand has to sit in the thickening snow disentangling his charcoal trouser legs from endless lengths of blackberry.

Higher up the vegetation is sparser so he angles upwards into the wind regretting the parka that's back into the wardrobe. He buttons up the consummately tailored jacket over the featherlight blue cashmere sweater and the fortuitous clean shirt, but climbing into a wind of this force is ultimately self-defeating so he slants back downward, sliding and falling, to traverse the shallower slope of the hill and, pausing to get his bearings, finds himself on the flank he looked down on just a few hours ago with the loch below and the forest beyond and no habitation in sight. Circling further he comes round the shoulder and sees above him the point in the path where they stopped and turned back just this afternoon. He scrambles up to its level surface already a bed of drifting snow with a tangible shift in his mood. Planning now, as far as one can plan in a blizzard in a wilderness and perversely confident. Above the path the rock face is sheer. Below is the hotel. At the side of the path is a boulder dragged here by a glacier or a giant with a flat perch on its surface. He climbs and perches.

Far below a dwindling column of smoke rises from the Achindarnoch Hotel. Two fire engines are there but the people have gone. They will be reconvening inside, warming their hands on hand-thrown mugs of herbal tea. Evaluating, drawing conclusions.

Charlotte will be keeping her distance. He feels a pang of regret, real regret, that he is not going to be able to talk this over with her. He should have asked her more about herself.

Shortly, he guesses, they will be serving the inclusive dinner he never got to taste, reconvening in the bar he never got to see. Press will arrive, first the local guy and later perhaps a TV crew. A bomb is a bomb or at least an explosive device. They will tell their tales and perhaps – for he is certainly missing – he will come into it. The sharp-suited stranger who showed up then vanished right after the bomb went off. A girl in a green dress is also missing, though perhaps not missed. He feels a first stirring of compassion for her. Someone may put one and one together and the police will want to talk to a man of medium build, six feet plus, dark hair, blue eyes, last seen in a dark suit and blue sweater. Charlotte will be questioned. He hazards a guess that she will know nothing. What will they make of her? Will the hair be a factor? They will look at the hotel register where they may or may not find a Charles Merchant.

Misinformation. How easily it starts. And how it tugs at what used to be his memory. The global reach of misinformation and its propagators must be delineated and kept apart to avoid the horror of a consensus of untruth. Where did that come from? Not a news headline, he thinks, but from the cloud that is his recent memory.

He will sit here a little longer. His tracks now will be totally hidden. He will retrace his steps to the empty side of the mountain and climb down to the loch, drink from it, then find his way to a road where, easily acceptable as a snow-stranded and well turned out motorist who has walked some way from his car, he will accept a lift as far and as fast from the Achindarnoch Hotel as the sod's law of passing vehicles will allow.

Chapter Three

When Sean calls Charlotte is in the bath. She scrambles out and grabs a towel then perches on the edge of the bed to listen to a rambling tale of snarl-ups and fuck-ups in the Earl's Court Road.

"Sean, this is very local."

"What? Oh yeah. Up north."

He says this in his idea of a Scots accent but at least he seems to know where she is.

"Nice, is it?"

"Snowing."

"Much doing there?"

"We had a bomb scare. Not a scare, an actual bomb. Which is *more* scary obviously."

"No shit. Cool. So what's the big story?"

"In the morning I'm catching a bus to Inverness. Train from there then, well, maybe another train."

"So you'll be back around when? Four? Five?"

"Sean, have you ever been to Scotland?"

"Sure. Fringe gig. Nice town Edinburgh but, you know, draughty? They want to build it higher, Edinburgh. Keep out those draughts."

"OK. If you ever looked at a map you'll have seen some space above that area. I'm in there. Near the top. It takes time."

"So, Wednesday night then? No I can't do Wednesday. Got a gig."

"Forget it. I'll call you when I'm back."

This is pathetic. Not the impulse – if you feel like you're falling off the map then phone a friend is a good option – but the people in her contacts file are electively and perhaps selectively peripheral. She should have a proper friend in there, someone who worries. The sort of person all those 'we're just getting into Waterloo' calls are aimed at. And just as soon as she's back in civilisation she will find such a friend.

"Charlotte? You there?" Bird in the hand though, Sean.

"Look Sean. There are some iffy people here."

"Seen them, yeah. Blue faces. Nasty turn of phrase. You want to be careful babe."

"Yes, well, that's rather the point. If I'm not back . . . if you don't hear from me by . . . OK make it Thursday . . . will you check that out?"

"What? You mean police and stuff?"

"Well perhaps not in the first instance. You could try phoning here. I'm staying at the Achindarnoch House Hotel. I'll give you the number. Write it down."

"I don't know, Charlotte. Haven't seen a pen in a while."

"Then go looking, Sean. I'll hold."

When he comes back triumphant and she's said it all twice she remembers gold lettering on a window pane and old filing cabinets presumably full of files, one of which will have her details and some hint of the background story so she gives him that number too. Then she dresses in the clothes she came in and slumps into the armchair by the window with the garden view to consider the events of the day.

There are ghosts here. Ghosts that may share her DNA. And, possibly, graves.

No one much mentioned graves that she can recall when she was growing up, but then no one would have mistaken her for a person halfway interested in dead people. What graves actually are, she thinks now, is a storage solution. The stones, the flowers, the grief, the guilt trips, that's just accessorising. Somewhere up here there is DNA in the ground that, if they were to dig the person up, would match her own.

So where are they, those graves? Who would know? It is odd – seemed odd from the outset which is why this trip so spooked her – that Saskia, flamboyantly, unshakably cosmopolitan

Saskia, retained enough of a connection with these parts to have left the senior MacMillan manning her departure gate. Although she never actually came here. Although she, Charlotte, believed that she, Saskia, never came here, the senior MacMillan believes her to have sat opposite him in his client chair, a man of integrity and a matter of record. The old desk diary would not lie.

The waitress finds her a table by the door, the last free table in the dining room. The conference people have taken up all but two in this vast room, two rooms in fact with connecting double doors. The other knitwear-free party comprises four men, smart casual and self-contained, none of them the guy in the Porsche.

The menu is weird, Mulligatawny Soup, Blanquette de Veau, Toad-in-the-Hole, a rather racy Chicken Maryland, Cabinet Pudding – as if someone back there in the kitchen has been toiling on through the decades, blind to pasta and ricotta and spinach. She sits back and feels an unfamiliar calm take hold of her. There is a shift in the ambience as if someone has turned down the volume of the room and she is sitting here next to the knobbly wallpaper and the oak panelling and her feet don't reach the floor. People are talking but not to her until someone leans over and says, "I want to see that plate cleared." She can see it, the plate, a giant plate with blue scenery all over it and something disgusting they actually expect her to eat. She'll push it around for a bit until they've lost interest then she'll slide down onto the floor and sit on the tiger-skin rug and stroke the tiger's head while they smoke and drink and argue. She will look up and ask how it got here, the tiger. Someone will say, "Jock shot it." Jock is the man in the picture. She listens to the wind howling outside and wonders if there are other tigers out there, crouching in the bracken. She wonders if Jock will come in with his rifle and another tiger folded over his arm.

By the time the waitress arrives wine is looking inappropriately adult and she orders Coke. For eats she goes for Crevettes Marie Rose and Sole Veronique and schedules Apple Charlotte for afters. When eating alone it is necessary to read. She reaches into her bag for the unsatisfactory paperback from the train but there are only thirty pages remaining and since she doesn't know if she can sleep without reading, it might be time to crack the book-free solo eating thing. You look around once then go back into the stuff in your head. That portrait on the wall, could it be Jock? You can watch the door but better not watch for Charles.

The waitress comes over bringing a pleasant looking couple who hover apologetically behind her. Would she mind? They are regular guests who don't usually bother to book only they didn't know about the conference, and it's their wedding anniversary. She smiles and they sit and now she has a family.

They have a farm not far from here. He is Archie, she is Catriona, Charlotte is Charlotte in a fresh version she is trying out. Archie is a giant with a bone-crushing handshake, Catriona, five feet nothing in a silk blouse and jade earrings and is giving out wafts of a familiar scent.

"Which anniversary?" she asks.

"Fifty-fifth," says Archie.

"Which one is that?" It's the sort of thing, she believes, that people do ask.

"Fifty-fifth," says Archie, raising his voice.

"The lassie isn't deaf, Archie. she means silver, gold, that kind of thing, don't you dear? You know, I've no idea. We don't make a song and dance of it, it comes round anyway. An evening without cooking that's got to be good, hasn't it? We've never bothered to book. Who are all these people, do you know?"

"A conference."

"What about?"

"There you have me."

"A douce-looking bunch right enough," says Archie. "Just a wee bit annoying. Not enough that you'd want to blow them up, mind."

"Oh yes," says Catriona excitedly. "The receptionist just told us. We didn't catch the news, we had an order to finish. Not too much damage done, she says. The big window in the function room, it used to be the ballroom, is blown out and the curtains gone. They'll need to redecorate. Who would do that do you think?"

"The laird now," says Archie. "There's plenty of folk might have lit the fuse if he'd been in."

"Now Archie. The lassie's not from around here."

"Even so."

"Anyway. For us it would have been an hour's drive near enough to the Wilderness Lodge if they'd had to close down here, near on a minute for every year and that's without the snow coming on . . . well, that or the Claymore and frankly I'd sooner heat up something from the freezer."

The waitress comes and they order and Catriona asks Charlotte where she's from and in a voice she barely recognises as her own she says, "My great-grandfather came from somewhere near here."

People that far back are fictions, not relatives, she has never connected with them and no one has ever asked. If they were alive you would have to go and visit them, two things not much practised in her family, staying alive and visiting.

"Really? Where was that, do you know?"

"It was called Tigh a' Chaoruinn."

"Goodness me. What was his name?"

"Lachlan. Lachlan MacPherson."

"Well now, there's a thing. Back in the day we heard a lot about him."

"You did?"

"My mum used to help out over there. Fine looking lad she said. Only turned seventeen when they eloped."

Eloped? She doesn't voice this but Catriona senses her surprise and pauses to choose her words: She says, "Christina was . . ." Not a day over fourteen? A right wee baggage? Ten years his senior? A bit of a drama queen? ". . . from here of course." Ah. Here. The mountain, the wallpaper, the ghosts. But here might not mean here, up here. Up here, here might be vast.

"Here. This hotel. It was a house then of course. This was Jock's place. Jock Ross. And of course he didn't approve so they went off abroad somewhere."

"Bohemia."

"Bohemia? That's a real place then?"

"Now the Czech Republic."

"Fancy that now. I thought that was in Paris, The Artists' Quarter."

As did everyone at school until she ditched her back story. Other people's ancestors went to Canada. She had to be making it up.

Christina? There was no Christina she could remember in her mother's telling of things. Cecilia and Saskia stepped straight out of a painting on the drawing room wall. But Saskia's letters featured a person known to them as Mother. No Father, just a Mother who to the best of her knowledge had never in her life gone down to the cellar. A creature of the drawing room who sang and painted and asked for her emeralds then forgot all about them. This, then, was Christina who, married or not, retained her surname, who grew up, indeed was probably born in this house and moved to Bohemia then Vienna. Eloped to Bohemia, how cool was that? Eloped because pregnant? In which case grandmother Cecilia, the eldest by two years, had been conceived in this house. Or more likely the garden.

She is chasing some shredded lettuce round the bottom of a glass with a hinged crayfish tail while she works through all this and Catriona is watching her anxiously. They will be wondering why she has come back. They will see it as back. It is totally not back. This is *terra* totally *incognita*.

"Is there a cemetery near here?"

As she says this the Zentralfriedhof in Vienna muscles in. From the flower seller at the gate they are buying sheaves of lilies to carry up the endless avenue to the Ehrengraben at the top facing across to the musicians on the other side. Catriona is saying something but she is hearing the clip clop of horses' hooves as the fiakers carry the old and the lazy and the important and busy to their relatives' last resting places in what they always tell her is the biggest cemetery in Europe. They arrange the lilies in an urn on top of whoever is in there and stand back to consider his massive pillared tombstone and bask in the status of having one's family tomb among the Elite Graves with Beethoven and Brahms across the way. Who was in there? Has Saskia joined them? What was she hiding under the floor of the cellar?

Catriona is offering her phone number. She writes it in Charlotte's diary then takes down Charlotte's in a leather-bound address book and asks her full name. "Charlotte," she says playing for time, "Kaufmann. Or Ross."

Her name going down in that book makes her feel traceable, accountable, logged. But is that necessarily such a bad thing? Seeing off the Sole Veronique while her new friends start on their oxtail soup she decides to skip the dessert and leave them to it. Neither will she pursue the cemetery. One cemetery in your head is already one too many. She says her goodbyes and discourages Archie from getting to his feet. She blows them a kiss. That's a first.

In the passage there is a portrait she won't stop to look at. There is a chair, the giant's chair, too high to climb into. The waterfall, the path, the sign . . . Saskia's will was here because Saskia's roots are here. You can fuck with history but you ignore geography at your peril. Who said that? She just did.

In the foyer the kilted proprietor is seated on a sofa opposite the senior MacMillan, a couple of whisky glasses on the table. They glance up as she passes but don't recognise her. She'd shampooed the pink out of her hair. It's as good as a disguise.

She has read herself to sleep and is dreaming of tigers when the noise wakens her, the sound of people being quiet, returning to their rooms. No stumbling, no whispering, no giggling. When the last door has closed as silently as an old door can and the plumbing gone back to sleep she looks at her watch. Half past midnight. She lets a few more minutes pass then gets up and dresses.

The door marked FIRE EXIT leads to a flight of stone steps which descends to a heavy door whose bar shifts easily. She pulls out a rock from a rockery and wedges it open then walks out into the kitchen garden of her great-grandmother's childhood home.

Beyond the small lawn are vegetable beds and greenhouses and an octagonal tool shed that's more of a folly with a verdigris dome. The nearest glasshouse is a conservatory with lacy white wrought-iron work and a pronged dome. All this she is seeing by the light of a full moon that hangs over the mountain and the waterfall.

The wind has dropped and the snow is now patchy and melting. Hugging Saskia's coat about her she walks past a camellia laden with pearly pink blooms reflecting the moonlight from its leaves. There is a giant rhododendron and some other stuff that Jock may have brought back from his tiger-shooting trip. She can hear the waterfall. The front rooms of the hotel must now have double glazing but back then they would have learned to sleep through it and wakened to its sound.

The mountain is bright in the moonlight and the remains of a fire are smouldering there, threads of smoke drifting across the moon. What were they at, these people? Sacrificing a small animal or perhaps the meekest of their number to a Celtic moon goddess? Or toasting marshmallows.

The entrance hall is still lit. A side window allows a view of two men standing there. Graham MacMillan turns away then the gravel crunches and a car starts. The kilted proprietor turns out the light.

She replaces the rock in the rockery, returns to her room and sleeps till her phone alarm wakens her. After a buffet-stripping breakfast of green figs and yoghurt, kippers, croissants and blackcurrant jam, fuelled for London on a one-stop strategy, she checks out at reception where the proprietor has been working on his attitude. He says, "I hope you enjoyed your stay with us. Perhaps we can look forward to seeing you again before too long?"

"Why not?" she says. "It's always a pleasure to visit the old homestead."

Chapter Four

There is daylight of a sort and the wind has dropped. While it howled and paced the perimeter of the forest he felt warm and safe; he is grateful to the trees and to the benign entity he senses here, a personification of good things in wild places, Mother Nature. Mother Nature? That trite, lumpen notion of bucolic femininity would never have crossed his mind. An earth goddess perhaps, a goddess of inclement places, never an apple-cheeked cliché, he doesn't do clichés. Something is muddying his mind. Yet he is still buoyed up by his ability to have got here through a chilly dusk and unnerving moonlight, a controlled descent of the back of the mountain, dropping to his knees on the bank of the loch to drink from his cupped hands, then the short ascent of the hill below the forest, all this without climbing boots or the high-end merchandise they would have you believe is essential.

His aim was to clear the open ground and reach the cover of the forest ahead of any pursuit. Speed was paramount and he was reassured, not to say surprised, by his physicality. But as he drew closer to the dense, rather banal, clump of trees they began to morph into separate verticals with dark spaces between, spaces that began to fill with things from his own head. Skeletal children wander hand in hand towards a malign presence and hungry creatures, neither cat nor dog, crouch in the still centre. He stopped walking but the person he was in his head continued. He closed his eyes and called back this other self and with his after all rather able brain took control of the forest, opening his eyes and staring it down.

This was not a forest, it was a plantation, a jumped-up vegetable patch that grew planks instead of cabbages, planks for flat-pack beds and bookshelves to be dispatched with Allen keys, sight-challenging assembly instructions and screws that had the capacity, when dropped, to roll under furniture necessitating the search for a tennis racquet or a putter to rake them out. What?

That thought lasted long enough to let him pick up speed on the final ascent and reach the cover of the trees where once again everything changed. It was a forest. Keeping it on his side, respecting it, he looked for a place where a man unsuitably dressed and uncertain of his immediate future might remain sheltered and dry while he got some sleep. He found a fallen trunk with a hollow beneath it and some sort of creeper supporting a layer of pine cones and needles to form an aromatic roof, crawled in there and slept. But wakening to find the soft thing touching his cheek was not an affectionate hand or a silk sheet but a mouse he jerked in the direction of upright and brought a shower of pine needles and a neck-crunching contact with the tree trunk.

So now what? He crawls out, stands up and takes a surprisingly short time to reprise the many schemes and acts of his recent history, shelves that for priorities, a pee and the need to eat, this need knocks everything else out of the court. He has eaten pigeons and rabbits but only when plucked, skinned and cooked by other people. He could not with confidence identify an edible plant and anyway that's totally the wrong thing. He needs to get the hell out of here. But the case against that piles in and he sits down on the tree trunk to consider.

There are no sounds of pursuit. But what sounds would there be in a place with no roads? Voices. Human voices. There are sounds all right, all of a creeping, crawling, rustling nature, but no voices. He stands up again but something with a heavy body crashlands in the tree above sending pine cones rattling down onto him as he hits the ground. The forest is definitely a forest, alien, primitive and not on his side.

To fend off the return of the skeletal children he will list the small British mammals, small Scottish mammals, that might be in here with him. Things you don't see much of, voles, pigmy shrews, hedgehogs, those things that turn white in winter, get a name-change and ermine, and end up in the Lords. Because of the cold factor they probably come from up here somewhere, although global warming is surely threatening the colour change. So which catastrophe is more likely, terminal ermine supply or imports from Siberia? Something higher up the food chain is moving around, red squirrel, wild cat? The sounds are really getting to him. He hits the ground again as the thing with the heavy body takes off.

The magic mushroom that tipped Chicken Licken into the sky-falling syndrome has found its way into his system and is targeting some urban aversion to where the wild things are. But it's people too. The man in the dining room window who pointed the gun that was not a gun and scared the shit out of him . . . and then the bomb blast . . . bomb, explosive device, whatever . . . could that really have blown him off his feet from that distance? He reacted, he was not felled. He knows absolutely that he is not a drug user, he is certain of that. This gives him an advantage, a one-upmanship on subjectivity, so much so that he would have thought his distaste and disdain, his total lack of susceptibility would be enough to override the effect, but perhaps that's just standard alpha thinking. So he's a standard alpha? If alpha surely not standard, and besides the agency is not his. This reads like induced paranoia.

He is running but no one is chasing him. Why is that? A young woman is dead, a woman with whom he apparently shared a bed. At that conference he drew attention to himself as he tried to find someone who would recognise him. And after the blast he disappeared.

He is hungry. He needs to eat. And there is discomfort around his upper left abdomen to lower left rib cage, he felt it when he wakened. He sends an exploratory hand there and finds a small but chunky object in his jacket pocket. The book.

At the flimsy fence that marks the far boundary of the plantation he stops to consider. When he reaches a road, as he surely must, he will loom up on the verge in a city suit with pine needles in his hair. Is he now so far from civilisation that a driver will unquestioningly stop for him? Or will they accelerate away at the mere sight of him? He climbs over the fence and moves on a few paces for a view of the morning ahead.

The loch is now far behind and below. Looking the other way the glen ahead seems endless. There's a dip here between the wooded hill he has just traversed and the next unplanted one, a dip carved out by a seasonal watercourse, a thin ribbon straggling down to the valley floor with a dead sheep pitched into its little ravine. The snow has drifted into patches but on much of the ground it has melted. He looks for the watch he doesn't have but finds his sharpened senses are filling in. It gets lighter earlier here after the equinox he recalls. He climbs down into the ravine above the sheep and drinks all he can then jumps the stream and climbs up the far bank. From the position of the sun he is heading north west. He is fit and rested, just inappropriately dressed. And the temperature is rising, no ice patches forming in the snow melt.

Moving on from the far bank of the gully, the view opening up as the light intensifies, he sees right away the figure of a man. He's about half a mile away, level with the next dip in the hills, standing still, looking down the glen in the direction he is going. A shepherd? *Pace* the deceased in the gully, he hasn't seen any sheep. A forestry worker? There will be all sorts of reasons for a man to be hanging around here, none of them sinister. Gamekeeper, hill walker, botanist, estate employee, estate owner. Most of these would involve some movement but the man remains still and even from this distance there's a familiar look to his posture. He is talking on his phone. So there's reception here? Or perhaps it's a walkie-talkie. In the distance he hears a sound, a motorbike, emerging now from the break in the hills, coming on swiftly, lurching and leaping and finally stopping alongside the man on the phone. The rider dismounts and takes up another classic pose. He is using binoculars, training them first on the slope of the hill opposite then slowly swivelling towards his position on the bank of the gully, by which time he is in it. He lets a few minutes pass then re-crosses the stream and climbs out on the forest side crouching low and running back to the fence, then as the bike revs and starts to come his way, the first man now on the pillion, he climbs back over it. With the bike still coming on he steps further into the shelter of the trees, buzzing with re-ignited energy, and hears behind him a sound of a different sort. A snarl. And he knows before he turns that the flat-pack plantation has morphed into the *mitteleuropäisch* horror-fest of his imagination.

    The wolf stands quite still, its lips or whatever it has in place of lips drawing back in another snarl. Behind this wolf is a second. A schoolboy grasp of wolf procedure tells him not to move. Ignore the bike, stare down the wolf. He reaches into his untapped skill set in the hope of discovering a tried and tested wolf stare. Nothing there, so this is a first, none of his forgotten past has been spent around wolves. Don't rehearse, he tells himself, just do it. He holds steady and tries not to blink. The wolf isn't moving either. As the *impasse* lengthens he taps into the British book of facts, last wolf shot in seventeen something. Are these its unsuspected descendants, a lone surviving pair? Two hundred plus years of ancestral evasion honed to perfection, the howling impulse totally suppressed, no more feckless breeding, no half-eaten sheep left lying or none that couldn't be put down to the Sutherland puma or whatever tabloid beast lurked in these parts. But however intelligent wolves might be surely they would feel a right to exist unapologetically that would surely preclude their survival. So these wolves have been introduced, a breeding pair, in it for the long term. Would that make them more or less dangerous?

    The wolf is also deep in thought, balancing the threat of an approaching motorbike against a man in a suit. It turns and with great dignity leads its partner further into the forest where he quickly joins them. And discovers that it's the wolves the men are after.

The man with the mobile vaults the fence but hangs back as the other, who is carrying a rifle, flattens sniper-style, close to the edge of the trees. The wolves will not be fooled. They will merge with the blacks and browns of the undergrowth and the stripes of sunlight, and the tranquiliser dart or the bullet – depending on whether these men are of the re-wilding faction or against it – will not be fired, but he slinks away, diverging just in case.

Presently the first man advances, making a lot of noise. Warning the wolves or saving himself. Perhaps he's out of step with his employer on the wolf question. Assuming their employer to be the estate owner. He moves back clear of the tree-line and gets on his phone which turns out to be a radio. He can't hear all of it but he gets the gist. He is reporting back to someone that the wolves have been located. Someone in authority here in the empty quarter. Someone who orders them back to base.

When they've gone he sets off again in the direction they have taken, confident now that there are people in these hills and that people who have motorbikes also have vehicles that require roads. But after half an hour with the sun strengthening but without much actual warmth in it and his mind going to whether he could catch, kill and skin a rabbit, he sees and smells wood smoke.

Set back into the hill on his left where a fast-flowing current, a small river perhaps, makes its way out of a defile between hills sits a grey stone cottage, rectangular, two-storeyed, side-on to this glen so facing the river. An infant river, exaggerated by the drama of its setting. Staying well downhill from its gable end he quickens his pace and is fifty yards short of it when he hears from above and ahead a rising whine. A drone. He is close enough to the cottage to commit himself to whatever lies in wait there, so, dropping the furtive demeanour he strides along the final stretch and hammers on the front door.

Dormer windows with red paintwork, a couple of outbuildings, a chicken coop and a four-by-four parked in front signalling a negotiable track arriving alongside the river from a more civilised glen at right angles to this, and as the door opens he remembers he has been here before. Under escort. In a jeep.

The man standing there studying him is also familiar, and there is a confirming glimmer of recognition in his face which stops short of hostile while drawing the line at welcoming. Guarded. Not about to put the kettle on.

The harsh but fair expression he remembers, the look of a decision maker. Tidy-haired, taciturn, fifty-something, dressed in one more version of camouflage. Behind him a fire is crackling up around some freshly laid logs and a tray sits on a low table. Whatever he was going to say is pointless now. He settles for a friendly, "Hi," and tacks on a smile that lets him take a step into the room out of sight of the drone. A strong protein smell is coming out at him, gross but delicious. The man steps back and nods him inside.

So much to compute, so much hanging on his manner . . . he likes the guy, likes and respects him, but can't pretend that his eyes are not going to the rifle propped in a corner under a calendar with lambs and daffodils. It seems important to establish his non-threatening credentials. "Don't let me interrupt," he says, indicating the tray where a bread roll is wedged open around a crusty pinkish-brown filling. The man is hesitating. Understandably. "Please." Charles gestures again towards the fireside chair and the bachelor breakfast, set out tidily on an ironed checked cloth. With luck there may be more of that back there in the kitchen.

The man frowns and, keeping him in view, edges towards a phone, a real phone with a landline, sitting on the dresser next to the rifle and dials a number. "He's here," he says, then turns his back so that Charles can't read his expression while the voice on the other end, faint, authoritative, perhaps with the hint of a foreign accent, talks at length. The man, his host as Charles is optimistically defining him, listens, shifting his weight from one foot to the other, not too keen on being talked at. He hangs up, hesitates, then turns and gestures towards the sofa which has begun to lose some of its appeal. He is to sit there, he imagines, until someone arrives. He is clearly unhappy. He has been given an order and he is a decision maker, not an order taker, so it's partly out of a desire to co-operate that Charles moves forward and sits. But he is thinking strategically now, reading what he can of the situation. The man sits down on the chair beside the tray which he pushes away. He should offer an explanation. "I got lost," he says. "When the bomb went off I got as far from all that as I could – there might have been another I thought – then I couldn't find my way back."

The effect of this is disproportionate. Surely he knew about the bomb, there is after all a radio and a small TV set in evidence but it seems this has hit him for six. His days will be spent outdoors and he won't do social media, he may not even have a mobile if reception is not reliable.

He is on his feet again, pacing about, avoiding eye contact. He stops suddenly and seems about to frame a question, then changes his mind. He turns towards the door, turns back, glances at the phone then with a curt "Stay here," he picks up the rifle and goes out, locking the door behind him.

Seconds pass, an engine starts, and almost immediately the phone rings. Charles let it ring six times before he answers. "Hi," says a young voice, "is my dad there?" On the wall above the sideboard and next to the calendar is a framed graduation photograph of an engaging looking young man. "You've just missed him," Charles says. "Can I give him a message?"

"Just tell him . . . you know how he over-reacts . . . tell him to cool it over Theo. He's unorthodox but he's doing a lot for us all. In particular he's doing a lot for me."

"I'll tell him," says Charles, then he crosses to the fireside chair where he sits down and eats the sandwich, some sort of square sausage he thinks, disgusting but undeniably satisfying.

He pours a cup of tea from the brown glazed teapot, adds a dash of milk from a small jug in the form of a cow, drinks the tea, then climbs out of the window.

Chapter Five

Birds are chattering in the trees that flank the hotel drive as Charlotte sets off to catch the morning bus. One of them peels off to shadow her as she walks, clattering through the lower branches until she reaches the gate. Retracing yesterday's steps along a High Street now busy with shoppers she arrives at the T-junction where the High Street and the town run out. On the other side of this minor trunk road crouches the bus shelter, holding the line between town and country. In fact it resembles a frontier post from a journey far back in her memory, one of the occasions when they drove to Vienna. There were armed guards and machine gun turrets, but perhaps those were on the far border. Behind the bus shelter are bare fields stretching away to the foothills of the next mountain range. She crosses the road and stands in the bus shelter.

In here there's a metallic beery smell and, with only an occasional car passing,

an uninterrupted view through the dingy pane of the war memorial which she is not surprised to find is a replica of the one in her head.

What is it like to live here? There's a fragility about the place that contradicts her first impression. People leave, her ancestors did, not for the New World but deeper into the old one. People leave but new people arrive. How did the town get to be here, in fact how did anywhere, feed yourself farming then specialisation, chosen or enforced, so retail, all the stuff that makes a community, butcher, baker, solicitor, guy in the big house who goes to India to shoot tigers, funeral directors. The funeral parlour in the High Street surely covers a wide area, you'd need a phenomenal death rate to have one in every village and surely it's a family firm, she should go in there and ask where did you put them, Jock and that lot in Achindarnoch House before it became a hotel?

With no bus in sight she crosses the road again and approaches the memorial with feigned disinterest. She will glance at the names, not study them. There are countless Macs, MacPhersons and MacMillans and below them a few Rosses. Higher up, hovering above the Keiths and the Kerrs is a solitary Kaufmann. Kaufmann K. An alien.

A man has emerged from the end of the High Street. He crosses the road and goes to stand in the bus shelter in the first-in-the-queue position. He is wearing a light-coloured belted trench coat and carrying a brief case and he stands facing the way the bus will come. She crosses back and joins him showing visible displeasure. They are of one mind when it comes to acknowledging a stranger, and with minutes passing it occurs to Charlotte that this is a city thing. Without the distraction of traffic sounds and people passing it becomes onerous. As she is considering breaking the silence a car that has just passed brakes and reverses and a peevish voice says, "You told me you were going back yesterday." Lamont or Lomond of the long hitch north.

In fact Lomond, Lomond like the loch as he reminds her when she's back in the familiar seat. He is boring and peevish but he is bound for Glasgow in an empty car and an empty bus passing through empty glens lost its appeal when it became a bus she would be sharing with that guy. They stop for a lunch she doesn't want and there's a wait at a garage for a lengthy repair but by nightfall she is in the concourse of Central Station, stiff from sitting and now cold from standing longer than she deems reasonable while they clean the train, tooled up with a fresh paperback, a bottle of spring water and an exorbitantly priced ticket for the sleeper train to London.

At last it's ready to board. The cleaning staff as they descend are swept aside by passengers, Charlotte reminds herself, perhaps without booked seats. She feels smug and recognises this as a first. The menace and the din of pull-along luggage finds her for a second in sympathy with her mother for whom rail travel was one long lament for the passing of those nice porters, but now she is in the right corridor of the right coach approaching her assigned compartment.

She finds her compartment, slides the door open and steps into the world of Travel Barbie. The top bunk is hers and there is so far no one she has to share the space with. She kicks off her shoes and climbs up and sits dangling her legs for a bit. This is good. She puts her shoes and her folded up coat on the rack at the bottom of her berth with her bag and the envelope on top. She comes down again and cleans her teeth at the cute washbasin, goes back up and thinks of the Vienna doll's house. Now she's the lady in it. An attendant looks in and offers a wake-up call with a choice of tea or coffee and biscuits. She opts for tea and digestives at six-thirty and finds herself basking in the calm of an ordered society.

In Vienna they let her play with the doll's house that had been Cecilia's and Saskia's when they were children. but they laughed when she asked if she could bring it home to England. It was too old, too valuable, unique and exquisite, designed for them by Theophil von Hansen himself. She dreamed of being in there among the gilt chairs and flower arrangements, the bookshelves with the tiny books. Its starched linen sheets not currently in use were kept folded up with the pillow cases in a tiny linen cupboard with some seeds from a stem of lavender. Were they ever changed? What tiny creature would do that? The other sort of furniture, Biedermeier they called it, was like their furniture in the morning rooms of the big house, though in the dining room they retained the gilt chairs as a bow to the past. In the day room of the doll's house was a side table with a Meissen tea service and the beautiful lady sat ready to pour.

Enough of that, she has a present to negotiate. She opens the paperback she bought at the station bookstall and settles back to read but her mind is elsewhere. She closes the book and leans forward to tuck the package with the letters securely under her coat. Saskia wanted her to have them, she doesn't know why but there will be a reason. She has just settled back with the book when the compartment door slides open and a tall woman in a headscarf and a belted coat hesitates in the entrance and nods in Charlotte's direction. She nods back – she has the impression that she is not an English speaker – then turns off her reading light to signal a no speaking policy and turns her face to the wall. The train starts – the woman must have caught it by the skin of her teeth – and from the sound of her breathing as she turns on the lower berth's reading light and sheds her outdoor things she had to sprint the length of the platform.

Very ready to put this whole day behind her Charlotte relaxes every muscle she has conscious communication with. She may have slept – must have slept, this is a sudden awakening – but now she is alert and listening. Someone is disturbing the neatly folded stack of things on the rack at the foot of her bunk. Loose change in the pocket of her coat gives a muffled jingle. Then comes the silence of someone not breathing, a silent ripple in the shared space. When she moves again – Charlotte hears the rustle of the envelope under the folds of cashmere – she is ready for her. She jerks upright as if coming out of a nightmare and indeed glimpses a nightmare silhouette as it drops out of sight. The image it leaves on her retina is hard to construe. The woman is still wearing her headscarf which has slipped to one side taking her hair with it. She is a he.

In the dimmed light of the compartment she can see that her coat has been roughly pushed aside and a corner of the envelope protrudes. Saskia's words come to her in Saskia's voice although spoken by a Scottish solicitor. 'In case the bastards get me.' The letters carry a message and here is a flesh and blood bastard sharing her sleeping compartment. There's a call button above her bed and a bastard underneath it. She presses the button.

When the attendant comes she draws the sheet up around herself and tells him that the pervert pretending to be asleep down there is a man masquerading as a woman who has just attempted to molest her. There comes an intake of breath and a rasp of laundry against a rough chin. Also for a second something like choked back laughter. His protest is delivered in the voice of a native English speaker, home counties, apologetic public school, Oxbridge or one of the runners-up and delivered with a composure that surprises her into looking down at him. He has ditched the scarf and the wig and is sitting up in his absurd bunk wearing a slightly crumpled half-unbuttoned blue and white striped shirt, while being falsely accused of grubby practices. He's looking cool. Even the way he averts his face looks accomplished. She tells the attendant she is prepared not to press charges if he is removed to where they can keep an eye on him. The attendant says that might not be up to her. The attendant is, however, plainly aware of the allegedly offending passenger's composure and of his own potential culpability in not having challenged him on the gender issue. Though that's a tricky one and no mistake. As her neighbour picks up his trench coat and his brief case and allows himself to be ushered out he has lost none of the containment of the man in the bus shelter.

When they've gone she locks the door and puts on her shoes and the Dior coat. She stretches out on top of the blanket, cradling the envelope. At Euston she spends the last of her money on a taxi.

The squat is disgusting. No one washes up when she isn't there. They eat takeaways or beans straight from the can. She would like to lay into them but there's no one home. She bags the rubbish, wipes the surfaces, mops the floor, then goes to her own room, the drawing room with its parquet and mirrors and brocade curtained floor-to-ceiling windows overlooking the square.

The trees in the square's railed garden have rumpled light green leaves, almost transparent in the early sunlight. There is blossom in there, cherry mostly, trite and urban in contrast to the pearly petals of the Highland garden, but everything is advanced in this southern climate, you have to give it that.

She settles on the sofa with her back to the window and takes out the letters. They have no context. Presently she makes coffee and carries her cup to the window. There's someone over there, leaning against the railings, holding a guitar, not playing it. A busker not busking. That's a crap place to choose with only residents passing and most of them ready to turn him in at the first offending riff. Sean always goes to the tube exit.

The thought that he is watching the house takes a while to form. Who would know where she lives and why would they want to? She's untraceable, it's the point. Her mother, despite her social connections, left the lightest of footprints and preferred to stay mobile. She never asked why. She knew, always, there were secrets, and that it was better not to ask. But might there be answers, is that what Saskia is telling her? The answers, if there are any, lie in Vienna.

She has always respected the things in this house. In the face of quite a lot of ridicule she shines the mirrors and dusts the frames of the paintings. But if she were to take just one thing, one only, and, if there was a pawn shop in the area - a rich person's pawnbroker *au fait* with painters - and if she was able to recognise such a pawn shop - would it have three balls even in Belgravia? - she might be able to raise the fare. The painting over the mantelpiece is too big. The little one in the corner of the girl in the yellow dress is her own favourite, maybe that means it's good.

The busker isn't doing anything, not even smoking. She has the feeling that he's taking care not to see her at the window. She walks over and stands close to the pane, flicking her hair, drawing attention. He goes on not looking then he hitches the guitar into performance mode and plays the start of something. It's pathetic. He slings the guitar over his shoulder and walks away in the direction of the tube.

She takes the painting off the wall, dusts it, finds a Tesco bag, then taking the long route round the square starts her search for a pawn shop. In another Tesco bag she is carrying the padded envelope stuffed with newspaper. The letters are in her rucksack under the things she'll need for a short city break.

There's an afternoon flight. She catches the tube to Heathrow.

Chapter Six

"Hector of Farr. He was *real?*"

The man in the wing chair, a tanned, urban, forty-something, is not dressed for the Highlands. Or not for inhabiting them. He is visiting, Charles guesses, and not for long, not so long that he needs to hide his amusement, long enough for his opinion to matter.

"Real enough."

The man answering him – bearded, expensively shabby and the focus of Charles's interest – is their host.

"Real enough for what?"

"A short film. The book."

"Ah. The book."

All eyes but Charles's go to the coffee table where a book with a pseudo-medieval cover is angled to draw attention, a clone of the smaller one still in his pocket. The one on the coffee table has a title, HECTOR OF FARR, THE SUTHERLAND SEER.

While the others consider the book he considers them. Gavin, the urban sceptic, is new to him. Their host, on the other hand, the bearded, earringed, presently equable man whom he recognised straight away as Ewan Cameron-Gunn, is the likely laird of these parts. A third man is so far silent and nameless. In profile he has the sharp intent look of an urban seagull but in his case without the urbanity.

For as long as Charles has been in this room no one has asked him what he's doing here. It seems increasingly likely that this won't happen. They know the answer to that even if he doesn't. But in case this proves to be false logic he should have some plot line ready to go and to that end he is trying to work out where they stand in relation to him and, more to the point where he stands in relation to them.

"A slim volume."

Gavin leans towards the book on the coffee table but stops short of picking it up. Ewan notes this and lets it pass. Gavin, Charles guesses, is famously economical with his responses. He is using these names in his head while he processes their owners, he is not about to flaunt them in direct speech.

Ewan who fortuitously so far seems to know him, presumably on an equally slender basis, is sitting in the fireside chair. This chair is strikingly upholstered in what appears to be a shredded medieval tapestry, something with narrative and a unicorn, a metaphor for his own short history, all forty-eight hours of it.

When Ewan leans forward to top up his own still half-full heavily engraved whisky glass from an antique decanter and fails to offer it around, Charles supposes this to be a coded rebuke to Gavin. Unless it's a whisky thing, you have your own pace, or a house-party thing, ditto. Sod that, it's a prep school level getting-back-at-Gavin thing, with only collateral damage to the urban seagull and himself.

Although Ewan knows him, there's a hitch to that. He knows him as Adam. This is agreeable and quite persuasive, a touch more familiar than Charles. If it was in his gift to choose, his preference would be for Adam.

Ewan takes a swig from his topped-up glass and leans towards Gavin.

"Slim. Yes. Necessarily slim. If bulk is what does it for you stick with the Old Testament. All prophets guaranteed authentic."

"Why 'necessarily'?"

"There *were* only a dozen prophecies."

Gavin fills his own glass. "What level of prophecy are we talking about here? The recession? Brexit? Or just the usual abstract drivel?"

"The Industrial Revolution. Climate change. Moon landings. The Sixties."

"The Sixties? He predicted they would follow the Fifties?"

"Counter-culture. The pill. Hippies. The prophecy that particularly resonates – in fact it's on the way to becoming the corner-stone of the whole project – is the Enlightenment. He predicted it."

"The Edinburgh Enlightenment?"

"He failed to mention Edinburgh. Possibly he wasn't as local in his thinking as you are, Gavin."

"So how exactly did he word it?"

"According to Wikipedia he said that men would cast off the shackles of superstition, raise their eyes from the ground and cultivate curiosity."

"In those words?"

"In Gaelic. Originally."

"And how accurate is the Wikipedia entry?"

"Very. I wrote it."

During this exchange a woman has come in carrying an ornate silver tray of edible items and their accessories. Savoury bits and pieces, dipping sauces, paper plates and napkins and a silver quaich containing wooden cocktail sticks. She pushes aside the book and lays the tray on the coffee table, then perches on the end of a moth-eaten velvet chaise-longue. Ewan leans forward and scoops up a random handful then concentrates on getting it down. He ignores the woman who is quite striking, slim and leggy, wearing a short orange wool dress. She stretches out her legs and crosses them, right over left. No one looks at her. Charles does but is careful not to be seen. Chauvinism-wise and aesthetically he's on her side but person-wise the jury is still out. He's hungry though so he stands up and crosses to the table where he collects a few cocktail sticks and impales some prawns. He runs them through the dipping sauce, picks up a radish, scoops pâté onto an oatcake, balances all these on a paper plate on top of a tartan paper napkin and returns to his chair, noting as he sits down the mud on his shoes and on the ankle area around the tear in his trouser leg.

Gavin has returned to the attack. "What," he asks, "is the Gaelic for shackles?"

"No idea, old man. Not a speaker. Beyond, obviously, topography. Sgurr. Bealach, that sort of thing."

The woman re-crosses her legs, left over right. They are long and clad in black opaque tights which make the well-bred sound of wool in friction. She speaks.

"What the guy basically said was they were getting it wrong. Like you don't pray for rain, you invent meteorology."

"*Advance* meteorology," says Ewan. "Meteorology's been invented." He throws a log on the fire and she presses on. "It's what their intelligence was for. The Scots."

"Weather forecasting?"

Ewan ignores Gavin. "*Is* for," he says. The girl takes this as a signal to continue.

"It's like they should already know stuff. Being born here. Scotland." Her accent is hard to place but it's from somewhere well south of the border.

"They should certainly know not to waste their time praying for rain," says Gavin. "Being born here."

"The intelligence is autochthonic," says Ewan throwing a glance, quite a fond one, at the woman – woman, girl, Charles can't place her age – perhaps to cue her out. "At least in places. Not the whole damn country. Anyway we're no longer planning to foreground that." Cued out or not she reaches for a radish and elucidates.

"Ewan had to freely interpret. He wasn't clear. The guy."

"Hector?"

"Yeah."

While still some way off being buddies with them – after all they're not even buddies with each other – Charles feels he is not so far manifesting as an outsider. The continuing affability of his host is helping. He also finds himself intensely interested in the topic. He would like to ask questions but that might show ignorance where he is assumed to have knowledge or put him out of role, and until he knows what that is he will remain the intelligent listener. So . . . Hector of Farr would have been a man of . . . the early eighteenth century? Late seventeenth? Or earlier? Perhaps authentically medieval. He has never heard of him, either in his current impaired state or, he feels, in the clued-up version he believes to be the real him. If he is a history buff he's passing on this one. But whoever and whatever Hector was he is the confirmed subject of the slim volume, and Ewan is its begetter if not its author.

"Which places?"

Charles finds he has said this. They all turn to look at him. It is his first contribution.

"Where do you suppose?" says Gavin.

The silent man is looking at him with disfavour. "North," he says. Charles thinks of the map on the leaflet.

"North of the central belt?" The man is preparing for a long answer.

"They are to raise their eyes from peatstack and from kelp, from machair and from glebe, from runrig and from baile, from cascrom and from ristle." So that's why the out-of-step guy is here. This is his subject.

"It's true, you don't get a lot of these in Edinburgh," says Gavin.

"To cut a long story short," says Ewan, "they are to diss soil and toil and embrace the intellect."

"The Enlightenment."

"Precisely."

"Call it what you will, old man, but precise it ain't."

As diverting as all this is, it is getting him no closer to his own enlightenment. When Ewan Cameron-Gunn, wearing a waxed jacket and driving a 4x4, passed him in the glen, he saw a gleam of light on the horizon. He was recognised. The 4x4 pulled up and waited. He walked towards it and got in, feeling that he had done this before, an idea encouraged by his recognising the driver and even knowing his name. No explanation seemed expected of him. They drove in silence, a slightly quizzical but never hostile silence, and he was content with that.

When they arrived at the stately pad, part fortified keep, part Victorian baronial, that too was familiar. He was repeating a previous arrival. But hanging over all this was a massive and he thought justified inhibition. Though he was for the moment in some ordained short-term social setting, planets in alignment, he was not among friends. If he were to loosen up and tell his tale in all its detail, the cold awakening in an unfamiliar bed in an unfamiliar room with an alarmingly cold and unfamiliar companion, a nuclear winter would come upon him. Someone would keep him talking while someone else got on the phone, an extension in an out of earshot room, and called the police. Even if he is not a physical danger to them, he is an odd-ball. He should have had sufficient panache to have kept this to himself. A guess informed not by his knowledge of the present company – he is fairly sure he doesn't know them that well – but by knowing the rules.

Gavin has assembled a starter collection of party food on one of the paper plates and returns with this to his wing chair where he unfurls the tartan napkin, Lindsay tartan, a Lowland clan, Charles believes, and tucks a corner into his shirt. You can mix paper plates and napkins with serious silver but you'd think they'd be fussy about the tartan.

"The film is still at the planning stage," Ewan is saying. "Though we have a possible Hector. And of course no shortage of extras."

"Aha! The Enlightened. I get it now." Gavin settles back and for the first time smiles. "And how many of them are there would you say?"

"More than enough last time I looked. They seem to be self-generating. You can count them yourself. They're coming over tomorrow."

"Is that strictly necessary?"

"I'm helping them to discover the settings of some of the prophecies. Bit of a pilgrimage in their eyes."

"On the estate and in felicitous locations?"

"On the estate, yes. There are clues in the prophecies."

"Four," says the girl in the orange dress.

Ewan frowns at her. "We're still working on that. There's a lochan, a broch, and a traditional river crossing with stepping stones in the shallows. We have these. Then there's a remnant of the ancient Caledonian Forest."

"But not the waterfall," says the girl.

"What I don't get," says Gavin, "is *why*. The estate chunters on and you with it. You don't need any of this."

"The North needs it. This part of the North. Loch Ness has the Monster, the south west has Burns, Edinburgh has the Festival and we have Hector of Farr. Or will have."

"Aha! So you invented him?"

"I did not invent him. He's in the tradition. The oral tradition."

"He is in the literature. The Gaelic literature." The man who delivered the impressive run-through of crofting terminology is clearly an expert. And Ewan clearly relies on him.

"But those people," says Gavin, "these extras as you see them, surely you are trading on their gullibility."

"I'm not the one who's doing that." There is a change in Ewan's tone. He is serious.

"They sound like – for want of a better word – disciples."

"They turned up here already converted."

So, Charles interrupts his own bemused reception of all this, these people are coming here tomorrow, the spokesman in the kilt, the lady in the black cape, the guy in the Fair Isle tank top. They are witnesses to his presence in the hotel, perhaps unlikely to connect him to the bomb, but subsequently, with the dead girl possibly discovered and identified as having checked into the same room as him – though he still can't get his head round that – he should not be here tomorrow.

There are other problems. He has the impression that he is a house guest. He has been staying here though, he feels, not for long. When Ewan picked him up in the glen he got the impression that he had gone inconsiderately AWOL. So he has a room in the house and will be expected to know where that is. It may even have some things of his in it. Adam's things.

"Look," he says, "I need a breath of fresh air. Can I do anything, bring in some logs?"

"We're OK for logs," says Ewan, looking at him with an amused and slightly quizzical expression, so he throws one of his pleasant not too valedictory glances round the room, walks out into the substantial hall and exits through the massive, slightly skewed but highly polished front door.

Chapter Seven

"Where to?" says the taxi driver in English.

"Ringstrasse."

"Where on Ringstrasse?"

"Opern?" The only point on the fabulous loop she can put a name to. The driver picks up on this.

"First time Vienna?" He lifts his eyes to the mirror and waits for hers to meet them. When they don't he stays on her case. "You want hotel? I take you good hotel."

"I don't want a good hotel. Thank you."

"OK. I take you bad hotel."

Watching the verges hurtle past and waiting for something to tell her what she's doing here she doesn't bother to reply. The driver is assessing her. "Where you from?" he says, his eyes still on the mirror as he hunts down the sports car in front.

"*Nicht so schnell bitte.*"

"*Schweiz?*"

"*Schottland.*" That's a first. Totally knee-jerk.

"*Schottland?* I know *Schottland.* Fighting skirt. Much fighting, *Schottland* men."

"You could say that."

"You take our life, yes, but our freedom, I don't think so." His sword arm rises from the wheel as he goes after a black Mercedes in the fast lane.

"Where are *you* from?"

"I? I from Turkey."

"Really? I thought you were turned back at the gates of Vienna."

"Please?" Just as well he didn't get that. He digs deeper into the *Schottland* seam, "Glasgow Celtic, Motherwell, Manchester United."

"Galatasaray, Suleiman the Magnificent, PKK."

His eyes flick back to the road and with the speed now tolerable she can relax. "Where is this hotel? The good one."

"Nice people. Nice accommodations. I fix you good price."

"Is it central?"

"Dead of central. Innere Stadt."

Images form in her head, some, she thinks, from actual memory. The verges have given way to architecture and this architecture to more architecture, passing now at a stately pace she recalls someone in the Vienna family, an uncle with a prefix of greats, like all the relatives, all distinguished, all great.

She has come this far on impulse, one thing more or less elbowing her into another, the pace of it not in her control. It's slackening now, much like the Danube at this point, letting itself be tidied into a canal. Nothing is straightforward in Vienna, least of all where she goes from here. When stuff stops happening you have to make decisions. Blue sky thinking. Or its deeper and darker cousin Blue Danube thinking.

The taxi is slowing. It dips into an offshoot that bends and narrows and they pull up under a swaying lantern at the end of a passageway hung with creepers. The driver twists to see her reaction.

"Here we find ancient hostelry."

"Undoubtedly."

"Bring to mind old times of Empire."

"Nailed it in one."

"Please?"

"Your English, it's amazing."

"I read. I read brochures."

He carries her backpack to the reception desk and fixes a price which she takes to be reasonable because how would she know. The girl in the yellow dress, now a short-stay resident in M. S. Redgrave's upmarket pawn parlour, was from the hand of an early Colourist. She is solvent. She hasn't checked the exchange rate yet but she hands the guy a swatch of notes, adds a few more, and he departs happy, wishing her a good holiday. *Is* it a holiday? It's not the word that comes to mind except for the lack of another. To whom it may concern, then, she's a tourist.

Her room is under the eaves, tiny, full of angles, with a lacy duvet heaped like meringue on the bed. There is a desk in the window alcove which faces out over the passage in front. The desk is painted in a grainy powder blue with flower garlands on its stationery drawers matching the narrow mirror-fronted wardrobe. There is a velvet button-back armchair in old gold with a cushion embroidered with the faces and names of composers wreathed in a bar or two of their music and on the walls are watercolours of pastures and palaces. She sinks into the armchair and experiences something very like tranquillity. She may become an art thief and just live here.

But she hasn't come all this way to feel tranquil. She takes Graham MacMillan's padded envelope out of her bag, empties the newspaper stuffing into the wastepaper basket, takes the chocolate box from her backpack and returns it to the envelope and puts the envelope in the bottom of the wardrobe. Then she sprays herself liberally with 4711 cologne from the glass shelf in the ensuite, the identical spray bottle her mother used, and goes out to square up to Vienna.

She walks for half an hour, noticing the names of the streets and the type of person who frequents them at this hour, foreign tourists as well as brisker dressier people she takes to be *echt Wiener*. The tone of the retail establishments is very niche. You wouldn't want to be running out of milk or loo paper in this locality.

The men's shops are ultra-niche, very loden, very European. This one has a coat just slung on the guy's shoulders with a Tyrolean hat hovering left and a designer laptop case right to sell its versatility, but what she is seeing is its foreignness. You have to take yourself seriously to wear a coat like that. When your ancestors migrate east instead of west it must mess with their identity. The guy outside the shop is not about to be their customer. He is slouchy cool, Atlantic, east or west.

His disaffection is catching. The streets are becoming a jumble and she is ambling, not exploring. Tomorrow she'll go looking for the house and for that she will need a street map. She finds one at a pavement kiosk. From another she buys roast potato wedges wrapped like flowers in a paper cone and is downing the last of these as the hotel comes into sight.

Yesterday's adrenalin rush flagged as she climbed the stairs to her room. She sat down on the top step to look around and locate herself. She was on a landing with four doors, one of them hers, another the preserve of a man who stepped out and looked startled to find her there. She stood up and smiled, flourishing her key to show her co-ownership of the landing but he hurried past her and down the stairs, taking her, she guessed, for an optional extra though not, one would think, in the family-run Pension Lehar.

She unlocked the door and the room was waiting for her, a corner of the lacy duvet folded back with her nightdress, another Saskia hand-me-down, arranged on the pillow and next to it a foil-wrapped chocolate that if you ate it *in situ*, would have you getting up again to clean your teeth. The Viennese and their chocolates. Also their chocolate boxes. She got up, ate the chocolate, took the envelope with the chocolate box out of the wardrobe, stuffed it behind the radiator, cleaned her teeth, double locked the door and got back into bed taking a moment to compare her present richesse with the top bunk of the previous night before she turned off the light and to the extent that's ever possible her brain.

She is wakened by something tapping on the window, the creeper, or something living in the creeper. It is full morning although the foliage is doing its best to hide that. The duvet crackles as she sits up, stuffed, she imagines, with birds of a different feather.

Showering and dressing she is surprised to find that yesterday's tranquillity has stayed with her. She feels she has a right to be here that is totally at odds with her usual passage through time and space. She got here on adrenalin and instinct, now she needs to be the person Saskia imagined her to be. She will be measured and structured in her quest to suss out the family secrets but god help anyone who gets in her way, in this city or, right now, in the queue for the breakfast buffet which the entire family has turned out to micro-manage.

A daughter in a dirndl shows her to a table by the window and helps her unload the half dozen starter items she has chosen and a twinkly-eyed uncle swathed in a black apron over a collarless shirt and waistcoat brings her coffee. Watching him pour, a man happy to dress in the style of an indoor retainer from less democratic times, it comes to her that she knows little or nothing of the disposition let alone the heart and soul of the people in whose city her ancestors chose to re-invent themselves. Her unquestioning acceptance of an obscure family history is looking careless. Also out of character. So why is that? She was discouraged from asking, diverted, she thinks now, rather than actively dissuaded, but whatever the thinking of her elders and betters she was left in no doubt that these were areas that only a gross and insensitive airhead would consider revisiting.

In an effort to ground herself she glances out of the window and sees a horse-drawn carriage pull away from the forecourt, the driver in a black cloak and black hat. The horse is also black. What is this? A film shoot? Something Freudian brought on by being female, slightly fraught and in Vienna? She is not neurotic, neurodivergent or any kind of head case, she is a tourist, and to root herself in that bunch she turns to look at her companions in the breakfast room, the loud Americans, the Brits stuck in their guide books, travelling, not touring. Out there though, in the heart of the city, Black Riders are cool.

What does she know of present-day Vienna? Nothing. But neither the coachman nor the daughter in the von Trapp Family costume nor the uncle with the coffee and the respectful manner seems to be taking their cues from the present. And

Saskia's old letters, years later still in her possession so they never made it out of the country . . . they are such a hot ticket that people invade railway sleeping compartments to get their hands on them. So not a call to rational thinking. Blue Danube thinking, maybe time to give it a go.

The facts are these. There is a Habsburg tinge to the family history. In the house was a dinner service, Meissen or Sevres, kept exclusively for when Franz Joseph dropped in for dinner. Emperor of Austria and a lot more besides, King of Hungary where they didn't see themselves as citizens of an empire, FJ in family terminology. They had a dachshund called FJ and she always thought they were talking about him. It wasn't until they covered the Habsburgs in the history class, briefly but reverently, the history teacher holidayed in Vienna, that she had a context. Glorious, Miss Russel said, out-gloriousing the rest of Europe, latterly in particular in the fields of music, medicine and architecture. All three of which, said Grandmother Cecilia when she reported back, were represented in the family.

Perhaps the architect built their house, one in an exquisitely proportioned sweep of limestone terrace, three or four storey, she never counted. Over the years they had shrunk inside it but in the beginning it was all theirs. And certainly at the time Saskia was writing those letters the cellar was still in their possession

What were they burying there? There is mention of jewellery and silver, some of it as tools for digging. There would have been the possessions that go with such a house, not, you'd think, amassed by the eloping Highlanders or not from a standing start, so acquired along the way.

There were two world wars, the first provoked by a Habsburg assassination, the second bringing widespread bombing. The house and the family survived both. At least the women did. Where were the men?

After the second came Occupied Vienna. The city was divided into four sectors, each controlled by one of the victorious allies, UK, USA, France and USSR. The Soviet Union didn't feature in their conversations, they stuck with Russia. The house was in the British sector, but Russian soldiers, still wired from heavy fighting, would go out after dark in search of the victors' spoils.

'This is the aftermath...' Saskia's bitter and sardonic voice came down the years from this occupied peacetime Vienna. But surely, Charlotte thinks, relocating herself in the hotel breakfast room, everything in post-Habsburg Vienna must be an aftermath.

She has a street map, she has the address, but does she have the right of entry? Did Saskia even own that last bit of the house? A door key would be useful. Christmas cards arrived but no longer with the printed address. Her own cards were addressed there but did they continue to arrive? And why was she so hell bent on getting out of Graham MacMilllan's office, a place clearly stuffed to the rafters with answers? Because she won't be talked at, because in some part of her mind she was scared shitless. What a boring vapid version of herself would call out of her comfort zone.

Where Saskia died and of what she hadn't thought to ask and this now seems remiss. Foul play had been floated in Saskia's breezy 'if the bastards get me,' but when you reach your nineties you can play games with your mortality and no one will think you are serious. And for her part she hadn't made herself easy to reach.

Perhaps she should have kept more closely in touch, but Saskia was always at the heart of things, fabulous city, fabulous house, money to burn, emeralds to bury, legendary liaisons still keeping her afloat while she, Charlotte, was peripheral and proud of it. Although, as of two days ago, less peripheral. A beneficiary. That word was used so perhaps not peripheral at all.

An hour later she is on the corner of its street, folding the map that got her here, the house with the fabulous stonework now concrete. In the figurative sense.

She crosses and stands in its shadow, re-crosses and stands back to take it in and finds as a burglar or any sort of furtive watcher must, that the house you're watching is watching you. Five storeys, many windows, all but the attic windows wreathed in sculpted leaves and flowers, so delicate they might have floated up there. The crescent shaped attic windows have the look of artists' studios. She crosses back and climbs the steps to the massive door.

There is a bronze address plate with names. Susanne Gerber, Markus Roschmann. Some of the names come with professions, *Architekt*, *Doktor*, Gutenberg Graphic, Aurelius Interventions, beneath that Marcus Aurelius. None of the names mean anything to her and Saskia's is not among them. Saskia Kaufmann – in this shape-shifting family was that her only name?

Her name would have been on the will, which, now she thinks about it, she never actually read. Across the desk MacMillan held it out to her but failed to relinquish his grip. She had hardly encouraged him. Just give me the gist, she told him, fidgeting in her chair and glowering out at the mountain, totally pissed off at all this. The gist was that she was Saskia's sole beneficiary, the catch being that there was no indication of what if anything she had to leave. He wanted to give her a copy but the photo-copier was broken and the guy who would fix it had a beat that covered a dizzying stretch of the county. They had to wait their turn. And until the Vienna lawyer got back to him he had no idea what was involved, only Saskia's direction that Charlotte should visit in person and receive the letters. But things have moved on from there. She is in Vienna, she and the Vienna lawyer. Does she really need an intermediary?

The door opens and a woman comes out. Charlotte says, "*Danke*," and takes the door from her. She is in a vast entrance hall panelled in liver-coloured marble with mosaic floor tiles. On one wall something with a face, a god or a goblin, spits water into a marble scallop shell and she remembers her mother pulling her away from it, Saskia's husky voice says 'at least he's only spitting.' A staircase with an intricate wrought-iron banister spirals up to a distant top floor and at this level is studded with medallions bearing a central gold rosette framing the single letter K.

But where exactly did they live? Upstairs. Not too far up because she remembers looking out of the windows and seeing street lamps and the tops of people's heads not far below. The windows ran from floor to ceiling. Her mother kept pulling her away in case she tripped and crashed clean out of their lives. She can see the carpet, a maze of dark shapes, only safe to walk on if you stay on the thin green line although the grown-ups tramped all over it. On the carpet is a red cushion. She's sitting on it, sitting in front of the doll's house. There's a chair in some slippery fabric with curvy legs and Saskia sits there smiling, smoking a cigarette in the long holder. Her hair is smooth and glossy. She is beautiful. When she leans down to hear what Charlotte is saying her hair touches Charlotte's cheek and just as she feels that familiar tickle a voice calls from somewhere in the house.

"In a minute," Saskia calls back, then to Charlotte, "Go and see what she wants, darling." Charlotte, terrified, goes.

Her neck has two ridges holding it up with a hole in the centre. She has claws for hands. She lies against a tower of pillows with letters sewn on them and she stares down at Charlotte out of yellow eyes.

"Who are you?" she says.

"Charlotte," says Charlotte.

"And what do you want?"

She doesn't want anything. *She* is the one doing the wanting. Then she sees that the confusion is not hers and that she can explain.

"Aunt Saskia says I've to see what you want."

The person with the yellow eyes laughs. It makes her cough. When she has finished coughing she speaks in what is meant to be another person's voice. "See what she wants. See what she wants." Like the parrot they have in a cage using Saskia's voice. Her expression changes. "I forget," she says. "Tell her I forget."

Was this their mother? Her own great-grandmother?

Inside the building a door closes. Someone is coming down the stairs, a woman in high heels. Charlotte observes her calmly before turning away and checking her watch or where it would be if she had one. As the woman passes she looks up again and they exchange brief smiles. She has established her right to be here. Encouraged by this she climbs the stairs to the first floor, which presents a fresh set of options.

The rooms she remembers were front-facing. They will belong to the apartments on the right. The name on the first door means nothing to her but as she steps forward to read the next one the door opens and a man comes out. She flashes off another smile and says "Frau Gruber?" The man points up to where the stairs curve away to the higher floors. She starts up the stairs but once the street door has closed behind him returns to his door. The plate reads MARKUS ROSCHMANN. Hand-written below is Kaufmann S.

Should she ring the bell? There may be a stay-at-home spouse, a child with a nanny, a housekeeper, all of those counter-productive. She should leave while the going is good and work on what she has got.

She descends quickly and casts another glance around the entrance hall. There was no outside staircase to the basement area, so access to the cellars must be from the ground floor apartments or from the back of the building. High above another pair of heels is descending. She opens the heavy door which swings inward and steps back out into the rest of Vienna.

Walking quickly, head down, deep in thought, she finds herself at the Opera House. They had a box at the opera.

There was no dissenting voice to those stories which would erupt at some internal cue, sometimes breaking off in some guarded response to another memory.

Survivor stories. To have survived an atrocity is noble but to have survived an extinct lifestyle is just untidy. Her grandmother, when she brought home friends from school, frightened them into silence. They didn't know how to speak to her nor she to them. Cecilia's friends – she was not to be called granny – first or second generation survivors, real survivors from improbable places too deep into Europe to have a coastline, were embarrassing.

The Vienna lawyer, how can she reach him? A name would help. *Ariadne Auf Naxos* is playing at the opera house and the Strauss name on a billboard rings a bell. The Vienna lawyer shared his name with a composer. Strauss or Mozart, probably not Mozart, certainly not Beethoven, perhaps Strauss because the name on the label of her jeans seemed to up the probability.

Between Schumann and Wagner a glass door swings open releasing coffee fumes. She grabs it and enters a very traditional café with dark wood panelling and waitresses in frilly aprons. There is a table behind a pillar next to an imposing wooden phone box. She orders a double espresso from a girl with real ringlets, not dreadlocks, and considers the possibilities.

The phone box may have a Viennese version of Yellow Pages, then she'll call the solicitors with composer names and tell their secretaries in English that she is the sole beneficiary of a client of theirs. Or she could just call Graham MacMillan.

She finds her diary and her phone but stops short of calling the number. She feels furtive, decidedly furtive. She doesn't want him to know that she is in Vienna and, glancing around the nearby tables, she doesn't want to be overheard. Paranoia perhaps but the man on the train may have an echo in Vienna. She looks again at the phone box. She could use her own phone but make the call from there. The waitress with the ringlets gives her change and when she makes the call Kirsty answers. She sounds unsurprised and normal. Her normality comes through cyberspace or whichever of the elements landlines use and, better still, Mr MacMillan, she says is out.

"No problem," Charlotte tells her. "I just need the contact details for my great-aunt's lawyer in Vienna. I've mislaid the note he gave me."

A short delay then she's writing down the phone number as Kirsty says, "Hang on a sec, that's him now."

"No need to trouble him. Got all I want. Thanks Kirsty." As she hangs up she is buzzing again. Not just the name, Herr Strauss indeed, and the number but also the address.

She unfolds the street map. Wilhelm J. Strauss's office is walkable, just off the Ringstrasse. She finishes her coffee, pays at the desk, and finds herself in front of another impressive building with another busy nameplate. He is on the second floor. She gives her name and asks in German to speak to Herr Strauss, and switching to English says no, he is not expecting her, but she is here from London and with time issues and something important she needs to talk to him about. She is buzzed in and gets into a lift already at ground level followed by a man who catches the door as it's closing. He smiles and raises querying eyebrows as he reaches for the panel. "*Zwei,*" she tells him.

The sleek brunette at the desk looks ready to freeze her out. She's about her age. In another world, a world in which her branch of the family had not returned to London she might have been sitting there herself. A Viennese legal secretary. She plays with the idea while the real secretary checks her out and switches to a fluent if frosty English. Herr Strauss is with a client. What exactly is this is about?

She really ought to get her on her side. She congratulates her on her English and tells her that a dear family member has just died. Fraulein Fröhlich, *fröhlich* by name if not by nature, says she has much practice in English as Herr Strauss has clients in many countries, several in the UK. Indeed two English clients have already consulted him today. And she is sorry to hear of Charlotte's loss. As it happens, Charlotte tells her, it is the deceased relative she hopes to speak to him about. Her beloved great-aunt Saskia Kaufmann. At this Fraulein Frohlich picks up a phone and relays the news in rapid German whereupon a door flies open and a beaming Herr Strauss sails out, carried on a wave of visible emotion. He wrings her hand then hugs her and with an arm still around her draws her into his office which is unsurprisingly empty of clients.

"Welcome," he says. "Many times welcome. So you are dear Charlotte!"

Chapter Eight

The calendar on the wall of Herr Strauss's office is open at May. How did that happen?
Yesterday must have been May Day, missiles trundling through Moscow and maypoles in Merrie England. Perhaps also in Scotland, and why is she thinking of this now when Herr Strauss is still speaking? He pauses to get her attention and she meets his eye but the calendar is still needling her, same blossomy street scene as the chocolate box, same smiling girl. Is it Saskia? The distress signal is actually *m'aidez*, not many people know that.
Half an hour now from the clock on the wall and they're still feeding her coffee and biscuits and info she can't digest. He has War and Peace length stuff to tell her and she has zero tolerance for being talked at. The Strauss client chair is close to five stars for comfort compared to maybe two point five for MacMillan's but it has no opposing mountain for distraction, no snowflakes to follow when your mind wants to take a walk.
At last he gets to his feet and herds her back into her heirloom coat. He takes her hand in both of his as he re-affirms his commitment to Clan Kaufmann, now sadly reduced to just herself. "As far as we know." He understands that she's having problems with communication. He gives her his card and says he is aware that she will have many questions which, if he can, he will be happy to answer, she has only to call. He asks where she's staying and seems to know it. And then Fraulein Frohlich - Klara - ushers her out onto the landing and after a tentative embrace scuttles back into the office.
She stands for a bit letting the buzzing in her head die down but the lift arrives without her intervention and its door slides

open to reveal the guy who shared the up trip. He smiles as before and side-steps to free up a few more inches of floor space. "I'll walk," she tells him and heads for the stairs.

When she reaches the entrance hall he is standing talking to an older couple,

talking in German, but she has already placed him as the blonde guy she saw outside the hat shop whom she'd tagged as a fellow Brit and whose presence here must be no more of a coincidence than the arrival on her sleeper train of the man from the Highland bus shelter. She has something someone wants and until she knows what that is she will put herself on as close to Red Alert as uncompromising cool will allow. But in the meantime a lot of dead people are clamouring for her attention.

She walks till she finds a pavement café, one with kerb appeal. It's the ambiance that matters, not the coffee, and when the waiter comes she asks for tea.

"What kind of tea?"

"What have you got?"

He reels off the weird list of fruit flavours, the usual abroad conversation about tea. She settles for English Breakfast. She sips it slowly and when her head is once more on the same page as her body considers her situation which has changed. With caveats and subject to due processes Herr Strauss believes her to be a 'supposable heiress'. She construes this as possible but improbable. Virtual in the sense of in another more ordered world. She could have asked him to be more precise but this way she retained some control. Her mind is free to wander.

Herr Strauss's belief in what he was telling her was in his eyes and in his manner. He deferred. He was plainly excited by the possibilities but fortunately for her personal integrity voluble on the barriers between her and any loot. Gaps in the record, documents missing, a small fire in a desk. Her great-grandmother Christina, she of the Highland tiger-shooting dynasty, had diversified after her elopement. She had married three times, 'married well' in Herr Strauss's words, becoming a substantial property owner. A right wee baggage sure enough. Aloud she said, "in Bohemia?"

"There also," said Herr Strauss. Here he glanced at her over his spectacles assessing, she thought, her knowledge of family history. Her face would have told him nothing as she detached herself and waltzed through a landscape of turrets with horses and geese. Might there be peasants? She would rally the peasants. Against whom? Against herself. It was his understanding, Herr Strauss said, that over the years property had been sold and, in areas under Soviet rule, commandeered. The turrets receded, the peasants led away the horses and the geese. Vying with her for what remained of these possessions would be, if such a person existed, a surviving fellow-member of Clan Kaufmann. For the moment none was known. There would be a search.

Christina – Herr Strauss referred to her as Frau Schmidt, the name of her final husband who like his predecessors had pre-deceased her – became in her later years heavily dependent on a number of people, people who increasingly ran her life for her. Her doctor, her accountant, her stockbroker, her chauffeur, her solicitor. A solicitor, of course, from a practice unconnected to his own and now, in fact, defunct. To these people she had given many of her apartments as well as some of her most precious antiques. The son of her previous solicitor had opened an antique shop. All this had changed when her daughter Saskia had moved back to the house. Moved back? Another question for the future.

"Your dear grandmother and her charming daughter, your mother, so sadly deceased, attempted for a time to trace the records. From England this was impossible. And of course your dear aunt Saskia had little interest in property."

"Great-aunt."

"Forgive me if I cut the corners. Your great-aunt. She retained at least as her main home the address here in Vienna."

The house, that at least was real. "Who is Marcus Aurelius?"

Herr Strauss laughed. "Why, he is our founding father. He is the Roman Emperor who founded Vienna."

"And who is Markus Roschmann?"

"Please?"

"Markus Roschmann."

"I know no Markus Roschmann."

"He has an apartment in the house."

"Roschmann."

"Markus. On the first floor. Was he living with her?"

At that Herr Strauss had winced. Winced and drawn back, whether from distaste or confusion she couldn't tell.

"I went there," she explained.

"Ah."

"His name is on the address plate. And in hand-writing it says Kaufmann S."

Herr Strauss leaned back in his chair and tilted his head. He had had enough of her, she thought. Then he sat forward, leaned on his elbows, and looked . . . animated. "I wonder," he said. "I wonder."

"Perhaps a pastry?" The waiter is hovering. "Or perhaps," he says, reaching for her empty cup, "you would like some more English tea?"

Her hands come up to protect her cup from another in the long line of waiters who reckons a person has outstayed her order. "No thank you." He steps away and as she watches him go the world swims back into focus, people all around her, people sitting, other people passing. She goes after the waiter. "On second thoughts," she tells him, "I would like a pot of green tea."

He moves off and standing there between tables she checks out her surroundings, box trees and bronze urns to mark the boundary, pedestrians filing past beyond. At a table close to where she is standing, sitting alone and reading a newspaper is the man from the elevator. He tilts his head and shoulders away from her. The waiter has paused at another table and she goes after him again. "With the tea I should after all like to try one of your famous Viennese pastries. I will come with you to make my selection."

Returning to her table followed by the waiter carrying her pastry she allows her eyes to light upon the front-page headline of the *Times*. She lets a little gasp of surprise escape her as she leans forward for a closer look. "Sorry," she says straightening and flashing a smile. "Bad habit. News starved. Travelling."

The man lays down the newspaper and indicates an empty chair. "Be my guest." Then he gets to his feet and fetches the green tea and the sugar-dusted *mille feuille* the waiter has just unloaded and brings them to his table.

She'll keep this brief. Friend or foe, he was following her. "So tell me," she says, "what's been happening in the wider world?"

"With specific reference to the UK?"

"You could start with that."

He is pleasant, amusing even, but when he suggests meeting up for dinner she turns that down. She's OK for drinks though and that is settled. At a bar of his choosing.

In the afternoon she visits the Hoffburg. The damask tablecloths, napkins the size of bath towels, the linen sheets, the silverware, the opera glasses are echoes of those in the family home. What she takes away is the image of the Emperor Franz Joseph's narrow single camp bed. An ascetic ruling an empire of waltzing hedonists. And giving credence to some of the family stories.

Chapter Nine

"Right then," says the man behind the desk stirring sugar into his instant coffee. "Fire away."

The man hasn't looked up yet so Charles takes a moment with his posture and his expression. He's not here to complain about fly tipping or potholes or whatever routine rant a local newspaper editor might expect in this part of the world, he comes in peace. Of course he has no idea how he looks, what state his hair and his clothes are in.

"Well," he begins. The man looks up. Was that too discursive a tone? "If you will bear with me I should like to take you back a day or two..."

The man sighs. "If you would start by telling me your name?"

"I'm afraid I can't do that."

Avoiding eye contact the man takes a sip of his coffee. The mug has a thistle entwined by a leek on the side that's visible. Might there be a rose and a shamrock on the other side or could this symbolise some Celtic origin myth? Perhaps it's not a leek, perhaps it's some sort of plaid.

"Well now..." the guy is putting on his grave face "... this newspaper has a policy. We don't print stories from anonymous sources. Not even if you're a ghillie from Balmoral or a whistle-blower from Cape Wrath. Our geographical spread is vast but our circulation is small and precise in its expectations. If you have a grievance, sir, you'd be better off taking it to one of the national tabloids. Unless it's a grievance that accords with the ethics and interests of our proprietor."

"Who is?"

"Someone whose anonymity we do respect."

They are at cross purposes here. He is assumed to have an agenda, probably to be some sort of nutter depending on how roughed-up he looks and how southern he sounds when he is simply trying to communicate. A bit maudlin, this. Stop self-obsessing he tells himself, forget about who you are, think about who he is. Take an interest.

"I'm afraid I'm a bit of a disruption to what's in your diary, pot holes, sales of work, fish prices." In deep water here, are they even near the sea?

"What do you know about it?" A little, Charles thinks. "Our fishermen send lobsters and langoustines to Dubai and Singapore, we have teachers with PhDs teaching one-class schools, our shops have world class crafts and along with the post offices and mail vans many are run by disaffected stockbrokers who have re-located here for the quality of life. There are estates the size of principalities whose owners could buy up the country. We are not short of stories but road repairs affect us all. And now I have a golf course planning application meeting to get to so I would ask you to be brief."

"I can't tell you my name because I don't know it. I've lost my memory."

"Ah."

"There is a name on a credit card but I don't believe it's mine."

"The credit card?"

"The name."

"And that would be?"

"Merchant. Charles Merchant."

"And how would you expect this newspaper to aid you in your predicament?"

"I expect nothing from your newspaper but perhaps from yourself a little human kindness. I have lost my memory and I hiked a very long way to reach a road where the man who was kind enough to pick me up told me he was a photographer on his way to an assignment and he dropped me off at your doorstep."

"Stevie."

"Look, I don't want to keep you from your meeting..."

"They'll turn him down, he's got enough golf courses as it is, a phone call will do it. What would you say to coming home with me? It's just down the road. Shona and I can sort you out."

"Well, if that's possible..."

"Just give me a minute. There are hygiene facilities through that door if you care to make use of them. I've a couple of calls to make and a few things to switch off."

There's a leaf or two in his hair and a scratch on his cheek but the face is now familiar and the clothes feel like his own. He is comfortable with this guy, hard to know why. Might the phone calls be to the police? If so that would be a kind of solution. He didn't kill the girl but someone did. Or might he be phoning the owner of the newspaper and perhaps of some of these mountains?

Just down the road is five or six miles from the newspaper office which is located in a village with the look of a town, four or five streets deep in its centre. The house, a modernised small farmhouse with extensions, is set back from the road up a hundred yards or so of track. A peacock is walking past the entrance as they approach. "Not ours," says Mitchell Carruthers who introduced himself at the start of the journey after asking Charles if he minds being addressed that way.

"Ewan Cameron-Gunn's?" Charles suggests. Lairds probably own peacocks.

"Grace MacKay's. Nice wee woman. Daft though."

Shona is wearing a paint-stained smock which she pulls off when she sees him along with the scarf holding back her hair. So the phone call was not to her. She washes her hands at the kitchen sink and switches on the kettle as Charles is introduced as a stranger who has lost his way.

"You're on holiday?" she asks.

"You could say that." He feels it is not his place to explain.

"The fact is," says Mitchell, "he doesn't know why he's here. He's lost his memory."

Shona glances at her husband to confirm he is serious then pulls out a chair and waves Charles into it.

"When did you last eat? Oh, maybe you don't know that. But you'd know if you were hungry. Are you?"

"Very." What a wonderful woman.

"So how did you meet up with Mitch?"

"Stevie dropped him off."

"If you see Stevie," says Charles, "be sure to pass on my heart-felt thanks." Their looks tell him he's over-cooking it. It's a habit he has. Somehow he knows that.

"There is a venison casserole in the oven," Shona says, "and there's early potatoes and purple sprouting broccoli from the garden."

"Did you shoot it yourselves?" Charles asks, taking an interest. They fall about laughing.

"You know how it is when everybody has blackcurrants at the one time and they're all trying to give them away?"

"Not really."

"Well that's how it is with venison."

"But this isn't the shooting season."

"You see that thing the size of a Morris Minor over there? That's the freezer." Distractions dealt with, Shona is back on his case. "So where exactly are you from? Don't tell me, you don't know that either. I'd say you're not from around here."

"Kingston-upon-Thames." They turn and stare at him and he asks to be directed to the loo.

When he returns to the kitchen Shona is serving the venison casserole but the welcome has cooled slightly. He can totally see why.

"It just came to me," he says, taking his place at the table. It's true but they may take some convincing.

"Do you think that's your home town?"

He doesn't, or not in a way that invokes civic pride or a memory of walking home from school.

"Perhaps," he says.

Meal finished, plates cleared, ice-cream turned down, they move to the sitting room where a fire is burning in the grate and a cat called Malcolm sits on the window sill watching the peacock pacing the lawn, turning on and off the security light as it passes.

There is a large TV screen on the wall next to the fireplace but they are making no move to turn it on. He turns down the dram that Mitch pours and then takes for himself and accepts Shona's offer of tea. His head must stay clear. Shona drinks home-made Cassis – the blackcurrant glut. At last Mitch reaches for the control to catch the late news. There is a Scottish news and neither it nor the national makes mention of the bomb incident – old news now – nor, more to the point, of the dead girl. Could he have imagined her? No way. The moment he saw her, reeling back from the sight before he pulled himself together to check her out, will stay with him for the rest of his life. Rising levels of apathy among young voters has a top spot. Too many sources of information, too little trust in mainstream news sources and now fresh evidence of disinformation is coming from new sources. A pundit points out that merely to question the reliability of the electoral system is to damage it. A former diplomat is being questioned over historical leakage of confidential documents in Vienna and an American actor who has swum Loch Ness to raise funds for a children's charity claims to have seen the monster.

"Well there you go," says Mitch and turns off the TV.

Shona shows Charles to his room which has a pair of blue and white striped pyjamas laid out on the duvet. "Get yourself into these," she says, "then put your clothes in the sitting room. I'll deal with them in the morning." And bidding him goodnight she goes off upstairs leaving him to check out his surroundings. The room is in the ground floor extension at the back of the house. Its window looks directly onto a mountain which begins its rise three or four fields away. Another tree-less mountain but with an undulating line of still leafless deciduous trees following the line of an invisible burn at its base. He is getting a feel for the elements of this landscape.

Though it's dark some light spills from an upstairs window and illuminates a garden with a washing line, a table with benches and what are probably vegetable beds with a small polytunnel and what may be fruit trees beyond. He takes off his shoes. After some thought he takes off his clothes and gets into the pyjamas. His impression is that he hasn't worn pyjamas for years. When the light from the upstairs window goes out he bundles up his clothes and carries them into the sitting room. He drops them on the sofa then squats on its arm to check out the laptop he spotted earlier. No need for a password, it hasn't been turned off. So . . . Kingston-upon-Thames. Not looking familiar, these street scenes. The name rings a bell but not the place. No messy accretions of a life lived or a place lived in, no privet hedges, no front gate. It's as bad a fit as Charles Merchant. Charlotte, he recalls, had issues with her surname. What would she have made of his departure? The cat on the windowsill is sizing him up for a prospective lap to sit on. He closes down Kingston-upon-Thames and returns to the bedroom.

What will they do with him tomorrow? Mitch will go to work, make some phone calls, toss around his name, but the paper is a weekly, so should he be tempted by the prospect of such an odd exclusive it will be a day or two before it's in print. He didn't tell him about the bomb, the dead girl or the Achindarnoch House Hotel so he won't go snooping around there.

Shona will be deployed to keep him happy and out of circulation. She paints, perhaps as a hobby, perhaps to commission but may be free to take him sight-seeing. He takes another look at the now darkened garden with a hint of moonlight somewhere indicating the bulk of the mountain. He could walk out of here and be well on his way before anyone thinks of looking for him but the prospect stirs no adrenalin. Miles of dark moorland and burns too wide to jump, thistles, brambles, large and unfamiliar birds, things that shouldn't be there. Wolves. He is beyond exhausted. He gets into the comfortable bed and sleeps.

Shona has hand-washed the blue cashmere sweater and brushed down the suit jacket. His shirt, socks and underwear are washed and in the dryer. When he pads barefoot into the kitchen, awkward in the striped pyjamas, she is mending the tear in his trouser leg. "Your things will be dry by the time you've had your shower," she says. "Do you like a cooked breakfast?" He doesn't normally he believes but there is nothing normal about all this and back from the shower dressed in the clean clothes that were waiting along with the mended trousers, the brushed jacket and the cleaned shoes he finds bacon, two eggs, and mushrooms awaiting him and Shona slotting what looks like home-made bread into a toast rack. Is this what married life is like? If so he's pretty damn sure he isn't married or in any such lavishly catered relationship which would anchor you with obligation till the end of time. But of course this is the opposite of a relationship. He is the stranger at the gates. A one-off.

"Mitch is away to the office," she says. "We thought you might like to see some of the countryside? That's if you've no other plans." They share a smile at that.

The blue cashmere sweater is still drying in the garden but Shona offers one of Mitch's which he turns down. It's not that cold today and anyway he really loves that sweater, he is sure now that it's his, that he bought it himself.

They step out into a calm, mild morning with clouds parting from time to time to reveal the sun. Shona drives a grey-blue Peugeot. Her hair is tied back in a chiffon scarf and she is wearing a jacket in a hazy light-weight tweed that echoes the colours of a northern sky. The fashion vocabulary lingers.

They head west on a single-track road and while its pinched dimensions constrain their progress everything else is vast. Space and light, an excess of these with the threat of more of this to come. The sun is up there but only as lighting for the clouds which have form and content and move across a sky that reaches to the end of the world. Shona knows better than to talk, she can sense his delight in the landscape but not the thing that's equally heady, he feels unconstrained. Unshackled. At liberty. Free to mess up. After a few miles she pulls off the road onto a tarmacked space on a cliff top. "Just for the view," she says. They are at the apex of a deep indentation which moves away from them, widening as it goes. A ragged tear in the land with an island in the middle and what must be the sea at the end. Can this be the north coast?

The north coast. The end of the British Isles. The Orkney Isles up there to the right and Shetland in a box next to them. But keep on going due north and it's empty sea all the way until you reach the place at the top where the longitudes come together. A child with an atlas and an adult with a lot of respect for the Vikings. It's the starting place of this big island. Self-knowledge, but still no self.

The road is still single track and they slide without rancour in and out of lay-bys to let east-bound cars pass. When a car pulls in to let her pass Shona gives a friendly wave. So she knows everyone, how nice is that. But the proliferation of foreign number plates breaks into his self-absorption and Shona growls under her breath as she backs up for a BMW that has pulled up just after a lay-by and waited without acknowledgement for her to reverse, then she reverses rather a long way to let a camper van full of Italians pass. They all smile and blow kisses and she blows a kiss back. "Is there a rule about who gives way?"

"There are national characteristics. Also human ones."

"You are very generous."

"It's that or bloody-minded. You choose how you're going to play it. Nice is easier to live with."

"But why is there so much traffic?"

"This is the NC500."

"What is that?"

"Scotland's answer to Route 66. Also it's the May holiday."

So no longer April. He doesn't voice this. He is presenting as wholly rational.

They pull in at last beside a building on another cliff-top, this with the sea breaking very far below and when Shona parks close to the edge he discovers he is prone to vertigo. He tries to welcome this as another piece in his personal jigsaw but when she makes for the picnic table closest to the edge he steers her towards one that's further inland.

A surprising number of warmly dressed people are sitting here eating and drinking and just happily looking around and when a waitress in heavy knitwear brings a menu he realises that for Shona this will be lunchtime. So rather than the coffee he feels is all he can manage he orders lobster bisque and a scone so that she can choose something substantial.

"Hector of Farr," he says. "Are we close to where he came from?"

"Who?"

"Hector. Of Farr."

"I know Farr but I don't know a Hector."

"I believe he is historic."

"Ah."

The lobster bisque is extraordinary and the scone clearly home-baked but how is he to pay for this? Shona may be planning to play host but he can't let her do that. And there's another thing. The credit card is burning a hole in his pocket. Could he make it work? The building the waitress comes and goes from is too big to be just a restaurant. It must be some sort of retail set-up, the first sight of retail in his present incarnation and he is itching to get in there and see what they have. He may have cracked the distinguishing element of being human. The need to shop. The waitress brings the dessert menu. He turns down these goodies but insists Shona goes ahead then excuses himself and makes his way inside.

It's a tourist-oriented Celtic nirvana with hand-knits and Scotch butter tablet, tweed handbags and tartan pashminas.

There are watercolours of the landscape, perhaps some by Shona, guidebooks, calendars and posters of the clans and their tartans.

There is also a stationery counter that has newspapers including a *Telegraph* with a headline that stops him in his tracks. He takes it to the counter recalling the change in his pocket. "I'm sorry sir," says a lady in a lavender silk shirt and amethyst earrings, "I'm afraid that Major Sinclair's *Telegraph* is not for sale." Spoken in the voice of the Shires, the English shires, not the Scottish.

"Ah. And is that the only one you have?"

"We have spare copies of the *Daily Mail* and the *Sun*. For the holiday weekend you know."

"Of course." He treats her to a silky smile and moves away to the posters with the tartans. He needs that *Telegraph*. He saw the headline and the byline was Ben Taylor. Better not to do things by halves, big spender versus distinguished local and wing it with the credit card.

He takes a cashmere scarf off its hanging rail, one that tones with Shona's colour scheme, retraces his steps and picks up a basket, adds a box of tablet, a poster of the clans and their tartans, a jar of rowan jelly and a paperback with a castle on the cover then, widening his horizons, sees against the wall a rail of men's outdoor jackets, padded, down-filled, not waxed but tending to countryside colours including that precise shade of olive drab that signals your social standing in places that don't have public transport. He lays down the basket and tries on the XL. There is a full-length mirror beside the rail. It's good. Then in a corner he sees a small table laid out with a range of familiar toiletries. A sheaf of purple heather in an opalescent vase stands guard over a collection of jars, flasks and sprays with a framed backdrop of moorland raised from tedium by a haze of that colour that it's hard to put a name to. In stylised block caps, FRAOCH, The Heather Collection. He takes one of everything along with the complementary purple toilet bag. On a bottom shelf he finds a selection of useful stuff, probably for the locals who may be fifty miles from a branch of Boots, maybe a hundred as the road winds. He picks up a toothbrush, toothpaste, a razor, a comb. There must be more he needs to get him through whatever is going to hit him next but he can't think of anything now, he is thinking only of the PIN number. He's owed some luck. Start with the mindset of the guy who chose it. For he is sure now that there is a will behind his plight, someone playing God. One reason for this is the name Merchant. An early job description shorn of ethnicity but perhaps with a hint of Near East, a featureless fixer ready to take up any identity that bring dividends. Theo? The date of a battle. Not 1066. Theo is dabbling in Scottish identity. Culloden? No idea of the date of that and wasn't it a Scottish defeat?

He is still rehearsing options as he heads to the counter with a full basket and the green goosedown number over his arm. He tells the dragon lady that he would also like to pay for the lunch.

"I'm afraid you'll have to do that in two transactions sir. The food counter is over there."

"Ah. OK. The thing is I'm pushed for time. There are people waiting at that counter. I have a flight to catch." Charlotte's cautionary suggestion of John o' Groats international airport flashes up but it seems she is melting.

"I'll see what I can do if you'll give me a minute," she says and walks across to the desk that deals with the restaurant. As she turns her back he rolls Major Sinclair's *Telegraph* into the inside pocket of his suit jacket. She comes back smiling.

"That's done for you sir. You can pay for everything here." She swivels the card display towards him and he pulls out Charles Merchant's card. Major Sinclair and his choice of newspaper. A Unionist. Bells are ringing. Union of Parliaments, 1707. The gods are on his side. About time too.

He thanks her with the killer smile and carries his booty out to where Shona is finishing her coffee.

"For you," he says laying down the cashmere scarf and the tablet. She looks confused, taking in the scale of his shopping. "So you are Charles Merchant after all?" Ah. Mitch told her about the credit card.

"Seems so," says Charles.

Chapter Ten

When they get back to the house Malcolm is asleep on the blue cashmere sweater which he has hooked from the drying rack in the garden. There is no sign of the peacock.

Shona reaches for her painting smock and Charles asks if there is anything helpful he can turn his hand to, for instance in the garden. Shona says not that she can think of, why doesn't he just relax, so he carries his shopping to the bedroom where he hangs up the suit jacket and removes the *Telegraph* from the inside pocket.

In the garden he reclaims the sweater from under a pissed-off Malcolm and puts it on, then he carries the newspaper to the chair under the leafless tree and, feeling absurdly furtive, settles to read it with his back to the house. There are scents and sounds inimical to concentration so he deals with these first. The grating and repetitive bird call is aimed at the cat so he blanks it out. The sporadic whooshing is wind, the sporadic rattle is the washing machine on a spin cycle and the chilly bracing green smell is the countryside. Bracing is good. He is braced for revelation. He unfolds the *Telegraph* which has MAJOR SINCLAIR clearly written above the headline

CELTIC SUPREMACISTS IN BALLROOM BLITZ
BOMB SCARE TURNS DAMP SQUIB IN
HIGHLAND BEAUTY SPOT

Ben Taylor's head and shoulders alongside his byline confirm his identity and celebrate his exclusive.

A picture below the headline shows singed curtains flapping in the draught from a shattered window and the story attests to how people attending a conference in the ballroom of a Highland hotel were evacuated shortly before an explosive device went off causing a small fire and damage to the décor. What was at first thought to be a Molotov Cocktail was described by a police spokesman as 'a home-made firework, a dangerous home-made firework that could have caused injury had there been people in the vicinity.' There was an anonymous telephone warning to the hotel shortly before the blast but no one had claimed responsibility.

It was unclear what the topic of the conference was to be as press were not admitted but it was thought to have been of a retrospective nature. One of the delegates, a lady who declined to give her name, said she believed the device was an attempt to silence the aims of the group though she also declined to say what these were. Many of the delegates were believed to be acting as extras in a history-based film being shot on the estate of maverick laird Ewan Cameron-Gunn to coincide with a book about the prophecies of a little-known, possibly mythical, medieval seer, similar to the seventeenth-century Brahan Seer, this one a native of Sutherland, who among other things predicted the dominance of people of Celtic origin. Many of his prophecies were believed by some including those attending the conference to have come true.

The Brahan Seer, from the Isle of Lewis, is said to have predicted the Highland Clearances and the building of the Caledonian Canal and to have brought off the double coup of predicting Scottish Devolution and the Channel Tunnel when he said that Scotland would once again have its own parliament, which it did in 1999, but not until people could walk dry-shod from England to France, which they did with the opening of the tunnel in 1994.

Ewan Cameron-Gunn had recently been accused of illegal re-wilding by some local farmers who claim that attacks on their flocks had left injuries consistent with those found in countries that retain a population of wolves, accusations he strongly denies, the denials backed up by others who believe that it is the new owner of another larger estate who is behind the experiment and possibly the misinformation regarding Cameron-Gunn.

The hotel had swiftly replaced the window pane and the damaged curtains in time for the May holiday weekend. Police enquiries were continuing.

A fizzing sensation in his head travels through his body, unlocking his grip on the *Telegraph* which drops out of his line of vision as Malcolm moves in. He leans to retrieve it and pitches forward with his head between his knees. He stays that way watching an ant climb a stalk of grass and inhales the clean green air while Charles Merchant relinquishes his hold on Adam Maxwell.

If he lets himself think about it he might solidify in transition, mind totally blown. He watches the ant reach the top of the grass stalk and turn its head left and right looking for some logical course of action. The grass stalk bends and the ant hops off and starts to climb another. When it reaches the top of a third grass stalk he, Adam, is ready to sit up and inhabit his new identity. He is an investigative reporter and Ben is competition. There was no mention of a dead woman in the story nor yet of a missing man. Ben knows him but Ben called him Charles.

Cancel Charles, he tells himself. Celebrate Adam. Take a trip round this fresh and altogether more agreeable persona. He has agency, he has ability, he has acumen, he has articulacy. He can do stuff. But there is still something missing, a day of his life, two days, a time gap. Searching for it is as unsettling as it is unproductive. He stands up, stretches, walks around the garden looking at things. Crocuses. OK, not the crocuses, zap the crocuses, see the mountain. Against the mountain a face is forming, the face of the man in the dining room window. He raises the hand that holds no gun and fires. And laughs at the reaction. That man, he was in on it. He waits for his pulse to steady then returns to the seat under the tree and picks up the *Telegraph* which he reads from front to back, cover to cover.

The gardening page does not travel well. Things down there, cherry blossom and magnolias are away ahead of things up here. He has written gardening pages. Also sports pages and fashion pages on his first local paper where you turned your hand to everything and phoned a girlfriend for terminology and colour names, occasionally inventing your own. His Medusa Hat for an unpopular minor royal who came to open a craft fair was copied by a national Sunday broadsheet.

The sound of a car breaks into his ramblings. Mitch is home. He'll let him catch up with Shona and just sit here being himself. But it isn't long before Mitch comes out carrying two mugs of tea which he sets on the grass while he fetches a small table and another chair. He looks down at the newspaper now re-folded front page uppermost.

"Aye aye. Nicked the Major's *Telegraph* I see. He'll have you in front of a firing squad for that."

"Bit of a character is he?" Local gossip, a tool to deflect questions.

"With political leanings we won't talk about."

"Right of centre?"

"Right of right. Suspected of being in cahoots with the extreme right in faraway places. Don't believe it myself. He's all talk and bluster."

"Where does he live?"

"Down the road. If you're that interested you could take the man his paper."

"Is there much of that round here?"

"You'll be thinking of the loonies and their bomb blast. This lot." He waves at the newspaper.

"Well, yes."

"There was talk of a posh guy that went missing. Funny you didn't mention a bomb."

"I guess it was after I left."

"Did you enjoy your wee outing with Shona?"

"Very much. This is a very different place from how I would have imagined it."

"And what way was that?"

"I suppose . . . a backwater."

"Just some names from the shipping forecast, Cape Wrath to Rattray Head. What could possibly happen in these parts?"

"Well, I suppose there was Dounreay."

"And then there's the war games at Cape Wrath. And on-off mention of a Spaceport."

"I guess that might make you the new place."

"It's a thought all right. Sometimes folk lift their eyes further up the map and see a lot of space and a sea coast they don't know. To folk stuck at the bottom of the map that can signal a fresh start."

"And how do you feel about that?"

"I bring out my newspaper and I keep my eyes open. What I'm seeing doesn't need to go in the paper. I'm still seeing it. They say you can get up to anything on these huge estates. They're bloody right. A local paper stays under the radar. Just gossip, recipes for scones and sales of work. You said so yourself. But we haven't lost our news values. We're on the spot when something breaks."

"You are indeed and I apologise for my crass remarks. You see, being in your office struck a chord. I'm another of your kind."

"I don't have a kind if you're talking politically. I'm non-aligned. An observer."

"My memory came back. I'm a journalist."

Mitch is looking at the tea in his cup, letting his reactions flicker across his face before he looks up again. "Are you indeed you smooth bastard." But before he can develop his thought an unearthly cry, blood-chilling and drawn out, comes from somewhere close. "Bloody peacock," Mitch says and they turn to look as it flaps its wings and becomes airborne for just long enough to clear the fence. It unfurls its tail and starts towards them. The cat stands and stretches and idles towards it swishing its own tail. "Now Malcolm," says Mitch. The cat sits down and holds its ground as a woman's voice comes from the field behind them.

"Hughie you wee devil. It's into the kennel for you if you don't stop your wandering. You'll need a run of barbed wire round the top of your fence, Mitch, if you're going to keep him out. Does he bother Malcolm?"

"Malcolm's fine with him, he likes a challenge. Charles, this is Grace. Grace this is Charles."

"Adam," says Adam.

The woman who has long straggling grey hair and wears a chunky hand-knitted jumper in a light aubergine over a skirt in one of the maroon tartans comes up and shakes his hand.

"Adam is it now?" says Mitch.

"And where's Shona?"

"Painting."

"And what's she on now?"

"A commission for the National Trust. Strathnaver."

"She's very clever, Shona. And what do you do Adam?"

It's Mitch who answers. "Adam is another journalist."

"Fancy that now. An old friend of yours?"

"Quite the reverse". It isn't clear whether he is refuting the time span or the friendship. "He walked into my office just yesterday."

"And where are you from, Adam?"

"Kingston-upon-Thames" says Mitch. "Although that's up for grabs too I expect."

"And which of the papers down there are you on?"

"I'm strictly freelance," says Adam picking up the *Telegraph*. "And now if you'll excuse me I have a paper to deliver to a man who'll be waiting for it. Can you direct me to Major Sinclair's house?"

"Torquil?" says Grace. "I'll show you. I'm going that way myself. Come on Hughie."

The peacock follows them laboriously, its tail re-furled and dragging, as they set off, westward, moving into the verge to let cars pass. As most of the cars slow and people lean out to talk to the peacock or take its picture they soon create a tailback.

"I don't know what they thought they were doing when they started calling it the NC500," says Grace.

"What does the NC stand for?"

"Numpties. Numpties with caravans, they're the worst. Folk who need a name for a thing before they'll try it. Like if everyone's doing it it's cool."

"Like Santiago de Compostela maybe? I mean if you're not religious that's just a popular walk."

"With a wee badge at the end of it. There isn't an end of the NC500, it's a circuit. What were you doing with the Major's paper?"

"I'm afraid I picked it up without realising it was spoken for."

"Well don't let him keep you with his nonsense."

"What nonsense would that be?"

Grace has stopped to rally the peacock. "Come on Hughie." Three cars have stopped and a girl leaning out of a window is trying to tempt him with a Mars Bar. He unfurls his tail and there are squeals from the cars behind. A driver heading east who has pulled into a lay-by blasts his horn. "Just you go on son," Grace tells him, "It's about half a mile along on the left. You can't miss it. He has a Union Jack at the gate."

It's an hour and a half later when Adam arrives back at the house.

"I told you not to heed his nonsense," says Mitch.

"Then you'll know how he is with an audience." Adam has no wish to get into a conversation about the Major's obsessions but he does want to know if he is in contact with the group from the conference who seemed, despite their misplaced sense of significance, harmless and home centred. He puts that to Mitch.

"No no. A different kind of daft. Torquil's a Brexiteer. You won't find many of these around here. The hotels would struggle to function without staff from Europe. Nice folk. Fit in well."

"And how is the Major about them?"

"I doubt if he knows where they're from. He's friendly with everyone but he's theoretically paranoid. Have you heard of an outfit called Gates of Vienna?"

He has. "Never", he says. "What's that?"

"Have a guess."

"It's where the Ottoman forces were turned back in sixteen something. Otherwise, Europe might no longer be Christian. That was the orthodoxy at my school."

"In Kingston-upon-Thames? Well, yes. I've heard he's in touch with them."

"But surely . . . up here . . . what's his problem?"

"His head's back in the Crusades. Was his way of life and now he's turned it into a hobby. With the Gerries defeated and the Ruskies hard to second-guess he's turned back a few pages. He's convinced there's a plan to settle the asylum seekers from Syria and Afghanistan in Caithness and Sutherland." At which point Shona shouts from the house that dinner's ready.

As she ladles out a chunky and fragrant soup she tells him is called Cullen Skink which brings to mind a small scaly desert creature but which tastes of finnan haddock, plans are forming in his head. It's time to go. There must be somewhere he can hire a car. He has the credit card. It's his. He set up the account for going undercover. Charles Merchant is the name he chose for more or less the reasons he ascribed to the people who worked him over, the people, presumably, he had gone undercover and travelled north to investigate, a trip of which he still remember nothing.

When Mitch tells Shona that the person formerly known as Charles is now Adam she asks how that feels. Good, he tells her. Though as often as not he is known to his friends as Max. He doesn't share that, there are only so many identities decent people will accept. Shona asks Mitch what is happening in the wider world. The usual, he says, famine, genocide, flooding, disaffection.

"And closer to home?"

"Road kill up on our traffic artery, pheasants mostly but yesterday they found a lynx. A guy's coming up from Edinburgh Zoo to identify it."

"Ewan Cameron-Gunn?"

"Ewan's not to blame. It's that other bastard."

"Which other bastard?"

Mitch looks down at the table. "How do I know you're not working for him?"

"I'm not working for anybody."

"Aye. We'll see. And a woman's body's been found in the forestry near that hotel where you were staying."

"Hypothermia?" Shona suggests. She turns to Adam to explain the vicious circle of scenery, spontaneity and the chill factor, people dressed for notional spring and without a map or compass walking round in circles in a place with no landmarks.

"They're waiting for a toxicologist," says Mitch. "They think she was drugged or poisoned."

Chapter Eleven

For her meeting with the guy from the café and the lift Charlotte decides to get there first. She needs to see him arrive, which he does ten minutes early and unaccompanied, glancing round the tables till he spots her. Her precautionary paranoia remains.

He is medium height, slim, good looking, not fabulous, wearing a padded jacket over a grey shirt and black jeans. She felt safe with him yesterday at the café table as she had not in the lift. Both impressions seem valid so no shift from red alert.

"Hi," he says, "can I get you another of whatever that is?"

"It's elderflower. I'll have a glass of something Austrian. White I guess."

He goes off to the bar and she takes a closer look at their surroundings. It's not so much a leisure hangout as an office pub, people de-stressing, putting off going home. Perhaps he has colleagues in the crowd. He returns with two chilled glasses. The wine tastes of outdoors.

"So," he says, "you're travelling. By rail?"

"Well, I flew here."

"Ah."

She could leave it but succumbs to the need to slap him down. "It cuts out France. And Switzerland."

"True. No point wasting time there. So, you're headed east?"

"East-ish."

"Hungary?"

"Perhaps. After Bohemia."

"Bohemia?"

"Today I visited the Bohemian State Chancellery. Such a beautiful building." The non sequitur makes him glance away and lets her take over.

"You of course will have been here for some time." His eyebrows rise. "Your fluent German. So you were not Herr Strauss's early morning English client."

"Herr Strauss is my solicitor."

"Then you're Austrian enough to have had need of a Viennese solicitor."

"I'm embassy."

"The UK embassy?"

"Of course. What else?"

"And you're a commercial attaché."

"How did you guess?" He has the grace to look uncomfortable.

"From my reading that's the usual cover for intelligence activity."

He shifts his chair closer to the table and glances round. When he faces her again he is un-amused. "I think you're getting a little ahead of yourself here. You're certainly getting ahead of me. God knows what you're reading."

She *is* getting ahead of herself. She has established firm ground so she should soften up otherwise this is going nowhere. "Espionage, fact and fiction, there's not a lot of difference I believe. And isn't Vienna the world centre?" Flagging up that her info is picked up here and there like everybody else's. He looks ready to go with that.

"I hope you're going to find time to take in the sights. And perhaps the opera." She bites back a mention of the family box at the opera house.

"I'm not sure I'll have time for that. I don't know how long I'm staying."

"Ah. The travelling imperative. I'm not sure I've ever understood that. When I get to a place I like I want to stick around. You must at least see the Stephansdom. And the Klimts and Schieles. I can show you around if you'll let me."

Certainly there is appeal in that. "Tomorrow if you have no other plans." She lifts her glass to cover her indecision and finds it almost empty.

"Why is the UK embassy interested in a heap of old letters?"

"Letters?" The word seems to puzzle him. "Are you sure I can't persuade you to join me for dinner? I know the places that have yet to reinvent themselves."

"I don't do dinner. In the evening I snack."

"That is also possible. Offhand I can't think of an atmospheric snackerie but I'm sure we could find one. This is a cheerless place I'm afraid. I'm not too up on bars."

The evening is calm and clear and the streets pleasantly busy. They walk without talking, giving her space to think in the traffic-free streets of the Inner City. When they turn into Wipplingerstrasse she stops walking.

"I know this."

"You came here, did you not, to look at the Bohemian State Chancellery?"

"I know it from before." Not just the buildings but the street name. Halfway along, it briefly becomes a bridge over a lower street. She would stop there, peering down, until her mother pulled her away. There was property here in Wipplingerstrasse. It was let to businesses.

The place they settle for is small and unpretentious with red checked tablecloths like a retro bistro back home. They are the only customers. A tall, cerebral-looking man in an apron brings the menu, but the air is heavy with unfamiliar spices and not to ask what is causing that would be wilful self-denial. "It is our famous goulash soup," he says. They agree on that and he brings crusty bread and a carafe of the house wine.

"And now the documents. Or letters if you prefer that." So they are no longer playing games. "I'm not going to dissemble. Their content may be relevant to certain issues."

"Relevant? Decades later?"

"There are ongoing issues."

"Issues. Such a useful word. How did we ever manage without it?"

"Perhaps because we were free to be explicit. There is a possibility that you are in some danger. Certainly I would think you are being observed. I don't know how much you know about your family history here?"

"They had a box at the opera."

"Before or after it was bombed?"

"It was bombed?"

"Bombed and rebuilt."

"Then before I suppose."

"Anything else?"

"In their house everything had a name. The furniture, the plates, the tapestries, Biedermeier, Meissen, Aubusson. They had a doll's house designed by Theophilus Hansen."

"In the swim, friends in high places. Were there people with names?

"I was young, I didn't listen."

"Do you know how they came to be here in the first place? What brought them here. To Austria?"

"I heard that someone eloped. Well, two people. Obviously."

"Really? How charming. I'm thinking maybe earlier . . ."

"Actually I heard they went to Bohemia."

"Also part of the Empire. I'm thinking late nineteenth century. Time of Franz Joseph."

"We had pictures of him on the wall. In England too. My mother had a fridge magnet. I found old postcards of him in uniform. On the back it said, 'Here's another for your collection.'"

"I guess he cast a long shadow. And so he should. After all they worked for him."

"Doing what?"

"Something in an area of expertise that was useful to him I imagine. He was hands-on. Possibly agronomy. That or engineering, very likely both. Scots were head-hunted for those." He spots the change in her expression. "I did a year of agronomy before I switched to PPE."

"Because of your ambition to be a commercial attaché. And why does any of this matter now?"

"They acquired property and influence that didn't disappear with the Habsburgs."

"Meaning what?"

"They could be players in the twentieth century."

"It's a big century. Which part?"

"World War II. More specifically post World War II."

"The aftermath."

"You could call it that."

"My great-aunt did."

"Was she here in Vienna at that time?" So he doesn't know about the stuff she thought he knew about. Stuff she does know about although she's no closer to understanding why any of it matters.

"She was. She was here in their house."

"Living in interesting times. What was she like, your aunt?"

"Fabulous."

"I mean, was she intelligent? Oh God. I mean . . ."

"I know what you mean. She was. Very. Look, I didn't catch your name yesterday."

He introduced himself at the café but she wasn't listening, she was tidying up the peasants and the geese.

"Martin. Martin Langley."

"Neat. CIA HQ."

"Old one. If we can return to the post-war period, and if you can sit through a short history lecture without feeling patronised we'll get to the point quicker. You'll know that Vienna was divided into four sectors by the occupying powers. Britain, American, France and Russia. With the war over, alliances were shifting. Russia was moving from its position as wartime ally to something less coherent, and prospects for peace in Europe very much depended on how it saw its role as its interests diverged from those of the . . . well what became known as The West."

"Not patronised, just impatient. The Cold War. Take it from there."

"OK, brute reality, things were grim. Hundreds of thousands of displaced people were living in encampments, trying to stay warm and fed, desperate for news of their families and their homes if these still existed. Other people, not necessarily criminal, perhaps just entrepreneurial, were making a living from that situation, and all of the occupying powers were trying to recruit reliable agents from that lot. Some, as you can imagine, were doubly recruited.

"British Field Security was looking for ways of tapping into the mind-set of its Russian neighbours. Given that they had been our allies we had few intelligence resources. The city was in ruins and rife with rumour and counter-rumour.

A Brit with local knowledge, fluent in German and passable in the other languages in the mix, also personable, clued up, reliable, and up for a name change and possibly a fluid identity, perhaps the most challenging prospect, was a gift from the gods."

The goulash soup arrives. "I believe we should give ourselves over to eating," he says and so they do that. Charlotte, with more to digest than soup, reconfigures her image of Central Europe, re-casts the peasants, and fills the landscape with encampments, people huddled around fires, flocks decimated to feed solders, geese hidden and kept for barter. It feels like something that happens here. Something that doesn't happen on an island.

The conversational lull seems to be over-extending. Martin tops up their wine glasses and leans forward. "Look, there isn't an end to this story, at least not one we know. There are holes in the record, in fact there is no written record. It's only recently that we have figured out what was happening. That's why we're looking at every avenue, every word of mouth, anecdote, bit of paper, so . . ."

He stops talking as a couple come into the restaurant. The waiter, chef, proprietor, perhaps all three, advances on them with the menu. They sniff the air and wave it aside. In English they order goulash soup. Charlotte says, "I don't believe he has anything else."

"You are surprisingly flippant after all I've told you."

"It's a defence mechanism. I've needed those."

"Have you indeed. I'm very interested in anything you can tell me about people in your family, in the wartime generations." She is about to explain that there are only previous generations and herself when his phone buzzes. He excuses himself and goes outside. The man in the apron approaches with the dessert menu but Martin returns looking stressed. "Look, something's come up. I have to go. Geoff's on his way, he'll walk you back to your hotel."

"I don't need anyone to walk me back."

"I think you do. I'll call for you tomorrow at eleven. We can do some sight-seeing and continue this. If you would bring the documents with you that would be helpful." Why that should be she is no closer to understanding and she is not about to find out as Geoff arrives and is introduced. He takes over the bill payment and they walk back to the hotel exchanging stilted pleasantries. He comes into the foyer with her and glances around.

"Just checking," he says and bids her goodnight.

In her room she takes the chocolate box from behind the radiator and sits down with it at the blue desk. The laughing girl on the lid meets her eye. It is Saskia, she's sure of that. What did she actually do, did she model, did she have a real job? It's a painting, not a photograph, perhaps she painted and sat for a fellow student. Her background was privileged, so perhaps she dabbled – art, music, dance, embroidery. She imagines her at the piano in the drawing room playing a Strauss waltz and junks the idea. She can't recall her ever touching a piano key. 'In the evenings we paint or play', this from the letters, or was it 'sew'? But then she was looking after her mother, Christina, and what does she know about her?

That she was up for an elopement. Saskia never married. Did she have relationships?

She smoked, she was clever, funny, deliberately oblique. The fault is her own, Charlotte thinks. She has shunted her too far back in time. In Britain women were building planes and flying them, parachuting into France to set up radio links. Could Vienna have still been stuck in its golden age?

Charles Merchant comes to mind, another person possibly landed with a name change. 'Same name,' he had said, a point that only someone who spent time with words would have picked up.

She puts the chocolate box in her bedside cabinet, unwraps the chocolate waiting on her pillow, eats it, cleans her teeth and succumbs to sleep.

Chapter Twelve

Late down to breakfast, only two tables still occupied and the buffet pillaged by carnivores, she picks up a plate and considers the nutritional prospects of the day ahead. The day ahead is unknowable. When you are in Vienna and the day ahead is unknowable and the Ottomans are at the gates you invent the croissant. Salutations to the croissant then, and there are two remaining in the basket while some Fruits of the Forest linger in a dark puddle at the bottom of the bowl. She takes both croissants, some plum jam, a slice of vanilla cake and the last of the fruit and a dollop of kefir and at the table declines coffee in favour of tea. Black tea or green? Or perhaps a fruit tea? Black. English Breakfast? Is there an alternative? There is not but it's important to challenge its arrogance.

She pours, drinks, eats and within fifteen minutes is back upstairs cleaning her teeth. The day seems mild, she decides against the coat and takes the chocolate box with the letters from her bedside cabinet. By ten fifty-five she is sitting in the foyer which is busy with people checking out and in. The Blue Danube is playing at around ten-minute intervals. When it has played for a third time and there is still no sign of Martin Langley she is not unduly anxious. The large padded envelope which held the chocolate box protrudes from her bag, the letters, meanwhile are under her mattress. The envelope to flag up her compliance and get them out of the hotel, the mattress because she is not yet ready to trust anyone.

Another coach from the stables of Castle Dracula is drawing up in the forecourt and a trio of giggling girls step down smoothing their hair and hoisting their bags into the foyer. Charlotte moves outside to widen her perspective. When the

Blue Danube strikes up again it's time to act. Call the embassy. Is he even at the embassy? It will not advance her peace of mind to find that the embassy have never heard of him.

The girls come back out to pay the coachman. He turns towards Charlotte and smiles encouragingly and she steps up into the carriage, perches on the edge of a seat which assumes a tendency to voluptuousness, then settled her bag and goes with the flow.

"Small tour?" the coachman suggests as the horses start to move and then they are off swaying and clattering, flying is what it feels like, with the horse airborne in front of them, surely headed for the rooftops. Free of the ground and the people plodding past down there, the detail of the buildings is at eye level. Perhaps the city was designed to be seen from a carriage. The view ahead is of the coachman's black cape and hat, his whip in silhouette. They are in another century, another empire, a borrowed personality, and when they pass the entrance to the Hofburg with a rank of coaches drawn up outside, there is for a moment nothing of the present in the landscape.

When the succession of streets becomes familiar she leans forward and tells the coachman that this is her journey's end. She steps down, adds what she hopes is a lavish tip in keeping with the borrowed personality and crosses towards the house in the expectation that someone – this time it's a man – will come out and hold the door for her.

There is music coming from behind one of the doors on the ground floor. Behind another a baby cries. On the first floor landing the door assigned to Markus Roschmann and as an afterthought Kaufmann S stands ajar, and from an open door further along the landing come voices, a man's and a woman's. She steps through the first door and walks forward along a threadbare oriental carpet over floorboards that do not creak towards tall double doors designed to allow the passage of a crinoline that are open enough to let a slice of sunlight fall slant-wise between them. She passes silently between them and the brilliant light from the floor-to-ceiling windows burns away the last remnants of caution as the drawing room in all its detail and entitlement opens around her.

The faded brocade of the wooden-armed chairs and sofas, the stuff they called Biedermeier, the curly table legs she always saw as buckling under the weight of the table top they were being asked to support. The patterns you could see in the wood of everything with a flat surface, always made out of fruit trees someone told her, cherry or walnut. The carpet with the secret maze, the piano, the tapestry with the hunting scene that filled most of one wall and beneath it the antique desk, perhaps the desk that had the small fire, all of this is reflected back to itself by the giant gilt-framed mirror. And under a tall scrolled table, partly obscured by a decorative hanging, is the doll's house. She drops her bag on a chair, scoops a cushion off a sofa and crouches in front of it. The key is in the lock. She turns it, the front swings open and there they are, the family who live there with their tiny oriental rugs, the dining chairs like those in the real house with their intricately carved backs arranged around a table set with a Meissen dinner service.

She closes its door, locks it, stands up and listens. She can still hear the muted voices from the other apartment so she crosses to the grand piano with its brocade stool and music open on the rest. On top of the dusty piano are photographs and the people in the photographs, caged up in their silver frames, send shock waves around the room. A teenage Saskia smiles up at a man, tall, slim, dark and undeniably handsome who smiles back down at her. Her father? Charlotte's great-grandfather? Why has she never seen a picture of him until now? And here is Franz Joseph, ruler of the Austro-Hungarian Empire and former employer of one or more of her ancestors, seated as usual in dress uniform and medals. And here he is again, surely, on an ice rink, skating. He and the man skating alongside him are laughing, laughing the way you do when you first put on a pair of skates, and yet again sitting on a grassy bank with three or four people and a picnic hamper. And on the wall is indeed the painting of Saskia in a street scene, the scene reproduced on the lid of the chocolate box. And as if to balance that a photograph of her, head angled to show the fall of hair here looking rather like a disguise, the characteristic cigarette in the long holder contrasted with the trousers she is wearing and the sardonic expression seeming to say that perhaps all this is cover.

In the corner is a glass-fronted cabinet displaying the dinner service they kept for when he dropped in for dinner. She is placing him at the table – would he sit at the top or as a guest halfway along where everyone could talk to him – when she senses that someone is in the house.

It's the silence. Although she didn't hear a door close the voices have stopped. She edges past the piano and steps behind the heavy fall of the curtain at the furthest corner. It smells of dust. She is possessed by an urge to look outside and sees the tops of peoples' heads in the street. He has come into the drawing room. The double doors, did she leave them further open? Would he remember? She did put the cushion back on the sofa, but had she displaced the photograph on the piano?

She can hear him breathing. Can he hear her? Best not to think about breathing. Although she can't see him she senses a heavy presence. He stands without moving waiting for the person who may or may not be in the room to betray his or her presence. And then she remembers her bag.

There is what feels like a pivotal moment not of her making in which he recognises or fails to recognise that he just saw a bag on a chair and then a phone rings and his footsteps move away over thick and then thin carpets, their sound changing as they reach a hard floor and the phone is answered in a deep voice almost simultaneous with the sound of a kettle being switched on. The voice, speaking in German, stops and starts to a background of a cupboard door opening and the clack of a cup on a work surface.

She steps out from behind the curtain and picks up her bag. If he noticed it its absence will totally spook him. She is now irredeemably sinister and feeling good with that when his voice grows louder and his steps move out onto the carpeted hall floor sending her back behind the curtain, clumsily this time leaving her a spy-hole. Still speaking he goes to the desk, takes a key ring from his pocket and unlocks it, folding down the writing flap and pushing aside a red folder to hunts through the pigeon holes at the back. He lays down the phone to scrutinise the document he has taken out, picks it up again and, talking continuously now, locks the desk, pockets the key ring and returns to the kitchen. The small silver key that glinted in the light from the desk lamp lit up a moment buried in the distant past. She goes to the doll's house, opens it and searches inside for the tiny linen cupboard. Here it is under the stairs with folded sheets and weighing them down, in plain sight when the cupboard door is open, a large silver key. "Our secret," Saskia told her when she saw her putting it in there. "They will search your lingerie drawer but they never look in your linen cupboard."

Markus Roschmann in the kitchen is talking angrily and the kettle is coming to the boil again. She unlocks the desk, picks up the red folder, puts it in her bag, re-locks the desk, and finding the front door still ajar leaves the apartment, the building and with a retrospective adrenalin rush the street.

Back at the hotel the receptionist hands her a message. Martin Langley, she assumes, with an apology and a re-scheduled meeting. But reading it as she starts up the stairs she sees Herr Strauss's letter heading and signature. Before she calls him back she checks under the mattress and puts the red folder alongside the letters. Herr Strauss has a surprise for her, a pleasant surprise he hopes. An old friend of Saskia's, a charming lady who is also a valued client, on hearing that Charlotte was in Vienna suggested he bring her over to her apartment in the afternoon. "She knew your dear aunt so well. She would love to talk to you about her." A meeting and a conversation, Charlotte confirms, that would give her great pleasure.

Viewing her small selection of charity shop tops she selects a pastel blouse with her mother's pearls. Herr Straus arrives in a grey velvet jacket and the glow of an adviser turned fixer. It was his idea to phone Frau Frühwirth to tell her Charlotte was in town. Frau Frühwirth, he explains as he drives, lives in the Landstrasse district not far outside the loop of the Ring, and is of an eminent family as of course was her aunt. As the architecture takes front stage again, stacking right and left in a creamy consistency that lightens it without taking the weight out of it, a never to be forgotten stage set for momentous events, Charlotte is trying to picture Saskia's dear friend – straight back, silver hair swept up, pendant earrings with amethysts echoing her lavender chiffon blouse, a small dog of some sort, a Pekinese or a Pomeranian, yapping at her feet against a backdrop of pastel silks, gilt chair legs and slippery cushions with a maid in uniform to open the door to them. A maid does indeed open the door, a tall girl, early twenties, wearing a white frilly apron over jeans and Doc Martins. "Hi," she says, "give me a moment will you," and she takes out half a cigarette, lights it, takes three or four quick puffs, extinguishes it against the sole of one boot and puts the rest back in her pocket. The accent is Essex. The room she shows them into is thoroughly disconcerting.

"Charlotte!" comes a voice from inside and they are led into a room that is distinctly avant-garde. The lady in the armchair, attempting to stand up while they all wave her down. "One has to try. Exercise and vanity. Mostly vanity. Do excuse me," she nods to a crutch beside her chair, "I fell off the ladder changing a light bulb."

Herr Strauss tut tuts. "For this you ask Camilla. You must not take risks."

"I told her that," says Camilla. "I always fucking tell her but she's a fucking war hero isn't she?"

"Sit here, Charlotte, where I can see you. Do sit down Willi, you can spare the time for a cup of Darjeeling. It was Sass who put me on to Darjeeling," she explains to Charlotte. "She was such a snob."

"Now Lydia," says Herr Strauss.

"She was English. The English are all snobs."

"Scottish," says Charlotte.

"Of course you're right. I'm told the Scots are never snobs. Forgive me, I like to tease her spirit who still visits me". She waves vaguely around the room giving Charlotte the chance to raise her eyes and take in the decor which dissolves instantly into the portrait of a male figure, starkers and splayed, above Frau Frühwirth's crisply scissored head. Camilla brings tea and cake and Herr Strauss and Frau Frühwirth start a long conversation in German which he breaks off to explain is of a business nature, then he sets down his cup and takes his leave, telling Charlotte there is an underground station nearby as well as a tram stop.

"I'll walk," she says and Camilla shows him out.

"Now," says Frau Frühwirth leaning forward and looking serious. "You and I can talk in peace about my dear friend who was not a snob but knew so much about absolutely everything that you had to put her down."

"Your English is cool."

"Cheltenham Ladies College. Is that cool? I remain in email contact with those classmates who are not gaga or dead. They refresh the idiom. I imagine you have a great many questions you would like to ask."

"Well," says Charlotte, narrowing her gaze to exclude the hovering pudenda, "the paintings?"

Frau Frühwirth twists in her chair and smiles. "My mother's. We have four Schieles. For a time Egon rented one of the rooms. When he was hard up he paid her with a painting. But you must want to ask me about Saskia. Or perhaps you prefer that I just tell you."

"I know nothing of her life really, I wouldn't know what to ask. Did she ever work? I mean at a job?"

This brings a hoot of laughter. "You could call it a job I suppose. She ran the house."

So, just a housewife after all. Not even that as there were

servants, at least for a time, to do the actual work. Her disappointment shows, for Frau Frühwirth interprets, "She ran the house and the people in it. Some of them anyway. Those who were placed there."

"Placed there? By whom?"

"Your British Security perhaps, or maybe something irregular. Official and irregular, or some group independent of them, they made it up on the spot so they could say it never happened. Just somebody's idea, maybe hers. She didn't tell me, I am not British and I was younger. Our friendship developed later."

"When was it that she did that, ran the house?"

"A little war, a little post-war. Mostly post-war. And of course always secretly."

"What sorts of people were placed there?"

"Both sorts, I think. I should say all sorts because of course they came from all those countries. It was a big house so it could be like many houses, people from different places maybe wanting, in the end, different things."

"You mean there might have been people not on the side of the West?"

"They were displaced. Perhaps they had a side, who knows? They were given a helping hand but maybe not a free hand. And of course there was watching and listening."

"But how did she get into this?"

"Her father, I think. She adored her father and of course he had to go out of her life with the chance that she never saw him again. I think that happened, that she didn't see him again."

"Why? Why did he have to go out of her life?"

"With the name-change. He was a very brave man."

"The name change? Her father changed his name?" Frau Frühwirth looks surprised.

"You don't know this?"

"What did he change it to?"

"Kaufmann."

There is snow falling, sleet swirling around and the war memorial with the granite soldier on top and Charlotte is reading the names. Kaufmann K, the solitary alien, and not an alien after all. A grandfather. Hers.

"My dear, I am afraid I have upset you. I am one of those people on those TV programmes who finds fathers and mothers who sometimes didn't want to be found and everyone cries. I am so sorry."

"Don't be sorry. Perhaps they told me. I expect they did tell me. Back then I didn't like to listen. But all our names were changed to Kaufmann."

"In case they came to check him out. He must not have a foreign family. And I think I may have spoken too much. Everything was secret. Perhaps it still is. I remember how it was, everyone spying on everyone else. There was so much cleaning up to be done afterwards, cleaning up and remembering to forget so that we could be normal again.

You narrowed your horizons and shut down your memory. I was just a child but I can't forget my mother's anxiety when the Russian soldiers went on the rampage. These were terrible times."

"The aftermath."

"That is one way of putting it."

"Saskia called it that in one of her letters. The letters she wrote to my grandmother, her sister. She wanted me to have them after she died. I don't know why."

"Ah. Then that's quite a responsibility she has left you. She gave me a hint of something of the sort some time ago. Something was troubling her. When I asked she said I couldn't help, I was no use. She said her whole family was no use, utterly hopeless in that regard. And then she said, 'maybe Charlotte.'"

"She said that? I don't suppose you have any idea what she meant by it?"

"She saw something of herself in you I think. She said you were a free spirit."

"She buried things. Physically I mean. In the cellar."

"My mother did that. Everyone did that. Austria may be full of buried things."

"It sounds too indiscreet for a letter. The letters were censored of course and somehow recovered after they were postmarked. People resorted to secret codes."

"Someone asked me about the letters. The word he used was documents."

"Oh? Who was that?"

"Someone from the embassy."

"Oh, which embassy was that?"

"The UK embassy here in Vienna."

"And how did you meet him?"

"He was tailing me." Her use of the word breaks the mannerly flow.

"Then that surely must mean this is serious."

"But what could be of interest so long after it was all over?"

"My dear it is never over. That much I do know. Here in Vienna we have spy exchanges. They say we are the world centre of spying. You must be careful. But you must go with your intuition as Saskia would have done."

"One other thing and then I'll leave you in peace. Who is Markus Roschmann?"

"That is a thing I have often asked myself. Who is Markus Roschmann?"

Chapter Thirteen

Half an identity is better than none, it gets you a car and lets you drive it, but it has fuck all to say about where you should be going and why. So he is simply heading south. The lure of the city is strong but there isn't going to be one of those anytime soon. Cities give you a break from skies and they sell the essentials. Phones, laptops, boxers, socks that are not hand-knitted.

He needs to check out land ownership in the Highlands. That was the story that brought him here and he can connect with the impulse and the intent, but not so far with the land. It's all around him, the land, owned or otherwise, streaming past without let-up on either side and he can't connect with it at all.

Is there land that is not owned? Just left lying from wherever this bit detached from another bit? Are there places that, if you do the research, don't show up in the records? Because, when you're here, it all seems as if it might be that way. Whatever was done to him back in that hotel seems to have zapped his business brain and left him exposed to the other side.

The road funnels south alongside a long narrow loch whose ragged bank reels past endlessly on his left. It is thanks to this road that he is able to proceed in a more or less southerly direction. The irritating absence of east-west roads, he has found, turns out to be a matter of geology. Those lochs along with the mountains that contain them are running the show.

Then there are the sheep. The dogged fertility of these verges throws up things that sheep, invariably single sheep, find attractive. Ater a glance around everything that's on offer they take a bite then chew it reflectively, perhaps running it past previously encountered bits of vegetation for toxicity and flavour, or perhaps thinking of something else altogether. They stand quite still, their four small feet planted on the crumbling tarmac and he respects them.

The road signs are unsettling. Deer with massive antlers are shown poised to leap out on bends. None has done that so far. There have been no other cars, bikes, tractors or pedestrians for a very long time and he begins to wonder why. Slow Animals and Children are now a potential hazard. The sign that warned of them was past before he could commit to memory the illustration. It's hard to see where they might come from, there have been no buildings since the start of this loch, but perhaps they inhabit a community somewhere up ahead round the next rocky outcrop. They may step out suddenly, small elfin creatures leading hedgehogs and tortoises, waddling ducks and three-legged cats and dogs. Where might they live? In a Broch. A Crannog or a Broch.

Where did the Picts live? Might they still be here? The Romans were so scared of them they built a wall. Two walls, by orders of two emperors after they successively failed to frighten them into passivity. And now the Celtic Supremacists. Is there nothing this part of the world will stop at to create its own agenda?

This road which he spotted and swung into in the hope that it would keep him out of the maw of the NC500 seems to be giving up on him. The loch is narrowing and the mountains that contain it are drawing together. There are puddles here now and drenched vegetation. He opens the window all the way and damp air and road spray surge in wiping the picture of the past hour or so clear off the slate. There has been a downpour but it has passed

He turns on the radio. Cybercrime continues to grow. A pundit says that in a rough divide of the population into those of liberal arts persuasion and those of a maths-science leaning the first think they are running the country, but the second know that they are. "Intellectual arrogance on the part of the first allows them to opt out of trying to keep up with technology and to see their failure to keep up as a generous nod to mere technicians. And arrogance it is. It is time they stepped up and took an interest."

Two cars are now catching up on him and he returns to road user mode just in time to stamp on the brakes behind a small red car which has pulled up before a sizable landslip. The cars behind him brake to a stop and when their engines are switched off the only sound is the rain and a bleak bird call, perhaps a curlew. The driver of the red car and his passenger are standing on the verge. He closes the window, pulls up the hood of the new jacket and joins them.

"I've phoned," the skinny boy in the cagoule tells him. "They're coming." His passenger throws her arms around him. Water squelches between them and diverts down the legs of their jeans. "Stop that," says the boy. "You're making it worse."

"I'm bloody perishing," says the girl.

"Get back in the car then."

The drivers of the following cars join them, each with a female passenger back in her front seat. They stand in a shifting cluster, hands in pockets, getting on top of things.

"*Who* are coming?" Adam asks. "Where are they coming from?"

"No idea. Cool with it though." A gale force gust tears along the loch and whips a few gallons of fresh water onto the road. They step over the ditch on the far side and move a few yards up the slope. Something huge lands on the loch's surface and takes off with a fish.

"Is that an osprey?" asks the man from the car behind Adam's. The accent is home counties.

"Don't ask me," says the boy, "I just live here."

"Possibly a sea eagle," says the man from the car behind that. "Did you notice its tail? If the tail was white it was probably a sea eagle." The holiday weekend, Adam reminds himself.

An alien sound comes from somewhere above and beyond and grows louder. They all look up. "Good God," says the third man. "It's a drone." It reaches where they are standing, hovers for a while, then leaves.

"Doing a reccy," says the skinny boy. "ASS."

"I beg your pardon?"

"ASS. Assess, Synchronise, Solve." The boy recites this in what is obviously a borrowed weighty tone.

"Really?" says the fourth man. "Where I'm from those bloody things are set to become the law-abiding citizens' TeePee. Target Practice. Tea Party if you prefer things in code."

"It's a courtesy." The boy is not about to hand over the floor. "He does it for free. Service to the community. His business is located here."

"Synchronised Solutions," says Adam. No one responds to that.

"So what are the options?" the third man wonders. "Back the way we came and join the NC500?"

"You'll be in and out of lay-bys all the way back," the boy tells him.

"I understood this road was unfrequented."

"You're not alone in that, it's on social media, plus it's a holiday weekend." They look where he is pointing and see two more cars have stopped.

"So what will happen?" the third man wonders.

"I dare say some local farmer will come along with his tractor," says the fourth man. "There's not so much. A few guys with spades could do it."

"You'll see," says the boy.

A sunbeam pierces the cloud layer and the scene is bathed in light. On the far side of the loch a red deer comes out from the trees and drinks. "Look at that," says the fourth man. A blast of Beyonce comes from the red car. The boy sighs.

"It is going to be a while though, isn't it," the third man insists.

"A snow plough would do it," the fourth man suggests. "I expect you need to have those handy up here."

"A snow plough would just shove it into the loch," the boy says. "Or into the ditch."

"True enough," says the third driver. "My thoughts exactly."

"That's them now," the boy says as the sound of machinery comes to them through the wind. From their slightly elevated position they can see some high-rise kit, emerald green in colour, approaching from the south jostling the lower branches of the trees. Then with an unfamiliar whirring sound the head and shoulders of this leviathan suck up the mass of soil and vegetation and feed it to somewhere in its rear quarters. In ten minutes the landslip has gone. The nozzle of something like a large hairdryer projects and turns the soil residue to dust which it blows to the side.

"Well I never," says the third driver.

"He's generally on top of it," the boy says and gets back into the red car. The music stops.

"Who's generally on top of it?" wonders the third driver.

"Who indeed," says Adam.

When he starts the engine the radio is still on its theme. "As long as the cyber creatives and mind guys are doing their own things there's competition, a diversity of thinking and outcome. Putting all the eggheads in one basket would not be good. There are rumours of someone already doing that – neuro-politics big time, possibly big pharma in there somewhere." Then it's over to Tomasz Schafernaker at the Weather Centre.

When he spots a petrol pump Adam brakes suddenly, raising an apologetic hand to those behind him. It's in the forecourt of a hotel. The clouds have lifted and the hotel's outdoor tables are busy, staff bringing out fresh seat cushions. There is a pleasing buzz of strangers connecting. He finds a space on the end of a table where three girls talking animatedly in a language he doesn't recognise nod a willingness to be joined, and when a girl wearing skinny trousers in one of the red tartans comes with the menu he orders roast lamb with roast root vegetables and rowan jelly. The girls continue talking and presently two men slot themselves in further down the table and ask for a rundown of the craft beers on offer. These sound like a snatch of the shipping forecast. With the arrival of their desserts the girls at the table look up and lower the linguistic drawbridge. Adam asks them where they're from. Norway, they tell him. He asks how long they're staying.

"Ah no," says the tallest one. "We do not stay. Only eat."

"You're touring then?"

"Not touring. Only cycling."

A girl with softer features and curly hair leans forward to interpret. "Touring is round and round," she explains. "We go straight."

"Due straight? This is the most relentless round and round slice of territory I've ever seen. When you're not going round a mountain or a loch you're going round a sheep. You can see why the Romans gave up."

"The Romans were in Scotland?" Exclaims the third girl. "I do not know this."

"South and east I believe. But I'm no expert. Where did your straight journey start from?"

"John o' Groats," says the tall girl. "We go John o' Groats to Land's End."

"I see. May I ask why?"

This seems to be taking things too far for a chance meeting. He often finds that, he believes. His curiosity has no end whereas for the casually met person it often has no beginning.

"Because we like to do this," explains the girl with the curly hair. The girl in the tartan trousers brings his lamb and he bites back the follow-up why.

"We cycle in many countries," says the third girl. "For instance Finland. Also Lithuania, Latvia and Estonia. Next year we do Iceland."

"So you were breaking out when you came to do Scotland."

"Scotland is Scandinavian," says the tall girl. "I believe that is so. The names tell this. Also the blood is sometimes common. The accent I thought would be easy for us to understand but I have not found it so. There must be other influences."

"That is true," the curly-haired girl agrees.

"Just you wait till you get to Glasgow," chips in one of the beer drinkers.

"It changes so much? We thought only in England."

"Nah," says another beer drinker, leaning forward to launch his own thesis,

an exit cue Adam is quick to take, freeing him to deal with the lamb and the bigger picture.

He is heading to a city to find out about land ownership in the country. More specifically to buy a laptop with which to do that. His coffee arrives and brings an edgy scent to the clean air, a reminder of the working environment, the inquiring mind's essentials. And perhaps a reminder, if he can make himself stand back, of how all this began. Like most things, probably in a pub. A rumour, something glimpsed or something overheard. He is trying to recreate that, a snatch of conversation, a repetition, surely, of what brought him north in the first place, when he has a sudden sense of foreboding.

Finding this oppressive he switches to the first thing he does remember, his awakening in the hotel bedroom. He tried to measure time loss by the stubble on his chin and by the body temperature of a dead woman. He has little memory of the stubble. Light, he thinks. And of the time it takes a human body to cool after death he has absolutely no idea. He is, after all, of the liberal arts persuasion.

The Vikings stand up and reach for their helmets. They wish him happy touring, and indeed going round and round is just what he has been doing. They unlock their amazing bikes from the rack under a tree and the curly haired girl turns to give him a wave before they vanish round a bend, their place immediately taken by a family of four, the parents noticeably flushed and their daughters and the dog wild of hair and eye. They settle on the benches around Adam and the older girl turns to him with the urgency of one bearing world-class news.

"We saw a wolf," she says and picks up the immediacy of his response. He did not commit the ultimate sin of glancing at her parents for confirmation. "Mrs White said there are no wolves in Scotland but there is at least one. Daddy's got it on his phone."

"Where was this?"

"In the bushes where we stopped for Abby to do a pee. It looked at us. It didn't run away."

"For once Holly is not exaggerating," says Holly's father. "It was not a fox."

"Should we tell someone?" Holly's mother wonders, leaning towards Adam. "Do you live here? Do you know who we should phone?"

"The police," says a male voice from the table behind Adam. He turns and sees a thick-set man with greying hair wearing business-like dungarees. "It's a police matter. It's time they got involved. It's Callum Mclean you want. I'll call him for you."

"Goodness," says Holly's mum. "Might it involve a court case? We're from Shropshire. We'd find it hard to take time off."

"He'd maybe just want a statement from you." He takes out his phone and taps a number. "Rhona, it's Jim, is Callum about? Hi Callum, I'm at the Treshnish. There's a family here up from the south who say they've just seen another wolf. Hang on. I'll ask. How far away from here would you say it was?"

"Maybe four or five miles."

"North or south?"

"South."

"The gentleman says maybe four or five miles south. Hang on. Callum says he'll be here in half an hour. He wants to know if you'll be here to give a statement. Aye, they'll be here. Oh and Callum, he's got it on his phone. That'll screw the bastard this time. Apologies for the language," he says ending the call. "This is a great favour you'll be doing us."

"Will they shoot the wolf?" asks Holly as Adam turns back to the table. "I don't want them to shoot the wolf. Daddy, delete the wolf on your phone."

"I'm sure they won't shoot it, Holly. Perhaps they'll take it to a zoo."

"I don't want it to go to a zoo."

"I do." Everyone looks at the little sister.

"It wouldn't be happy in a zoo, Abby."

"I don't want it to be happy."

"Then you don't love animals."

"I do so love animals. I don't love wolves that come out of the bushes when people are peeing."

"Thank you Mr . . ." Holly's daddy calls across the tables.

"Jim."

"Brian. Brian Fielding. This is my wife Judith."

"Charles," says Adam. "Charles Merchant." Just in time he remembered he was using the credit card.

"How do you do," says Holly. "I'm Holly Fielding and this is my sister Abby.

Will they shoot it with a tranquiliser dart? I don't mind if they shoot it with a tranquiliser dart."

"I'm sure the police officer will know what to do when he comes Holly. Now let's have a look at this menu."

"I wouldn't be too sure of that," says an imperious female voice from somewhere behind. There is a rumble of assent. "How would you have felt about a lynx?"

"A lynx?" says Mrs Fielding. "I have really no idea. I've never seen a lynx. Why do you ask?"

"Because we're hearing that he has lynxes lined up too."

Enough already with the lynxes. Adam gets to his feet and excuses himself as the woman behind him starts to explain. "Re-wilding. He's obsessed with re-wilding. He won't stop till someone gets killed."

"Or the police man up and get involved."

At the reception desk he asks if they have a single room for the night. They do. It will be ready in half an hour. He uses the

Charles Merchant credit card to pay for his lunch and walks outside continuing round to the back of the hotel which is in fact the front, the former front of a substantial house with tall windows and a portico-ed entrance up a short flight of steps. The windows look out onto another loch, a small one with a rowing boat tied up at the foot of another flight of steps. He walks back and forward on the grassy bank placing himself and the hotel in its wider setting, essentially a hollow between ranges of hills that are stacked in decreasing heights until they reach this low-lying fertile spot, a breathing space between two ranges accessed by two glens. A staging post. Did stage coaches operate this far north? Surely not. They would have had horses of their own, or ponies. And farm carts, some of them. Anyway, enough to go round.

He has not offered up his own wolf story. If they questioned him about it he would be back in the madness of the lost identity, the dead woman and the bomb. He walks back round the building, waylays the girl in the tartan trousers, orders a pint of something local and carries it to one of the now vacated tables. And the pint in his hand and the relaxed gathering of strangers out of doors stirs something that is pleasant, agreeable, interesting and which is widening into a context.

Chapter Fourteen

It was at a table much like this in a pub garden by the Thames on a crisp sunny day in late autumn that his thoughts first turned north. A Sunday lunchtime fluctuating fixture with Quentin, long-time friend, now in PR. Quentin had brought along his son Jeremy, a third-year astrophysicist at Keele. Quentin's *Sunday Times* lay folded on the table and Jeremy scanned it while they talked.

"Holy shit," he said suddenly. "That's the guy." He was looking at a picture of people at a charity auction where someone had just bid a six-figure sum for a dinner date with the star of a drama series. The face he recognised was in the crowd, a lean handsome face with a smooth dark fall of hair, from comparison with those around him a man of less than average height.

"Who is he?" Quentin asked.

"The guy I told you about. The one who took over the shoot last year but didn't make an appearance till this year. Folk around the village near the estate thought he was lying low. The new owner."

Quentin explained that Jeremy had a regular holiday job grouse beating on an estate in the Highlands. Fresh air, people-watching and sizeable tips. Quentin had got no further when a rather striking woman with a pronounced French accent, half of a couple sharing their table, leaned across and said, "Excuse me, I couldn't help hearing and so I have to ask, I am anxious you understand, you say you have a job *beating* grouse? Why is this?"

"Please excuse my wife," the husband said. "She runs a wild animal charity. If you wave a wasp away from your glass she will tell you it is a redundant male wasp who deserves your compassion and some of your drink."

Jeremy explained that he was not employed to beat the grouse, only their cover, the undergrowth that sheltered them. Why, she wanted to know, could they not be left in peace? Were they such a threat to the environment that they had to be exterminated? They were game birds, Jeremy explained, bred for the purpose. It was their karma to be shot.

"They look after these birds only to shoot them? This must be stopped. I shall look into it."

Jeremy told her that grouse shooting was a staple of the Highland economy, an important source of income for the estates and of employment for people in remote areas of the countryside. People from many countries were prepared to pay large sums of money for the privilege of shooting them.

She shook her head and squared her shoulders. To divert her, her husband weighed in with a question. "What is the diet of these birds in this remote place? What do they eat?"

"Heather," said Jeremy. "Heather and pine needles."

"Hah!" The husband roared with delight and slapped his wife's shoulder. "I knew it. The English sense of humour. They were teasing you, my dear."

Later, when the French couple had gone, they returned to the subject of the new estate owner. "Tell Adam," Quentin said, and Jeremy explained that this was his third season working on the estate, but this time it was in the process of changing hands. The long-time laird whose family estate it had been for generations was in the Caribbean and the prospective new owner was renting it for the season. It was he whom Jeremy thought he recognised in the crowd.

"Where is he from?" Adam asked.

"Hard to say. Not the UK but an English public-school accent on top of another. Not the States or Australia, not France, Spain, Italy, Holland or Germany. Elsewhere is the best I can do. His name was Theo. Everyone called him that and we were told to as well."

"And the shooters?"

"Guns. That's what they call them."

"The guns then, what were they like?"

"Scary."

"Scary inept or scary dead-shot?"

"Scary ept . . ." here he had left the thought trailing while he consulted his memory and in his troubled expression fired Adam's curiosity.

"Jeremy?" Quentin prompted.

"Sorry. Back on the moors with those people . . ."

"By 'ept' you meant?"

"Been there, done that, didn't buy the T-shirt."

"Where were they from then, these guns that kill without human involvement?"

"Couple of oligarchs or something of the sort. Trio from the Emirates I think, maybe north of that. The Stans, the Caucasus, that sort of place. I don't know really. They were not inclined to chat."

"So what would be a normal set-up?"

"Retail magnates, Tory peers, Labour peer, sports stars, Yanks . . . people with money but otherwise normal. They came in bunches as often as not."

"So these were not a bunch?"

"From the sizing up that was going on, no. No overt signs of hedonism, easy on the single malt, easy on the food which was fabulous. No problem there, all the more for us. No excesses I could see unless you count an excess of not relaxing."

"Who does the cooking?"

"The usual house staff were there, the head gamekeeper and the ghillies. Though the oligarchs brought their own chef."

"Why would they do that?"

"For precautionary reasons I'd guess."

"A load of laughs it sounds like." Adam was cooling it now, signalling a flagging interest to cover the totality of his engagement. "How were they on the actual shooting?"

"Quick learners. I don't think any of them had seen a grouse before. They looked surprised when they saw what the dogs were bringing back."

"What did they think they were shooting?"

"Duck? Clay pigeons? I have no idea. In the end I wasn't there that long. Their appetite for shooting had reached its limit. They paid us off, paid us for the full season but the guests were all staying on. The had other fish to fry."

"Those being?"

"Intel real and fake, mind bending, practice and use of. A lot of hard tech. They had professionals lined up who were expected imminently. That's when they became keen for us to leave. The guns were the customers. I got the idea they were setting up some sort of centre of excellence. It was notionally under wraps but I picked up a few chapter headings."

"How did you do that?"

"Nasty habit of listening when I know I'm not supposed to. But basically us hired hands were assumed to be thickos."

Back home that evening, a home that remains a total blank in his memory, a place that, sitting here amid glens and mountains, is a sort of trig point rather than a place with bookshelves and armchairs, he unfolded his own copy of the *Sunday Times*. The face in the crowd that Jeremy had spotted seemed tantalisingly familiar, the face of a man who, when out and about, has no stake in being recognised. In character with that, Jeremy had not remembered or had not known his name.

The wind has dropped and the sun picked up. He has no plans. He seems to be on holiday. He should go for a walk. He lays down his glass, still half full and goes to the reception desk to ask about his room. It's ready. He goes out to the car, now one of only three parked there, and brings in his luggage, the canvas bag he was given by the eventually pliant lady in the shop on the cliff top containing the heathery grooming accoutrements, the tartan poster, the paperback with the castle on the cover and his suit jacket. These he deploys around his first-floor room which has a window overlooking the small loch. He feels absurdly happy. He has a place of his own and now he is furnishing it, the simplest of human pleasures. He hangs the suit jacket on the suit hanger in the wardrobe, arranges the toiletries on a shelf in the ensuite and lays the rolled poster and the paperback on the bedside table. Then he goes back outside, finishes the beer, and takes the road south, the road the Norwegian girls took that leads ultimately to Land's End.

The road is well surfaced, no longer single track, lightly wooded on either side with rowan and birch. The leaves have not yet fully unfurled and their near translucence filters the sunlight between the slender trunks on his right while to the left the loch glimmers between the trees. On both sides there is undergrowth, grouse habitat if this were a shooting estate.

How agreeable would a wolf find it to live here? There are rabbits, no need to go in search of sheep. They would though. A scent in the air, a tingle down the spine, a race memory of teeth tearing through wool, the challenge of a head higher than yours, a mass worth bringing down, even without the joy of the chase. The need to be nomadic, to sniff the horizon, to second-guess. And would this woodland be agreeable for people to walk in or walk beside if wolves might be watching them? He knows the answer to that.

Were there bears here too? Lynx? Boar? Such things live on in Europe, in the forests and in the folklore, and where they have left their possibility will linger. With wolves and forests and folklore come peasants. That was another thing Jeremy said – the guns from, he thought, Eastern Europe or Western Asia were disconcerted by countryside without peasants.

If there were bears here they could catch salmon. They do that in Alaska, scooping them from waterfalls with paws like spoons. Could they fish in the loch? There will be trout. Salmon need the pull of a current, they need to stay on the move. Boar might be happy rooting through woodland. But would a thing with a tusk pass lightly among children picking blackberries, and how would they be with dogs? And might not lynxes kill the last of the wildcats?

Wolves and bears and peasants belong in land without end, in the immensity of middle Europe where people and animals flow east to west across borders drawn in the air and to look over your eastern shoulder may be prudent. The sea changes everything. On an island you forget that life is intrinsically dangerous. The sea has washed away the instinct.

He is walking on the tarmac, stepping into the verge whenever he hears the approach of a car and after what seems like half an hour – the shop on the cliff-top did not sell watches – he hears the distant sound of voices. In the absence of all but notional people his senses have sharpened. He can feel the north coast at his back, a straight line, finite. As something passes through the undergrowth to his right, a silent shadow moving ahead of the voices, there is a sense of mutual awareness and respect.

The voices grow louder, the trees rustle and Jim who called the police comes out of a thicket with Callum in uniform coming behind.

"Did you see it?" Jim calls.

"See what?"

"The wolf."

"No." This seems to give them the excuse to stop. They are out of breath and a following pack that includes the Fielding family and the Glasgow craft beer drinkers comes out onto the road plucking leaves and burrs from their hair and clothes.

Holly Fielding comes over and says confidentially, "Everybody saw it. Now they all believe us."

"OK folks," says Callum. "Game over. If you would all be good enough to retrieve your vehicles from those lay-bys before they cause an incident I think we can put the rumours of the non-existence of a wolf to rest."

A voice in the crowd mutters, "I told you it would attract the tourists." Another voice says, "Hardly what Theo had in mind."

Theo. The name overheard from the men in the hotel bedroom next to his, Theo who knew nothing of agronomy and everything there was to know about exceptionalism. Theo who the son of the man in the cottage whose breakfast he stole asked him to tell his father to cool it with. The man in the adjoining hotel room and, like a long-delayed echo, from Quentin's son Jeremy, the disaffected grouse beater. He watches the small crowd pass in twos and threes but whoever was speaking has fallen silent. The name and its echo persist as echoes do. He has met Theo and may be about to meet him again.

In his extremely pleasant room with a view of an angler setting up on the bank of the loch he takes off the blue cashmere sweater, folds it and puts it in a drawer, reclaiming his urban self. Straightening he catches a glimpse of himself in the mirror that rocks him back on his heels, and takes him to another hotel bedroom where the man in the mirror in a shirt and suit pants was new to him. His hand goes to his chin. He is in need of a shave, he has a bathroom full of heathery products and is once again passing as Charles Merchant. How much has really changed?

He showers, shaves, washes his hair and, liberally heather-scented, puts on the suit jacket and goes downstairs to the dining room where the girl in the tartan trousers, now in a black dress, seats him at a table for two alongside a wall. Alongside a wall would not be his choice. It's a direct challenge to his identity, the wall at his back is non-negotiable. He de-stresses. The need for anonymity is surely still as strong and his ever expanding personality had better not forget it.

The dining room is busy, irritatingly so. He declines desert and coffee, the irrelevance of the people around him is making him question his decision to stay. The residents' lounge similarly lacks appeal. He searches out the public bar whose door opens onto a blast of talk and laughter, and at the bar orders a single malt. He stays at the bar, for which he is now over-dressed, compensating with an approachable expression and listening in for some snatch of conversation that may throw him a cue to join in. Along the bar they are talking of a film shoot somewhere nearby. One of the group is an extra, he gathers, explaining the hair and the beard.

"Have they got a Hector yet?" someone asks the extra.

"Ewan's going for a real actor for that. Can't be doing with our accents. Says we don't take it seriously."

"Is this – forgive me for interrupting, I couldn't help overhearing – is this the Hector of Farr film project?" They shift around to include him in the group.

"Do you know Ewan then?"

"I do indeed. I was at his place only the other day when he was talking about it. Where are they filming?"

"Around the estate. Fergus here is a warrior."

"Warrior or Sceptic. Maybe both."

"You have a speaking part then?"

The idea provokes howls of laughter "He does it with his eyes," one of them says. "Show the man your sceptic look Fergie."

Fergus, who is wearing a pink GNR T-shirt, hands his pint to one of his pals, draws himself up to full height, squares his shoulders, looks Adam in the eye and starts a contortion of his face that moves through surprise and outrage to end in a pout. Everyone falls about laughing. Someone comes from behind the bar and mops up the beer spills on the floor.

Adam orders a round for his new friends. He will go along to watch the filming and reacquaint himself with Ewan, with whom he must remember to be Adam, a guy who has twice walked out on him. To avoid recognition, hence a link to the hotel and the body, by the conference people, whom he will henceforth call The Farr Centre, he will comb his hair forward and wear the green parka.

Someone further along the bar calls for silence, pointing to the TV set above the gantry. In an extraordinary array of fancy dress there they are, The Farr Centre, the lady in the cape and the Celtic cross and the man with the ginger beard whom the reporter is questioning. "You mean you managed to lose it, the original calf-bound volume of prophecies your movement is founded on?"

Adam's hand goes to his jacket pocket. No book is there.

"We did. And now it has come back to us."

"How did that happen?"

"One of the ghillies found it in clump of heather by the edge of a burn. He contacted us today through Mr Cameron-Gunn." He holds up the book that lived for a while in the jacket he is again wearing.

"Can I ask how you came to lose it?"

"Just before our conference was so dramatically interrupted by the explosive device, a gentleman in the audience, a stranger to us, who had found his way to our gathering by means only he can know had for that reason been passed the volume. We felt there was some significance in his being there. He was holding it when the fire alarm went off and we were ushered out of the building. At that moment snow began to fall, extraordinary for this time of year. One moment he was there with the snow swirling around him, the next he vanished. But the book came back to us."

The reporter says, "You present yourselves as apolitical environmentalists and small 'n' nationalists only concerned with maintaining the integrity of the Highlands as a unique and pristine environment and in preventing exploitation... exploitation of what?"

"Of our wind and our waves."

"What do you say to the charge that you are politically naive and open to manipulation by certain landed interests?"

"I say that it is those critics who are politically naive. There is some argument about the interpretation of the prophecies but it is clear that he was referring to the flow country and the peat country and the mountains of the Caledonian Orogeny as well as remnants of the ancient Caledonian Forest in his warnings. There have been attempts to drain the wetlands to plant forests for the benefit of investors in the south and we fear that the incomparable power of our winds and our waves may be harnessed for the benefit of industry in the south."

The drinks he ordered are on the bar. He gives his name, Charles Merchant, and asks the barman to put it on his room bill. He is now a character in their mythology.

"Slange," his new friends say. "Slange," he replies. It's spelt slainte, something he knows from his life in the real world. As they start to talk about making the national news he is once again working on how to keep out of it. Then the girl in her green dress swims up from where he has buried her and hangs there, floating at the extremity of his line of vision, staying there as he finishes his drink and moving ahead of him as he takes his leave of the company and heads back upstairs. He has given little thought to her. Little if any compassion. She was very young. And something connects them. He owes it to her to find out what that is.

The radio in his room has the late headlines, mainly extreme weather events. As he reaches out to turn it off he hears, "A toxicologist's report on the young woman found dead in a remote area of the Highlands has been unable to identify the drug that caused her death. It is thought to be of a series designed to distort memory being developed in an illegal laboratory somewhere in Eastern Europe for counter-intelligence and election rigging purposes as well as industrial sabotage. 'Not something you can cook up at home' a spokesman said. The identity of the woman has yet to be established. Her identity might go some way towards pinpointing a location in Scotland where it might have been accidentally ingested or injected. A recent death in Vienna is believed to be attributable to the same drug."

Chapter Fifteen

Last night's disagreeable dinner table is perfectly acceptable for breakfast. It has narcissus in an opaline vase and, propped against that, a flyer for a castle in the area, open to the public. It is not the one.

Last night as he turned in, starkers again – the cliff shop had T-shirts, he should have bought one – he picked up the paperback with the castle on the cover. Skimming it, he thought, would quieten his brain enough to let him get some sleep. Instead he found familiarity flickering in the back of his brain, flashes of recognition along with a memory of repetitive trudging, long walks up wooded drives from the lay-bys he turned into, the strongest impression of that being dogged repetition. The colour plates and tales of clan warfare secondary to the sense of being there.

Two of the castles illustrated flashed a memory of being admitted. Steep stone staircases leading to massive fortified doors. The first brought a member of the household staff to the door who invited him into the carpeted interior to explain that the family were away from home. The second brought an actual family member and led to a pleasant chat with a clan chieftain in an antler-free study off the drawing room. He apologised for his unheralded visit and explained that he was in the area checking out the most dramatic castles prior, were he agreeable, to a formal visit he hoped to make for the book he was researching on inhabited castles of the Scottish Highlands. With this visit as reference he approached the next, a ferocious fortified keep with languid English-influenced extensions, clearly photographed for the paperback while still in the hands of its previous owner, an owner by inheritances.

He had tried to talk himself in from a gatehouse that was a faux-baronial gun turret overlooking the approach to its impenetrable gate with close circuit cameras angled in all directions. He answered the voice that challenged him electronically from the distant national monument with an apology for the unannounced arrival due to his failure to find a phone number for the castle which he hoped to feature in his forthcoming book. The voice said that would not be possible. He launched into the longer spiel but soon realized there was no one listening. The cameras swivelled to watch him leave and confirmed him in his plan to reinvent himself as an aspirant insider, a customer for the specialist services. He laid down the paperback and turned off the light but sleep was off the menu. By the time the sun rose over the mountains across the loch his pulse had slowed and he had turned another page in the chapter of his missing days and nights.

The girl in the tartan trousers comes to take his order. He had planned to surprise her by identifying her tartan – from the poster he thought MacLean of Duart – but today she has switched her allegiance to a different clan and with it a different colour palette, this one with green predominant. Perhaps a sept. Septs seem a big thing with clans. He orders poached finnan haddock with a poached egg and is attacking it with the gluttony of the sleep-deprived when the Fielding family arrive at the adjoining table and greet him as an old friend.

"I'm putting you in my essay," Holly tells him.

"Are you indeed. What is the title of your essay?"

"The Wolf in our Midst."

"An appropriately enigmatic title. Where do I come in?"

"You were the first person I told and you believed me."

"I certainly did. Does it happen often that people don't believe you?"

"Mrs White won't believe me when she reads about it."

"It's lucky you have that picture on your father's phone. You can let her see that."

"I can. I think I'll wait till she reads my essay and doesn't believe me before I show it to her. We didn't have a picture of the parakeet."

"You saw a parakeet?"

"In a tree in our garden. I expect it had escaped from somebody's house. Daddy was at the office and Mummy had let her battery run out again."

"Ah."

"To be fair a wolf is more unexpected than a parakeet."

"That's true. So you won't be too hard on Mrs White then?"

"I expect I should try to see the wolf from her point of view."

The girl formerly in red tartan trousers, brings them plates of grilled kippers and when they've worked their way through those and Adam has consumed the last of his toast Brian Fielding asks if he'd like to join them. He would.

They ask him if he is on holiday. He weighs up the options for a man in charcoal knife-edge suit pants holidaying alone and they are not appealing. Without climbing boots or binoculars or a fishing rod or a treatise on Hutton's Unconformity he would seem odd. Odd or sad.

"I'm writing about the Highlands."

"Really? Writing a book?"

He signals to the girl now in green tartan trousers for a top-up of his coffee while he summons up the pile of books or virtual volumes on geology, agronomy and anthropology he would have had to digest before heading up the M1 with a satnav set for somewhere that the bossy carping voice would scold him for improvising his way to. "Nothing so demanding. An article for a magazine."

"Do you know anything about the filming that's going on? Something historic I gather."

"Notionally historic might be the way to see it." Wilfully historic is how he would put it. "It's rather a modest private project I think, thought up by a local land-owner to attract the sort of tourists who are into Highland mysticism. It's based on a medieval seer who may or may not have existed."

"What's a seer?" Holly wants to know.

"Someone who sees into the future."

"That's impossible."

"Why do you say that?"

"Because the future hasn't happened yet."

"Ah. You're a sceptic."

"What's a sceptic?"

"Someone who tends not to believe in unlikely things. Like Mrs White."

"I am not like Mrs White."

"Being a sceptic about seeing into the future is an OK thing to be. I don't believe in him either. Or not his prophecies. I'm sorry I brought Mrs White into it. But there are people who want to believe in things that other people are sceptical about. Maybe he has predicted things they want to come true. I've only heard of a few of his predictions."

"For instance?" Judith Fielding says.

"A mighty chasm is to open in the sea between the British Isles and mainland Europe."

"Ah. Brexit."

"Mostly they're environmental things. And a great plague."

"Ah. His followers must feel vindicated. But there's always a plague. Whoever is writing these things will be having the time of his life."

Her husband shakes his head. "Whoever is writing these things will be having a visit from MI5."

"Do you know exactly where the filming is taking place? It might be fun to watch. Do you think that would be allowed?"

"Given that the laird who is behind it is aiming for maximum publicity I'm sure they won't be turning people away. It won't be a coincidence that he scheduled it for a holiday weekend. I should be able to direct you. I have visited the estate." Though not of course by the conventional route.

"Were you thinking of watching it yourself? If so perhaps we could go together."

The green parka and the Fielding family. No more skulking. "Let's do that."

Half an hour later the Fieldings' Volvo with Adam sporadically navigating turns off the main road and crunches along an unmetalled track under trees. The track runs alongside a burn and continues for some time with occasional digressions round vast puddles that reflect the trees and the sky. When it turns away from the burn and breaks out of the trees there is a barrier with an arrow pointing left to where a great many vehicles of different types are parked before a high wall. Spectators are clearly expected. A marshal indicates where they should park. Behind him a wooden board nailed to a tree has a rather beautifully painted image of a tall bearded long-haired man in robes holding a staff in one hand and a scroll in the other. Beneath that in stylish capitals it says

HISTORIC DUNCHATTAN ESTATE
HOME OF HECTOR OF FARR

"I thought Farr was on the north coast," says Brain Fielding.
"It is. I imagine the suggestion is that he was born on the coast but generally inhabited a wider stretch of the landscape. Perhaps he was employed by the estate. Perhaps by an ancestor of the laird Ewan Cameron-Gunn if they go back that far."
"I don't think he would like to be tied down," says Holly. "It's in his name.
Far and few, few and far are the lands where the Jumblies live."
Beyond the tree with the board the house comes into view, from this distance, impressive. Not a castle but an early laird's house with additions. On his previous visit, he came from the opposite direction and in the company of people, saviours or jailers, who had picked him up in the glen some hours after he climbed out the window of the man with the gun, a man

who had reported his presence to someone looking for him. "He's here." Nothing if not definitive. Someone was looking for him. The Wolf Man? Or some still unidentified other who operates in a corner of his brain, someone of less than average height with the perfect but fathomless features of an actor, the face in the crowd in the *Sunday Times* photograph, the face of a man possibly answering to Theo. Whether he has woven him out of straw or chipped him out of immutable granite, this is the man who is looking for him and who must now become the hunted.

In the back of the jeep seated between two guys of the sort you didn't argue with he had Ewan lined up as the Wolf Man. But Ewan had known him as Adam which pointed to an acquaintance pre-dating the invention of the tiresome Charles. Of the wolf epidemic Mitch Carruthers had said, "it's not Ewan, it's the other bastard," then totally clammed up in the face of further questioning. What could make a man of his calibre feel and try to hide such patent fear?

As they approach the house people in robes, children among them, are milling about in front of the most dramatic part of the façade along with cameras and girls with clipboards.

"Can I be a child actor?" Abby asks. "I've always wanted to be a child actor."

"You know my views on child actors," says her mother.

"She always talks that way," Holly confides to Adam. "As if she was about forty-two. She's only five."

"That's enough Holly," Judith says.

"Do you know the laird then?" Brian asks.

"Slightly."

One of the girls with the clipboards approaches and directs them to a small rustic bridge that spans the burn. On the other side the ground rises quite steeply and a number of people, upwards of fifty, short of a hundred, have gathered there to watch the action. The mood is festive and in the absence of information they have begun to toss in suggestions and write their own script.

"Why aren't they wearing kilts?" someone asks. "I should have thought they'd all be in kilts. The men anyway."

"Kilts would not be authentic." This in an authoritative Scots voice.

"Perhaps the kilt had not been invented by . . . whenever this is supposed to be," suggests a woman. The man with her says, "Does anyone know when kilts were invented?"

"I don't believe invented is the correct term. No one sat down at a drawing board to design those things."

A man with an American accent wearing a Stetson asks, "Does anyone know when tartan was invented?" It seems no one does.

"I have to say that's a bit of a disappointment to me."

"It wasn't invented," someone tells him. "It happened."

"My great-great-grandfather Alexander MacKay arrived in North Carolina in eighteen forty-six and he was certainly wearing a kilt. We have documentary evidence."

"Perhaps in those days they wore tweed," says an English-accented woman's voice. "Tweed doesn't drape." Another Home Counties accent. "That's an absurd suggestion."

"But is draping necessarily authentic? Does it feature in the records?"

"When was tweed invented?"

"Not until the eighteenth century," says the authoritative Scot.

"Tartan drapes. You can get a pashmina in it."

"Tartan is not a fabric. It's a pattern."

"It's a hell of a lot of patterns. I went into one of those kilt places in Edinburgh to ask about a kilt. I'm a MacRae on my mother's side. I wasn't that committed, it was more out of curiosity. I thought the guy would show me a sample. It turns out there's a choice. There's ancient and modern and weathered and dress and hunting. What's that all about?"

"Know what you mean, pal." The Glasgow craft beer drinkers are in the crowd.

"You're Scottish. Do you wear kilts?"

"Sure. Weddings, funerals and the Six Nations."

"Same kilt?"

"Only got the one."

"So why all the optional schmutter?"

"I'm on your side, pal. Bad for the image. Guy goes 'Fancy a bit o' huntin', Donnie?' Donnie goes 'Aye, ok. Hang on till I change my kilt.'"

"Tweed was the Hi-Tech of its day."

"Nobody's going to argue with you there. My grandpa lived and died in it."

"If they wore robes they would have to be made of wool or linen. Cotton hadn't been invented."

"I guess whoever's on wardrobe detail would be going for a scholarly look. Scholars wore robes. I guess Hector was a scholar."

"Can we assume he wrote down the prophecies himself?" Adam is startled to hear his own voice. "Someone else might have done that. The clan chieftain maybe."

"When were the clans invented?"

"Scottish literacy dates from the early centuries. It is not impossible that the man, who I believe is unlikely to have existed, could write."

"Which early century?" asks the man in the Stetson.

"There were three universities in Scotland in the fifteenth century. After the Reformation it was decreed that there should be a school in every parish."

"My great-great-grandfather was literate when he landed in North Carolina. He found work right away as a clerk keeping records."

There is movement in the crowd, some new arrivals from the car park and a couple from among the cameras now crossing the bridge. They are greeted by several in the crowd and some from further up the slope come down to talk to them. Then the couple start to make their way along the crowd, stopping here and there to talk, rather in the style of a royal visit.

"Why hallo there." It's only when she addresses him that Adam recognises the
girl in the short orange dress. She's in boots and a jacket.

"Hi," he says. The man making his way through the crowd knows him as Adam while to the Fieldings he is duplicitous Charles. He has to take control. But as Ewan, earring in place and swathed in a plaid, approaches he says only, "We meet again," and turns to the Fieldings, inviting an introduction. They tell him they are enjoying their first visit to this part of the world and Holly tells him about the wolf. He listens with genuine interest and asks for the details.

"Nice guy," says Brian when they move on. "Whatever his motives."

The man in the Stetson leans over and asks Adam if this is indeed the lord.

"Laird," says Adam. It does make a difference.

The man reaches out a respectful hand to detain him. "Sir, may I introduce myself? I am Alexander MacKay the fifth of Raleigh, North Carolina. My great-great-grandfather was a native of Sutherland from where he travelled to found the company of which I am today the president. This is my first visit to your fine country. I certainly hope it won't be my last."

Ewan says that he shares his hope.

"Can I ask how far back you trace your family?"

"About six hundred years." The crowd has fallen quiet, listening, "Not as tranquil as it sounds. We stole the land from the MacIntoshes – they are part of Clan Chattan hence the name of the estate – then they stole it back but we stole it back again."

"You've got one of those names, sir, well two of them I guess, that doesn't begin with Mac. How does that work? Are you still a clan?"

"Or two clans," someone in the crowd suggests. Everyone laughs.

"Like, do you have a motto and such?"

"The Camerons have a very fine motto. Sons of the Hound come here and get flesh."

"I'm going to write that down right away. Back home I'll get it on a plaque or something. Guy I play golf with is a Cameron."

"They're from further south. We interbreed you know. As for the clan Gunn . . ."

"Sir, I would not ask any more of your last name than what it already does. It celebrates the Second Amendment."

As Ewan and the girl formerly in the short orange dress move on, the American returns to his theme. "Did these guys have crests as well to go with the mottos? You know, like a coat of arms?"

"They did," says the man who knows everything. "The Gunns have a hand holding a sword."

"I guess you could say the sword was the Lee Enfield of its day."

"So the dagger would be the Beretta," someone says. "For close encounters."

"Right enough," says one of the Glasgow guys. "And the claymore was the Kalashnikov."

"As a matter of fact the clan Gunn does have a motto of its own," says the man who knows everything. "*Aut pax aut bellum.* Either peace or war."

"Symbolising judgement, do you think? A pledge to fight only when the cause is just?"

"Symbolising hedging your bets more like."

On the other side of the burn things are happening. The extras in their robes, men, women and children, have gathered in front of the house and have taken up a listening posture. A splinter group, the sceptics perhaps, stands on the bridge. A tall man with a commanding presence heightened by the staff he is carrying steps forward.

"People of the land," he declaims, "the land that is father and mother to us, the glens that were carved from the mountains for us, the sweet water that tumbles into our lochs, the sea that is our frontier and our friend, I say to you that a time is coming when all this will change." The sceptics shake their heads and stamp their feet. The bridge sways. "I say to you that the sea will come upon the land and that spring will come in winter and the ptarmigan and the hare and the stoat will lose their winter coat."

"Global warming," someone says.

"And the people are paying no heed for their heads are turned by silks and sweetmeats, by gaudy raiment from the east."

"Primark."

"And machines will send out things that will make their way even unto our doors."

"Amazon."

Someone is making his way through the crowd behind them. Adam feels the ripple of people letting him through, then suddenly there is warm breath in his ear as a voice says, "Don't look round," while a hand dips into his pocket. When he judges it clear to look he sees the back of a man in a dark jacket reach the fringe of the crowd. He tries to find a way across the burn and turns far enough for Adam to recognise the face in the dining room window of the Achindarnoch House Hotel, the face of the guy who pointed his finger like a pistol. Finding no stepping stones he makes a leap and lands short of the bank. He scrambles out and disappears behind the trees.

In his pocket there is a scrap of paper.

Hector has moved on to civil unrest ". . . and in a time of great suffering the leaders will falter and fail and east will be turned against west and north against south . . ."

Ewan, is back in the centre of the crowd. He puts a hand on Adam's shoulder. "We should talk," he says.

". . . so I say to you consider the salmon . . ."

"For God's sake not the bloody salmon," Ewan says. "I told him to delete that, I don't know who wrote that."

". . . for the salmon in its travels thinks only of home and returns always to the place of its birth, nay to the very pool of the stream of the river where it spawned, the spawn of a union only of its own kind so that its blood line is never compromised..."

"I didn't write this crap," Ewan says. "Someone is sabotaging this."

"I guess Hector's copyright has expired," Adam says. "Not a lot you can do about that."

From somewhere higher on the hill behind them comes the unmistakable crack of a rifle. Hector of Farr drops his staff and subsides. Everyone freezes. Into the silence.

a man's voice says, "When was the rifle invented?"

A woman says, "Nobody's screaming. If it was in the script wouldn't they be screaming?"

Across the burn the men in robes are bending over him and the women are pulling away their children. Shouldering his way through the sceptics on the bridge Ewan kneels beside the fallen prophet.

On the hill behind there is a scuffle as the Glasgow guys bring down a man whose right hand is being competently twisted. He relaxes his grip on an unwieldy and ornate weapon. The man in the Stetson picks it up. "Wogdon and Barton," he says. "Late eighteenth. Manufactured here in England."

"This is Scotland."

"I beg your pardon, Ma'm. Manufactured in England. One of a pair of single shot duelling pistols. It fired a wax bullet."

Adam takes the piece of paper from his pocket. A mobile number is written on a scrap torn from an A4 sheet with the letter heading SYNCHRONISED SOLUTIONS. Next to the phone number is written, 'Call me.' Across the burn Hector of Farr is sitting up.

Chapter Sixteen

Leaving the house of Frau Frühwirth, taking the distancing steps required of a departing guest, Charlotte finds a blank piece of wall and leans against it. She is in a part of Vienna she doesn't know, but then she knows very little of Vienna, only those paths trodden by her family of whom, in turn, she knows next to nothing. She needs to get to know Vienna and she needs to get to know her family. The first requires that she should walk, the second that she should sit down. She walks until she finds a café and on the point of going in spots a news-stall with a foreign section and a front-page photograph that stops her in her tracks. She buys the *Daily Mail*, goes into the café and when the waiter comes asks for a coffee of the type most popular with the café's Viennese patrons. By the time her coffee arrives she has taken wing to the North Highlands where she crash-lands in a familiar glen.

MOUNTAIN GIRL'S DEATH LINKED TO LONDON STREET SLEEPER TRAGEDIES. The headline is as arresting as the photograph. The unidentified girl found dead in a remote glen in the Scottish Highlands wearing only a green satin dress has now been examined by the toxicologist working with the Metropolitan Police on the mysterious deaths of three homeless men in London. It is believed that traces of the unknown drug implicated in their separate deaths have also been found in the dead girl. Police Scotland believe her cause of death to have been a 'designer' drug similar to that involved in the London deaths. The source of the drug is believed to be somewhere in Eastern Europe.

There is an artist's impression of the dead girl's movingly

young and pretty features, her party dress and slender chin necklace. She is so much the creature of Charles Merchant's account that she replays with him now the shock of her discovery and the further shock of her disappearance. Where is he now and what must he be feeling? There are currently no missing person reports that might relate to her, says a police spokesman, and no one in the area has come forward to identify her. When found she was wearing only a sleeveless dress thought to be of Romanian manufacture.

The girl who was so real to Charles and so peripheral to her now reproaches Charlotte from the front page, fragile in the line drawing, fragile perhaps in life. They have changed places, she and the girl, the girl now in the Highlands and Charlotte in the that vast unknowable land mass that from the UK is Eastern Europe.

At Charles's bidding she had gone to his room to look for her, but she had gone. Dead people don't go. No wonder he was so spooked by Charlotte's failure to find her. A drug and a dress, both thought to have been manufactured in Eastern Europe.

Eastern Europe, seen from the UK, is a place of shifting borders divided by the less familiar mountain ranges that separate people of exotic origins speaking languages no one else knows, a habitat of vampires and werewolves. To the more prosaic mind, the aspect of her conflicted self that Charlotte tries to keep uppermost, they are delineated by whichever empire they were once a fragment of, Ottoman, Russian, Habsburg. And sporadically behind the werewolves, Russia squaring its shoulders.

Folding the newspaper she looks again at the place where the girl was found. She can identify it absolutely as the further glen she and Charles looked down into when they walked up the hill on the sign-posted path by the waterfall. Why had she gone for a walk with a man she had only just met and who presented nothing but warning signs. The walk was her idea, she was totally taken up with how the landscape was talking to her. She was working on instinct and her instinct was to trust him. It still is.

Back at the hotel there is a message from Martin Langley, "Call me ASAP", and a mobile number. The chocolate box with the letters and the purloined red folder are still under the mattress. The folder contains lists, incomprehensible lists as well as handwritten notes scribbled on yellowing paper that suggests decades of distance. She puts it into the padded envelope, calls Martin Langley and leaves a message. She is returning the chocolate box with the letters to its place under the mattress when he calls back from the foyer. He can't have been more than a street or two away. She puts the padded envelope now containing the red folder in her bag, drapes a scarf over it and heads back downstairs.

"OK," he says, "Let's go."

They are outside before she can ask where they are going and the answer is cryptic, "To see Dave." Dave is within walking distance and neither of them is inclined to talk, Charlotte because her head is full and Martin, from the look of him, something similar. Passing an apartment block entrance it seems they might stop there but Martin touches a button without turning his head and walks on. They circle the block and when they come back to the entrance the door opens and they climb two flights of stairs, Charlotte now under a caution of silence but onto that anyway.

A door opens as they reach it and they go straight into a pleasant but soulless room with modular furniture and a deep pile grey carpet, and since there are no civilised exchanges with Dave, just a nod of recognition, she inspects the books on the Ikea shelves which are middle of the road in the extreme or as extreme as middle of the road can get. There is a photograph in a silver frame which looks like the one it came with. When Martin and Dave have exchanged thoughts or whatever silent communication they deal in, they wave her towards the sofa and wine is poured, white, rather pleasant, like the wine in the bar where they met. The mood is perceptively mannered but from the armchairs comes a fizz of testosterone like power cables sparking in the rain.

"Is this a Safe House?" she asks to get the conversation going. No one bothers to answer.

"The letters?" Martin says, his eyes on the draped scarf. "You have brought them?"

She shakes her head, "No, but I have brought this." She pulls out the red folder, denying herself a flourish. After all she has no idea what's in there. They look confused as is their right but Martin reaches out a hand.

Her decision to hang on to the letters was a split-second reaction to doing the right thing. The right thing was not *per se* right, or not in her experience. You had to push it around a bit till you knew what you were getting yourself into. If the letters were just letters she was going to be out of all this, back with twinkly Herr Strauss and his castles in the air. The converse was equally true. If the content was important no one was going to say congratulations you have just prevented World War Three. Without the letters she could be seen off to a life of relative stability or sent the way of the girl in the green dress. No reason to think that way but then what does she know about anything. Need to know turns out to be huge but not as huge as the process of finding out. Basically she's in it for the danger. The letters are keeping the danger in her life.

After ten minutes with the folder Martin passes it to Dave. When he looks her way she can no longer read his expression. The laborious politeness he employs to deal with her waywardness has gone. "Where did you get this?"

"I found it."

"Found it where?"

"It was in a desk. I came across it so I took it."

"Can we stop playing games. It's doing my head in."

"I went to my great-aunt's apartment. The door was open so I went in. The guy who seems to live there came back. I didn't like him. I don't think Saskia would have liked him poking around in her desk. I thought it might be important to him so I took it." Martin's face is blank. That's not surprising. "It was an impulse."

"Did this guy have a name."

"Markus Roschmann. At least I assumed he was Markus A Roschmann. Does that mean anything to you?"

"Not at the moment. Have you any more surprises for us before we get onto this?"

"It's important then?"

"You could put it that way. Where is this desk?"

"Where it always was. Under the tapestry in the drawing room."

"Could you put it back there?"

"What? Now?"

"When we've made a copy. Did this Markus Roschmann know you were in his apartment?"

"Her apartment. No. Not unless he saw my bag. I hid behind the curtain."

"When was this?"

"This morning."

"So he may not know it's missing yet," Martin is addressing Dave who gets to his feet and takes out his car keys.

"On it," he says.

When he has gone Martin turns to her with his professional charmer smile nailed back in place. "And how soon may we hope to see those letters?"

"How soon do you want to have the folder returned?"

Half an hour later she and Martin Langley are sheltering in a doorway from a sudden shower. When it stops the streets are now reflecting the lights and lanterns of the inner city from surfaces that see no traffic. When Dave left to have the contents of the red folder copied Martin suggested he walk her back to the hotel. And the letters, she thought. The rain shower gives her a moment's respite but she is losing the urge to disoblige. Nearing the hotel they pass a flamboyant fast-food van with HABSBURGERS in gold lettering on its purple painted side.

"When did you last eat?"

"That might have been at breakfast."

Without consulting her he goes to the window and orders two. Handing her one he says, "If you're vegetarian pretend to eat it. It's to get us past the hotel. It's being watched." Wrapped in a napkin decorated with gold crowns the Habsburger is totally disgusting but she has a go at it. The aim is apparently to demonstrate that they are not going into the hotel.

Round a couple of blocks and passing a line of bins they junk the burgers and he accepts her offer of a wet wipe. "Where exactly," he asks, "have you put the letters?"

"Under the mattress."

He groans. "OK. I'm going to have to ask you to get them out right now."

"You're not coming with me?"

"We've only known each other for two days. It's my guess your tail would find that out of character."

"You think I have a tail?"

"You certainly have one now."

"So, what is likely to happen when I come out of the hotel with the letters?"

"It's likely you'll be apprehended on some pretext before you reach the bottom of the stairs. That's why you're going to drop them out of the window. Where is your room?"

"Right at the top. Top front. Under the eaves. Second left."

"Does the window open? Some hotels have their windows fixed shut not to compromise the air conditioning."

"It opens."

"Right then. Let's be practical. Take a pillow case from one of your pillows and put the letters in there. Knot the open end. I'll deflect the guy, probably just by letting him see I'm onto him. When he's moved on you'll drop them. We'll need a signal."

"You could whistle something. Mozart or Strauss if that's easier."

"Can't whistle. Never could."

"How does a coughing fit grab you? Or you could retch. Those things were disgusting."

"I'll cough."

"OK."

"And now we part company."

Walking back to the hotel, not looking round to see her tail, she is messaging Saskia in the afterlife. Message received. Not understood though. Nowhere near that.

The man who shares her landing comes out of his room and ignores her. Inside she drops her bag and opens the window. Apprehensive now she slides a hand under the mattress but the letters are still there in their box, Saskia's confirmed face on the lid now with an edge to her smile. She removes the pillow case from the under pillow. Do they do a laundry count and will they think she's nicked it or might suspicion fall on the chambermaid? It will come back of course on some occasion she can't imagine. She considers taking the letters out of the box. She doesn't want to lose it. But they still need its protection. She scribbles a note on the writing pad in the desk, 'Box to be returned with contents,' puts it in the pillow case, knots the loose end and waits by the window for a coughing fit. It's a few minutes before she hears a polite cough repeated three times. She slings them far enough out to clear the creeper. Then she sits in the armchair just long enough for the anti-climax to kick in. What next? Thanks to the red folder she has not yet reached her Use By date. She closes the window, washes her hands and heads downstairs to see what is left of the hotel's running buffet.

She is half way through a peppery stew when she starts to think about the silver key, the key to the desk in the drawing room that held the red folder. Did she return it to the doll's house or could she have left it in the desk? What will Martin Roschmann do if he finds a second key? And how will she be able to put back the red folder which is clearly what they are going to ask of her?

She lays down her fork and composes herself with a few deep breaths. That sometimes seems to work. Then she pats the pocket of her skirt. It's there. Sloppy thinking though. She must be tired. She transfers the key to her purse, finishes the stew and goes back upstairs to a bed that no longer has anything hidden under the mattress but once again has a chocolate on the pillow. She eats the chocolate, cleans her teeth, thinks of the grindings of intelligence or whatever they like to call it and falls fast asleep.

Chapter Seventeen

Herr Strauss calls in the morning. He is anxious, he says, retrospectively anxious, about this Markus Roschmann. He recalls a phone call from Frau Kaufmann – "your dear great-aunt" – some months before she died. She had just agreed to take a tenant, "a lodger I think you call such a person, living in the same house, yes? Paying some rent?" Charlotte confirms that that's a lodger. "Only I believe that in this case he was not to pay, he was to be helpful to her. She called me because she wondered what I thought of such an arrangement."

"Can you remember what you told her?"

"I can't I'm afraid. I told her that it seemed a wise solution to everyday problems like those of her dear friend Frau Frühwirth who as you know fell off a ladder changing a light bulb. For her Camilla has been wonderful. As long as she knew his background and knew from others that he was to be trusted. She told me that he had been introduced to her by a gentleman she knew from her theatre group. This was a group of mainly older people who met to go to theatrical productions and concerts and who met later to discuss them. He was a gentleman who had had a business importing luxury foods into what we must now call the Czech Republic. His business had become unsuccessful due to the bureaucracy involved with unusual food items and so he had returned to Vienna to investigate other possibilities for his expertise and contacts in other things not normally available in Austria."

"Returned to Vienna? Surely if he was Viennese he would have had family or friends he could have stayed with."

"That is true. Again I reproach myself. Perhaps the gentleman was a Czech citizen. He was looking for some accommodation while he did this research. He was prepared to do any work that Saskia required. Carpentry he could do. Also electrical work, painting. The house of course required more maintenance than it had been given for some time. It is only now when I think about it that I wonder why she asked my opinion. She was a lady of independent mind. Perhaps after all she was uneasy in her decision. I blame myself for not asking to meet the gentleman. And this was Markus Roschmann. I had forgotten the name, but yes. I shall try to make enquiries but if as you say he is living in the apartment this is most irregular. I think for your safety you should not go there again."

At the breakfast buffet, a reliably colourful start to her day, Charlotte finds she has no appetite. She picks up a croissant and is playing with it when the coffee uncle asks if she has plans for the day. There is no answer to this. "Perhaps Schönbrunn," she says but she has no heart for that. The rogue lodger has moved into her head.

Frau Frühwirth too had seemed uneasy at the mention of Markus Roschmann. Like Herr Strauss she had not met him. Over coffee and half the croissant she plays with the idea of rounding up Saskia's theatre group for cross-examination but a gaggle of dotty old culture vultures being over-helpful in exaggerated English is too much for this hour of the day.

Back in her room she calls Frau Frühwirth who insists she come round immediately to share coffee and the delightful cake that the wonderful Camilla has just brought out of the oven.

Camilla answers the door with a cigarette in her hand. She steps into the street and takes several deep drags before stubbing it out and tossing the end into a pavement bin. Then she ushers her again into Frau Frühwirth's disconcerting drawing room where she takes care not to sit square on to the Schiele. The cake is produced, a surprisingly elaborate thing of tiers and icing. Camilla is asked to join them and pours the coffee as Charlotte congratulates her on the cake. "Yeah," she says, "they put me on a baking course when I was training for day release."

"I want to ask you about Markus Roschmann," Charlotte says when her mouth is clear of cake. "Was there ever a suggestion that you might meet him?"

"I ask myself often why I did not," Frau Frühwirth replies. "I asked Saskia to bring him round for dinner one evening but he was busy. Perhaps he was not anxious to meet friends of Saskia."

"What did she tell you about him?"

"Only that someone brought him to her theatre group. She had mentioned already that she was thinking of employing someone two or three times a week to help with things she was finding it hard to do. A woman I imagine. She had in fact said that a man might be better for the work she had in mind. She thought to advertise, but choosing the right words for such an advertisement, an advertisement for a man, might be a kettle of worms. We laughed at that. And so she had almost invented such a man before he came along. He had recently arrived from Czechoslovakia which we must now call the Czech Republic but which I still like to call Bohemia."

"Bohemia? My ancestors eloped to Bohemia. Christina that would be, my great-grandmother, and Lachlan whom I am trying to reconfigure as Karl. Why would they have eloped to Bohemia?"

"Perhaps because of Christina's grandfather."

"Her grandfather was Bohemian?"

"Ultimately, yes. But of course Lachlan came from Scotland. He worked for our dear Franz Joseph to whom his sister became close."

"The dinner service."

"Yes, the famous dinner service."

"And the photographs."

"One could say the family were in his favour, and of course his sister was married for a time to a physician who was with the Austro-Hungarian army which our young emperor led in person at the Battle of Solferino. The last reigning monarch to lead his army. Along with the leaders of the other side, of course."

"Would Markus Roschmann have known all this?"

"Perhaps. He might have thought he was connecting with some influence. Old influence of course, but maybe also some new. He was importing local delicacies from many small producers in many countries, the Cornish pastry, the pudding made of blood, the stuffed stomach of Scottish sheep, the soup made with the fin of the shark and many other such things as were not found in the country of our neighbours and for which of course it was necessary to have a great many licences and getting these licences became unprofitable as well as boring. I could find no problem with that. He wanted to import-export something else. Maybe some antiques."

"Of which of course Saskia had many."

"That is a concern. But perhaps he was amusing. Saskia would be inclined to trust him if he was amusing."

An amusing importer of haggis and black puddings. Is this the enemy she has been raising an army against? "It sounds as if she was taking his problems on board. Maybe too much so. She also told Herr Strauss about this."

"That is what I thought. I said so to Camilla, did I not?"

"You said Saskia seems to have fucked herself up with this dodgy lodger guy."

"I don't think I put it quite that way."

"Whatever."

"Do you think he had some sort of hold on her?"

"That didn't cross my mind. It's hard to see what hold that could be."

"Her war experience? Cold War rather I suppose."

"Ah. Perhaps. Though she hadn't mentioned that for some time. What is it that brings him to your attention now?"

"He's living in her apartment. He has the key to her desk."

"That is quite wrong. Does Willi Strauss know about this?"

"I don't think he knew until I told him. He said he felt retrospectively anxious about him. Like you do."

"Ah. Hindmost sight."

"Unless he has the right to be there for some reason we don't know about."

"The deathbed marriage you mean."

"Well, no. That had not occurred to me."

"I shall phone Willi after half past twelve. When Klara goes out for lunch he likes to eat a takeaway and watch an opera on his computer. Klara told me this. Sometimes it is not an opera, in fact she thinks it is always not an opera. He likes to watch English football. She found a Tottenham Hotspur scarf in a drawer."

"Thank you. That would be helpful. Shall I call you in the evening?"

"Certainly my dear. Camilla, wrap up a piece of your divine cake to give Charlotte. Goodbye my dear. Forgive me if I don't get up."

Her phone buzzes as she is making her way to the tram stop. It's Martin Langley. "Where are you?" he says.

"Making my way back from a coffee and cake appointment with a contact. Why do you ask?"

"Your friend Herr Roschmann has just left his apartment. Now might be a good time to return his folder. You do remember his folder?"

"Of course."

"I didn't know you had contacts in Vienna. Where exactly are you?"

"Landstrasse. Corner of Lagergasse and something that might be Haymarket."

"Stay there. I'll come and get you."

Ten minutes later he draws up and they drive at speed to a street round the corner from the apartment. The oblique way of arriving, it must choreograph your whole life, always turning up just round the corner from the place you're going to.

"How did you get into the building when you went there before?"

"Someone came out. They held the door for me."

"I usually deal with that by buzzing a ground floor resident and telling them I have a delivery for someone who isn't answering."

"Let's do it your way."

He takes out an envelope he may carry for that purpose. He comes out and holds the door for her and she is halfway up the winding staircase to the first floor when it occurs to her that this time the door will not be ajar, but then there is the proximity of the friendly neighbour. Her name is Hilde Schwarzkopf. She buzzes Markus several times, shuffling impatiently outside his door before she buzzes Hilde who pops out straight away, a brassy blonde defying her name. She tells her that Markus was to have left something for her to pick up but he seems to be out. Hilde fetches the key and hovers in the outer doorway while Charlotte goes to the drawing room, replaces the folder, relocks the desk and, looking for something of bulk and outline she might conceivably have come to pick up takes the photograph of the emperor and the picnic basket from the piano top, puts it in a carrier bag that's lying on a chair and comes out to thank Hilde profusely. The man who crosses the road towards the house looks a candidate for the man she glimpsed through the gap in the curtains but she takes her time walking round the corner to the car. After all he had not seen her. "Well?" says Martin.

"Well what?"

"You replaced the folder?"

"Of course. Now are you going to tell me exactly what it is I've just been doing?" "Not yet."

"So I can look forward to a time when I'm permitted to know if I've been risking my life for my country or doing something altogether less reputable. Tomorrow? Next week? Once I'm safely out of the country?"

"With any luck, this evening."

"And perhaps you will also have something to tell me about the letters?"

"That is ongoing. There may be a progress report."

Progress report. Up a pay grade there. People reporting back to her. "Can I offer you a piece of cake?" she says.

"What? No thanks. I'll call you. Five-ish. Maybe six."

He drops her round the corner from the hotel where there is a message from Herr Strauss. Would she call him. Climbing the stairs to her room her phone buzzes. Which of the three people she knows in Vienna, might this be? It's Sean. "Been a while babe," he says.

"Give me a minute, Sean." She opens the door, drops her bag and sheds her coat. "Yes, Sean. You were saying?"

"Just checking on you like you said. You still in Edinburgh? Been a bit of news there. Scotland that is."

"Yeah. Well I guess there are things happening all the time even there. No I'm not in Scotland right now."

"Back in London then?"

"Vienna."

"Vienna? That's in Germany."

"Austria."

"Yeah well."

"And I'm in good health you'll be glad to know. You too I hope."

"I wouldn't go that far. OK though."

"Glad to hear it. And thank you for calling."

"Well, you know, just checking like you said."

"It's good to know I can rely on you Sean."

While they've been talking she's noticed some changes. They've put another pillow case on her lower pillow, the window is slightly ajar and the creeper outside it has been pruned. Also someone has been up to what Saskia liked to warn her of, rummaging in her lingerie drawer. Lingerie is pushing it, a couple of bras and half a dozen pairs of cotton briefs, but they've been pushed to one side and not replaced.

She calls Herr Strauss. He would like to have a talk with her about Saskia. Frau Frühwirth called him. He understands from what she told him that Herr Roschmann is indeed living in the apartment. If she can come to his office in the afternoon they can talk about what steps might be taken.

What does she really know of Saskia's relationship to Markus Roschmann? Nothing. Perhaps she had feelings for him, perhaps he was one of the good guys, perhaps he had a right to stay in her apartment. She takes Camilla's cake out of her bag and contemplates it, then she puts it in her tidied-up underwear drawer – a surprise if they come looking, and surely they will have the decency not to eat it.

En route to the hotel's salad bar she stops at reception and asks the girl on duty if someone has been in her room. The girl says yes, the guy came to prune the creeper. Could he not have done that from a ladder outside? Normally yes, if it was under the regular arrangement, but since it was in response to her complaint about it tapping on the window he did it via her room. On whose instruction would that have been? She doesn't know but she'll check.

There are few takers for the salad bar, most people out and about in the city. The guy from her landing is there. They ignore each other. She eats quickly and stops at the reception desk where the girl is apologetic. No one seems to know where the guy who did the pruning came from. He turned up at reception in overalls and carrying shears and asked for her room number. Housekeeping let him in. Is there anything missing from her room? Fortunately no, she says, but she had not complained about the creeper, for which reason she expects a little vigilance on their part.

Back in her room she catches the BBC news headlines. Three out of twenty eight-year-olds questioned in a recent survey did not know that chickens came from eggs and that milk came from cows. After severe flooding in Yorkshire, fish have been seen swimming down a residential street. A family was filmed dangling fishing rods from bedroom windows. A wolf shot by a farmer in the Northern Highlands after it killed three ewes in a frenzied attack is thought to have ingested a neuro-toxic substance. "This is not normal wolf behaviour," said a zoologist. A toxicologist's report has been ordered. And now Herr Strauss calls back. After all he will not trouble her to come to his office. He has made a decision, he will go to Saskia's apartment in the company of a valuator to make an initial assessment of her possessions for tax purposes. He will then be in a position to question Herr Roschmann. If he has a contract from Frau Kaufmann he must show it. If his continuing tenancy is the result of a simple misunderstanding he will ask the gentleman to find other accommodation. If he has no contract and reacts unreasonably the police will be mentioned.

So now she has time on her hands. Time on her hands does not feel good and she also has a feeling that her movements might be subject to other people's restrictions. If only for that reason she must go somewhere. And the place that flashes up is the Zentralfriedhof, the vast cemetery where some of her family are buried.

When Martin calls he is detectibly excited. "Where are you?"

"On a tram. I'm going to visit the family grave in the Friedhof."

"For Christ's sake, that's miles away."

"It has been a longer journey than I expected."

"Don't go in there. There's miles of it. Get off at the main gate and I'll meet you there."

Certainly they do seem to have been passing it for some time when the driver announces that they're at the main gate. There is a flower stall outside the gate and people are selling trinkets, perhaps religious, perhaps not, and postcards. Inside the gate three of the carriages with their black-caped coachmen and black horses are lined up, so vast is the expanse of the cemetery.

It's a spot where if you stand about, people approach you. A man offers his services as a guide to the musicians' graves, someone else offers her a guide book and postcards. This feels like Eastern Europe now the Middle Europeans who lived here are dead. And here at the gate is a time warp. When Martin arrives she is very glad to see him.

"Well," he says. "Are we going in there or aren't we?"

"This might not be the time."

"Do you know where to find the family graves?"

"All in one I think. It's on the main drag, right at the top. The Nobles' graves."

"That's miles away."

"I could come back later."

"Then I suggest we find a café where we can talk. I have news. Do you have a tail at the moment?"

"I don't think so. Should I have?"

"Anything is possible but perhaps attention has shifted from you now that you are not in possession."

"They would know that? She thinks of the pruned creeper outside her window. "There was a guide who approached me and a postcard seller."

"Those would be genuine. Tails don't fraternise."

Martin had also come by tram. They catch another back to the Ringstrasse and find a noisy café where they can talk.

"I've been doing some work on Markus Roschmann," Martin says when their coffees arrive. "He is a Czech national, name of Matyas Rozek. Born in Pardubice. There is no record of a food import business. For his day job he is an antique dealer, but it is looking likely that he is on the retail end of a niche pharma lab that's probably behind those deaths in the UK."

"Niche?"

"Drugs designed to order. He exports high value antiques that require copious paper work and a personal courier. He is meticulous about the documentation and couriers them himself with the drugs on the side. He has also been fingered here for intelligence. The lab is likely to be in the Czech Republic as is his allegiance if he has any. He may or may not have Russian masters but he is as likely to be a freelance as anything else. His allegiance would be to the highest bidder."

"So the antiques business might explain his interest in Saskia."

"It could. However, it is more than likely that he too is after the Kaufmann File."

A contained response would be cool but cool is difficult right now. Displacement tactics while she tries to digest what has become indigestible.

"There is another name on the address plate outside Saskia's place," she says. "It's the guy who runs Aurelius Interventions. Marcus Aurelius. Does that mean anything to you?"

"Too right it does. He's the Roman emperor and founding father of Vienna."

Chapter Eighteen

"Schönbrunn good?" asks the coffee uncle at the breakfast table.

"Schönbrunn maybe tomorrow," Charlotte says. "Or today." After all she has nothing planned.

"Perhaps Belvedere?" he says but Charlotte's phone buzzes. It's Martin. "Your friend Herr Strauss has just gone into the house with another man. We think Markus Roschmann is there. Paul is watching. Do you know anything about this?"

"It might be the valuator."

"It might be dangerous. Perhaps you should come in case an intermediary is needed." Intermediary now. Another promotion. "We'll be at the café opposite the house. Take a taxi. I'll pay."

At a café table diagonally opposite the house Martin introduces her to Paul who has already ordered her a flat white.

"Here's Arielle now," says Paul. A girl is coming down a side street carrying a broom and a basket of cleaning products. She buzzes and is admitted. This is Arielle, summoned by Paul to be the eavesdropper everyone ignores, currently spitting mad at the absence of gender neutrality. "It's the visibility issue," Paul says. "It works both ways. It was her or Dave." There is a burst of non-gender-neutral laughter at this. Is Dave a slob or just too visible? He is very tall.

"So," says Martin, "you knew that Herr Strauss was planning this visit?"

"Not today, no. He must have found a hole in his diary."

"And the man with him?"

"That would be the valuator. He was to do a rough assessment of Saskia's possessions ostensibly for tax purposes. Herr Strauss thought that would make his visit less confrontational."

"He was a pretty confrontational looking guy, the valuator. Paul said six-four or thereabouts."

"With shoulders. The build was awesome. Pure rugby league."

"Perhaps he had that in mind."

"And you say Herr Strauss's only concern was to find out if Markus Roschmann had a legal right to be living there."

"That's right. If he has a written contract he isn't planning to evict him. Just now at least. Just let him know that the contents are being listed."

"What do you know about Herr Strauss?"

"Probably less than you do. You were hanging around his office when I arrived."

"Around it. Yes."

"You let me think he was your solicitor."

"Perhaps."

"Now that you've seen the letters you will know there is no point to this."

"Not at all."

"They hadn't even been posted. They've been sitting in a filing cabinet in the north of Scotland for years. At the most they're amusing. Then suddenly they're hot. Why?"

"We thought we'd found the Kaufmann File."

"The Kaufmann File?"

"That's what we thought was there. When we heard that an estate was being handled from the north of Scotland it seemed to explain why it had never turned up."

"So what is the Kaufmann File?"

"You've already got more out of me than is reasonable. You have quite a talent for that."

"It's got my name on it. Doesn't that give me a need to know?"

"It's got someone's name on it. You are not Kaufmann K."

Martin's phone buzzes. "Right," he says, then to Charlotte "We'll get back to this. Herr Strauss is leaving."

When the door opens three men come out, Herr Strauss, a big man in a suit and Markus Roschmann, a true gentleman showing out his guests. There are affable exchanges and handshakes. Roschmann goes back inside, the door closes and Herr Strauss and the valuator walk off down the street.

Minutes later Arielle comes out with her cleaning kit and vanishes round the corner. Charlotte watches her go. "She isn't joining us then?"

"A cleaning lady who joined a couple of Brits from the embassy would be very unusual."

"I guess I haven't been taking this seriously. He would be watching her from the window, or someone else might be. Your tails. Singular or plural." From somewhere round the corner Arielle calls Paul.

"Well?"

Her answer is audible. "That's the cleanest bloody staircase in Vienna."

"And?"

"You saw. Bosom pals. No blood spilled."

"Good job. Drinks later."

"What do I do with the cleaning clobber?"

"Find a space in a cupboard. We might need it again."

"Count me out for that."

"Understood."

Charlotte says, "So he conned Herr Strauss?"

"Or he had a contract. Or Herr Strauss knows more than he's telling you. This may be an area where you could help us out. I imagine you're expecting him to get back to you."

"He'll do that. I'm the sole beneficiary."

"Are you indeed. That's quite a hand you have there."

"And perhaps a right to know."

"Perhaps. Right now I have work to do. Can we meet later? To eat perhaps. Bearing in mind your preference for an evening snack."

"I could do dinner."

"Right. Best not to meet at the hotel."

"That's another thing. Someone was in my room on the pretext of pruning the foliage outside my window. Of course there was nothing for him to find."

"That's interesting. Let's meet at the gawdawful bar where we met before and move on from there. If Herr Strauss has got back to you by then I'll be very interested to hear what he has to say."

She is back at the hotel when Herr Strauss calls her. He sounds very pleased with himself. "I have been to see Herr Roschmann. A charming gentleman. He welcomed us in. and insisted we take tea with him. He has a contract. He showed it to me and it was very convincing. But then he added some more stitches – embroidered it I think you say. He told me about the deep feelings he had for your dear aunt, an affection he believed was reciprocated. He said . . . he actually told me this . . . that they had discussed marriage before she was taken ill. I am very happy to say that I hid the fury that was coming over me. I made the performance. I made the performance of a man deeply moved. This person is half her age and not at all cultivated. And you are right, his accent is not of Austria. As you know your aunt was a lady of great intelligence and her character had very little of the softer side. What attachments she may have had in her long life, these attachments were never enough for her to give up her independence. Now that I have met this very unpleasant man I will make plans."

"I'm happy to have my impression confirmed, but I should tell you there are some developments. He is also being investigated on, I believe, intelligence grounds. Perhaps there's a link to her own background. Post-war I mean."

"Ah. You know about that. Of course, Frau Frühwirth would have told you. I shall wait. I shall do nothing. I am still her loyal servant."

After the call she sits in the armchair with the cushions embroidered with musicians' names. There must be time for an opera, or a concert at least.

She takes Camilla's cake out of the drawer and looks at it. It is too beautiful to eat and besides there will be dinner. She puts it back, showers, shampoos, puts on Saskia's silk shirt that was a last-minute packing decision and arrives at the bar on the heels of Martin Langley.

"I have news," he says. "Tomorrow we're digging up the cellar."

"Where the silver was buried. Can you really do that?"

"There is an emergency. The main drain has a leak. The ground floor residents will have to vacate their apartments for however long it takes."

"Is that legal?"

"We have documentation and three plumbers. We understand the cellars are only used for storage. No carpets are involved."

"And this came from Saskia's letter?"

"That and the others. Those addressed to her from London."

"From my grandmother. I didn't read those. They were too boring."

"Nonetheless they contained coded instructions from British Intelligence in London."

"They did? Perhaps I should work at developing a more open mind."

"Though the reference to 'Colin's stuff' is the most promising. There's a chance that's the Kaufmann File."

"I take it I'm now in the loop."

"In *a* loop certainly. With a right to know. A limited right to know at the moment. I suggest we talk about that over dinner."

"And where are we going for dinner?"

"The Hotel Sacher. OTT but appropriate I think."

The waiter at the Sacher who takes the Dior coat handles it with respect. It has come home. They often talked of eating here. When they are seated and Charlotte has scanned the paintings and the chandeliers she says, "Appropriate? In what way appropriate?"

"This was British Army HQ during the years of occupation. Graham Greene hung out at the bar." When the wine list arrives he glances at it then hastily tilts it her way. She waves it away. He is less confident around her now.

She says, "No fizz. That grassy white you ordered last time at the gawdawful bar was good. Something like that". At Martin's suggestion they order light mains and no starters to leave room for the fabled *Sachertorte*.

"OK," he says. "Time for straight talking. Your relative from Scotland who was reinvented for his intelligence work would have been a witness to the early attempts at information gathering, many of them failed attempts, some with loss of life."

"British attempts?"

"A front seat at some of those, but probably a glimpse of what the other three occupying powers were up to. And later the more successful attempts, sometimes as a participant. The Soviets may have thought he was working for them. The Americans were sure he was theirs. He was working for us but without the structure and security that would normally be assumed. Also his family were here."

"After they'd moved from Bohemia."

"Well now. That's news to me. That would certainly have widened his range. The wider his range the more useful he would be. And the more a danger to himself. His survival might ultimately have depended on his record keeping. Information that could be used to protect his family and himself."

"The Kaufmann File."

"When he disappeared that was a cause for anxiety on several counts."

"He disappeared? He didn't die?"

"Well, by now . . ."

"He'd be a hundred and thirty something, I know, I haven't lost my marbles. It isn't known, then, when or where he died? I saw his name. It was on a war memorial in the Highlands.

In the area he came from. His Cold War name, Kaufmann K. Strange that they didn't use his real name."

"Which was?"

"Lachlan MacPherson. Why is no one in my family called MacPherson? We are either Kaufmann or Ross. Ross was his wife's name. They eloped, they had two daughters, perhaps they didn't bother to marry."

"Do you know what he was doing in Bohemia?"

"Someone suggested land management. Perhaps that was you."

"Lachlan MacPherson would have been tricky and perhaps too visible. Ross trips off the tongue. Speaking of Ross, what did Herr Strauss have to tell you of Roschmann?"

"Total phoney with fake documents. He claimed that he and Saskia were to be married. Herr Strauss is ready to have him removed but only when the time is right for that. I hinted that he was in your sights."

"So totally trustworthy Herr Strauss."

"And now that you've seen the letters, who is Colin?"

"There was a British army captain of that name in Field Security. Another Scot. We're working on the assumption that your ancestor passed on the file to him for safe keeping before he decided to disappear."

"And why is it important after all this time?"

"It's important for what it may rule out."

"For instance?"

"A picture of a time when there were few rules to play by. To know that that is not graphically recorded would put quite a few minds at rest. If some things are there in detail then all the better it's in our own hands."

"And if it shows other people behaving badly that too might be useful?"

"You're pushing it again. I'd prefer to say also in safe hands."

"Because I still have to get my head round why Saskia went all the way to Scotland to leave her estate in the hands of an elderly family solicitor. She hadn't been to Scotland in a decade, so I understood. And when she was there she didn't even contact me. Though that might have been difficult."

"I'd say that something had alarmed her and that she had cause to be alarmed. She had historic links to British Intelligence, didn't she?"

"In some capacity, yes. I've only just learned that."

"It might have been time for lateral thinking. Once the documents were known to exist and as long as no one knew where to look for them they would have become her own insurance."

"But you knew about them from the start. From right after her death. You knew the location of what you thought was the file. Your guy on the London train certainly knew what he was after."

"I don't know what you're talking about."

"The guy who conned his way into my sleeping compartment on the Glasgow to London night train and tried to snitch the letters from the rack in my top berth."

"Someone did that? News to me."

"Disguised as a woman. I called the attendant."

"Ah. Ethan."

"You know him then."

"He's freelance. Ear to the ground. Unorthodox. I didn't know he was our source. First we knew was when you turned up at Herr Strauss's office."

"Then why were you hanging around outside the hat shop near the hotel."

"I wasn't. Well not in that context. I didn't know you'd recognised me."

"So, another star on my case sheet?"

Chapter Nineteen

When they watched *The Third Man*, which was often, too often in Charlotte's opinion, her mother would pause on the two graveyard scenes, the first when the man who was not Harry Lime was disinterred, the second where the real Harry Lime took his place. "That's our grave," she would say. "Or pretty damn close to it." It is the film rather than family visits that Charlotte now uses as sat-nav to get her to the grave. Entering the Zentralfriedhof, one of the biggest cemeteries in the world, through its main gate, she morphs into the scruffy unimpressed adolescent, pulling petals off a lily and closing her ears to another recital of the great and the good who are buried here. The central avenue, relentlessly long and straight, leads eventually to the Ehrengraben, the 'elite' graves, where the father of Christina's final husband secured a prime position for himself, his descendants and their partners, facing across the avenue to the musicians' graves, and the promise of a convivial afterlife.

Such people should not be approached without offerings. She retraces her steps to the flower stall outside the gate and taps into her grown-up vibe. Something with roots. Something appropriate. 'At the archduke's, my cousin's . . .' So lilacs. She chooses a plant already in bloom which the stall holder wraps in imperial purple and, squaring her shoulders, brushes aside the sellers of postcards and memorabilia who mistake her for the tourist she no longer is, sets off on the long walk.

The substantial gravestone she is heading for has many names on it, the Rosses turned Kaufmann mere interlopers. But perhaps that's in the nature of graveyard geopolitics. Who of her family is likely to be there? Christina alongside her final husband who is no relation and Saskia, always assuming she has already made her way here and is not in some transitional place of contemplation.

When she gets back to the UK which must be soon, she will reclaim the painting of the girl in the yellow dress, put it back where it belongs and make her way without delay to the Highlands. The only problem with that is liquid assets which have not yet come up in conversation. In the absence of liquid assets she will be forced to use her wits. Then she will go looking for a northern cemetery, a proper cemetery with crumbling stones you have to scrape the moss off to read.

The grave is getting closer. It will be on the right. Up ahead there are fresh flowers, possibly Saskia's. Who would send them? The theatre group, Herr Strauss. Frau Frühwirth. How little she knows of Saskia's circle, a circle, after all, of mainly dead people. Which thought brings her to the grave which is indeed ablaze with flowers confirming Saskia's arrival, a location marker like balloons outside a party house, as well as a mark of respect and affection. Copious and extravagant, filling the allotted space, elbowing out the squat and forceful shrub growing in the plot to the right which has sensed a dynasty in decline. Next time she comes she will bring secateurs.

Saskia's name is not yet on the stone. There is space for it below Christina's but she will end the line. Christina's name is given as Christina Ross. The names above it are long and Germanic, interspersed with professions and honours, *Handelsman, Realitätenbesitzer, Architekt, Baurat*, the name preceding Christina's is tagged with Knight of the Order of Franz Josef. The sense of their presence is physical. She would like to believe that the sense of her own presence might weigh enough to register in return. Sometimes it's respectful to suspend disbelief. So to Saskia, treating the coffin as a chaise longue where she will lounge in perpetuity, cigarette holder in hand, she says, "Got the message." And only then becomes aware of a man standing in front of the adjoining grave, the one with the forceful shrub.

She unwraps the lilac, discarding the wrapping and the plural, and looks for a place to put it. There is an empty urn and the blossoms stretch out and settle. They should have water. A hand holding a brass watering can reaches towards her from the grave to her right. "*Danke,*" she says and waters the plant using all the water. She turns to apologise for that to the owner of the hand, a trim thirty-something holding in his other hand a single weed, holding it too obviously to establish *bona fides* as the son of the dead person next door.

"Fraulein Kaufmann?" he says with a small teutonic bow. "May I offer you my condolences on your sad loss." He puts down the watering can, drops the weed and reaches out a hand. She thanks him and shakes the hand, turning away immediately to look at the names on Saskia's flowers, but finds it hard to blank him out. Here is Herr Strauss's wreath, and next to it Frau Frühwirth's. The flashiest most dominant wreath trying and failing on grounds of taste, sensibility and empathy to promote its sender as principal mourner carries in block capitals the name Markus Roschmann.

She pulls back before her fingers touch the card and wonders if the man intruding on her private space might be him. But no. Twice glimpsed but not forgotten. This is not a good place to be right now. She senses that if she starts to walk away he will join her. She hesitates and her phone buzzes,

"Where are you?" says Martin's voice and she moves away.

"At the Friedhof. At the grave." She starts to move down the avenue aware that the man is close behind her.

"I think you may have company. Act on instinct. I'm coming to get you."

There is no one nearby but coming back from the area of the musicians' graves is a family with young children. She goes back to the grave, picks up the plant wrapping and hurries toward them as if from the man's perspective they might be friends. Reaching them she waves the wrapping paper and makes a display of trying to find the words in German for where are the litter bins, hopefully with an overlay of 'help me out here'. "*Wo kann ich...*" she says, flapping the paper in their faces. Let them think she's crazy, hope they stay polite. The mother helpfully tries to take the wrapping from her, signalling that she will bin it. Charlotte resists. She makes a performance of looking round for a bin. They point ahead down the avenue in the direction of the gate and allow her to walk alongside them. When they reach the bin she thanks them profusely and ditches the paper, glancing back to see that the man is still in her wake. What could he do in a public place? Quite a lot. What can she do? Become a litter obsessive. Unfortunately this is not a country where people eat on the move and drop the wrapping, but a puff of wind lifts a solitary sheet of newspaper and she chases it down, seizes it triumphantly and puts it in the next bin. She is now being noticed, no one likely to approach her, and if the man does that he will have an audience.

Another family comes past and she attaches herself to them, keeping a little distance, until they reach the gate by which time she has only a couple of minutes to wait before Martin pulls up with a racing stop and throws open the door.

"Problems?" she asks as he does a racing reverse.

"Developments. Good and not so good. Were you approached back there?"

"There was a man tending the next grave."

"In working clothes? A gardener?"

"Sports jacket and jeans. He did pull up a weed."

"Did he speak to you?"

"He offered me his watering can."

"What did you do?"

"I took it and watered the plant I'd brought. Why? Was that an error judgement?"

"Did he say anything?"

"He offered me his condolences. He knew my name."

"OK. Much as I thought. What happened next?"

"You phoned. What developments?"

"We found some buried treasure."

"The silver."

"There was rather a lot of silver, all of it monogrammed and in need of polishing. A salver or two, tea services, some small stuff."

"And?"

"A soup tureen. Oh and also some papers. Rather a lot of those."

"Colin's stuff."

"I would say so."

"Is it as you hoped?"

"And then some. Back at base they've been glancing over it. They'll start working on it tomorrow. Meanwhile I guess it's still yours."

"Really?"

"On the face of it as sole beneficiary I would say so. Of course you might have to prove it was your great-aunt who buried it all and what right she had to it and in the meantime the papers would have disappeared and the silver ended up in Sotheby's."

"Let's get this straight. You as a representative of the UK government or in some shadier capacity are trying to bribe me with my own inheritance to let you make off with Colin's stuff."

"That's about it."

"Fine with me. Do I get to know what's in it?"

"There you go again."

"I know, it's above my pay grade, but as a gesture."

"We might have to kill you. Look, while we're talking this way, what are your plans?"

"I should get back to the UK."

"Why not home? You never say home."

"I haven't really got one of those."

"So, having dealt with whatever domestic arrangements you are lucky enough not to have, you might return to Vienna?"

"That's what I'm hoping."

"OK, we need to talk. Anywhere you like to suggest? Not that bloody bar though."

"Since this sounds ominously philosophical what about the wheel in the Prater?"

"You must be joking."

"I am."

"Thank God for that. Someone might join us. Where else?"

"Demel?"

"We might have to queue and since it's all about patisserie we wouldn't do much talking. Perhaps one of the art gallery cafés. We could see the collection first. Have you seen the Klimts and the Schieles?"

"A Schiele. Just the one. On Frau Frühwirth's drawing room wall. She sits with her back to it but it's rather taxing for her guests."

"But he was amazingly versatile for one who died so young. He died in the Spanish Flu Epidemic. As did Klimt. Schiele's work is in the Leopold in the Museum Quarter. We could talk in the café there."

Martin parks and calls someone. They are on the edge of a vast paved space with detached buildings arranged around it, the Museum Quarter. He is being considerate. There is an agenda. Call made, he retains his pleasant expression which is starting to spook her, and they stroll, really stroll, among the buildings in a manner she can only put down to deflecting observers.

"OK, so what was the urgency of getting me out of the Friedhof? And did you fix the leak?"

"Leak?"

"In the cellar."

"We came out with drenched overalls leaving a damp bit of floor neatly patched. The reason I called you was that we had an interested observer outside the building while we were working there. We picked up his phone conversation. He was speaking to someone who seemed to be at the Zentralfriedhof."

"But why would I still be of interest to them?"

"You might be useful as a bargaining chip."

"You mean they'd kidnap me? What would that do?"

"Cause embarrassment when your disappearance became a police matter and we were found to be implicated. I really think you should start looking out for yourself, or let us do that for you. Maybe time to enjoy Vienna."

Enjoy? What's this about? Aloud she says, "You're right. I haven't seen any sights except the Hofburg."

"And the Bohemian State Chancellery."

"So tell me, which Habsburg decided there would be enough stuff to fill all these museums and galleries? These are old buildings."

"They already had the stuff. They were the ultimate collectors, generations of them organised expeditions and brought back fossils, rock samples, artefacts, plants from more or less everywhere. If you see just one museum make it the Natural History. The buildings? Well, some of them were the imperial stables. Six hundred horses were stabled here. Down there, that's the back of the Hofburg, so this was its backyard."

"They recycled. Franz Joseph knocked down the fortifications which were restricting the growth of the city and created the Ringstrasse, and Johan Strauss junior knocked out the Demolition Polka. You get the picture."

"I'm still trying to work out the family link with Franz Joseph, the idea that he might drop in for dinner."

"He was totally hands-on. His working day started at five. Joseph Roth looked back on his reign which was being sent up by the younger writers, himself included, and found himself mourning its passing. It was unique."

Unique, Charlotte thinks as Martin takes another call, polar opposite of cool. What did your family do? Made themselves useful to the Emperor Franz Joseph. Emperor? Emperor of what? The Austro-Hungarian Empire. You're making it up.

A world where you needed horses the way you needed candles . . . Some time should be spent there. Half of Europe was once Habsburg along with chunks of the New World, chunks as large as Mexico, all this with an HQ in a country that doesn't even have a coastline. And they were Holy Roman Emperors, Grand Masters of the Order of the Golden Fleece, how uncool is that? Freud is still cool, Mozart never lost his cool, only their country did that. And what has this to do with her current status, someone who needs careful handling in case she rocks the boat? Something to do with identity or lack of it, she and the Habsburgs both. Well, time to fight back.

Martin finishes his call and they continue their stroll to the Leopold Museum where she rates Schiele at least equal with Klimt and they adjourn to the museum café where they order coffee and a modest pastry apiece to display their tourist credentials.

"Well now. To business. As well as mending the leak which was under the apartment of an elderly long-time resident who made little use of his cellar and whose apartment we are redecorating by way of compensation, we took the chance to have a look at all the ground floor apartments. The apartment which was designated as an office of Aurelius Interventions was particularly interesting. Herr Roschmann's other interests were in evidence there, a small pharmaceutical operation linked to a lab in the Czech Republic which is thought to have been the source of whatever killed the homeless men in London and the Romanian woman in the Highlands. There is a UK end to this. Hints of traffic to and from the Scottish Highlands."

"Ah."

"It is entirely due to your initiative that Markus Roschmann came to anyone's attention. Can you remind me how your great-aunt came to meet him?"

"He was introduced to her by someone in her theatre group. He was a new member."

"A theatre group? That might be fruitful."

"In what way?"

"As long as he can be lulled into thinking he is not in our sights we might find a fellow theatregoer to join the group. A mature theatregoer, Patrick for instance." A man with a flat white and a meringue on a tray is passing their table. Martin hails him, he expresses surprise and diverts towards them. "Charlotte, this is Patrick. Patrick, this is Charlotte. Do join us."

Older, distinguished looking, up a grade or two from Martin no doubt. Odd choice, the meringue, but perhaps it's cover. "Miss Kaufmann," he says, "you have caused something of a stir in certain circles in this city which has seen more than its share of turbulence. You have been here how long? Less than a week. If you were to stay any longer we would have to take on extra staff. You have given us a great deal to work on. We have been wondering what plans if any you have for a longer return to Vienna."

"I'm coming back. That's for sure. When and for how long I can't say. It depends, for instance, on whether I have inherited my great-aunt's apartment and if I could afford to stay."

"If you were to consider doing some further work for us in an informal capacity you would certainly be able to afford to stay here. For some time at least."

"I don't do proper jobs. I fail to respect how things are done."

"Music to my ears."

She can't do this, sit and listen, and something's bugging her. This link to the Highlands. Does she still owe a promise of secrecy to Charles Merchant?

"Look," she says, "there's something I have to ask. This mystery drug, can it cause loss of memory?"

"We've heard that," says Martin quickly. "The buzz is that it's a tidy solution so long as it's permanent. No need for terminal solutions, just wipe out the memory. Why?"

"In the Highlands, before I came here, I almost met the dead Romanian girl. Her body at least." She has their attention and Charles Merchant is surely a long way clear of being a suspect, whether or not he knows that. "I met a man in a bar. He had lost his memory. He didn't know who he was or where he was. He had wakened in a hotel bedroom with a dead girl in bed beside him. He asked me to check on her but she had disappeared."

Now she's losing them. They look away as she talks, avoiding eye contact, re-assessing her as a reliable narrator. "Go on," says Martin.

"He wanted me to help him. I checked into the same hotel and looked in his room. The body had gone. He thought it was a plant and that more or less confirmed it."

"And this was in the North Highlands? Near the place where the body was found?"

"Yes. And near the solicitor's office where I had gone as a condition of her bequest to hear about Saskia's will."

"Have you any plans," says Patrick, "to return to the Highlands?"

"Sure. Right after I get back. I want to research my family history. Go looking in cemeteries."

Martin and Patrick exchange the sort of glance they probably don't know women interpret. Her future is being decided, they think. Patrick hasn't touched his meringue.

"If you're not going to eat that . . ." Charlotte says. He pushes the plate towards her.

"So when are you thinking of returning to the UK?" Patrick wants to know. "We'll book your flight. Just let Martin know."

"I just have to tell Herr Strauss I'm leaving. Otherwise there is nothing to keep me here. What have you done with the silver?"

"We'll keep it under lock and key. Talking of which we found something else." Martin takes an envelope out of his pocket and lays it on the table in front of her. The contents are hard and quite heavy. She starts to open it but Martin puts out a hand to stop her. "We thought you'd prefer to open it when you got back to the hotel."

"I'd rather open it now if you don't mind."

"Just don't flash them around then," says Martin.

She opens the corner of the envelope and holds it out of

sight, on her knee and under the table. The emeralds are dazzling. "Christina's emeralds! I wondered if they'd turn up." From either side a hand reaches out to stop her pulling them out. "Beautiful," she says. "But not really me."

"I'm sure you'll find a buyer," says Martin. "Perhaps Sotheby's or Christie's."

"Perhaps I'll keep them for a while. Just to look at."

Chapter Twenty

The weight of the glass in his hand and the scent of the single malt belong in a world Adam has been too long away from. The room is familiar but the sense of impending danger has gone. The tattered upholstery of the fireside armchair where he now sits opposite Ewan Cameron-Gunn is as reassuring as an old sweater. Ewan throws a log onto the fire and asks the girl with long legs to leave them alone for a bit. She goes without argument.

"When we found you," Ewan says, "in the glen, you had the look of a wounded stag looking for a place to die. Why was that?"

"I was not myself." Keep it brief. Let it unfold. "Hadn't been myself for a day or two."

"Because?"

"I had lost my memory."

"All of it?"

"Pretty well. I knew I had met you before. I just didn't know the context."

"And now?"

"I know not to be afraid of you. I didn't then. I was living on the last of my wits. How did we know each other? I still haven't figured that out."

"You came to see me. Guy Harkness called me and asked if I could help you with a story you were researching."

"Did he say what the story was about?"

"Not in any detail. I imagine he was respecting your hope of an exclusive."

"How did Guy Harkness know me?"

"I know how he knows me. We were at Clare together. I

don't know how he knew you. Perhaps because you were both broadsheet hacks."

"Ah. The name means nothing to me. There are bits still missing."

"He described you as a former colleague gone rogue. His term for freelance I imagine. He said you were onto something in the Highlands that needed informed local gossip. He thought I could help."

"And did you?"

"I believe so. I've regretted it ever since. These are dangerous waters you've chosen to swim in."

"Are we talking about a man by the name of Theo?"

"Alas yes. His name is seldom articulated."

"Why is that?"

"He has spies."

"What do you know about him?"

"Nothing. And I know more than most."

"Have you met him?"

"I have been in a room that he was also in."

"What is it about him that you put it that way?"

"His is a slight and sinister presence. Something of the night in play there. Certainly nothing of the outdoors."

"So why would a man like that buy an estate in the remotest part of the Highlands?"

"I think you've just answered that. How did he come to your attention?"

"I was following up a lead. Not so much a lead as a hint. The son of a friend I was meeting for Sunday lunch spotted a face in the crowd on the front page of the *Sunday Times*. He identified him as the new owner of the estate where he had a holiday job grouse beating. The new owner had spooked him. He thought the grouse were a front. For what, he didn't know, but Jeremy had the impression he was dealing in the dark arts of cyberpolitics, neuropolitics, the creative use of disinformation, ways to manipulate people. Teaching these he thought. He had monosyllabic staff, not English people, possibly experts in this and that who did the actual teaching. The grouse were a shop front to satisfy the locals. He underrated the locals. He underrated local knowledge, curiosity, a mind-set he had no experience of.

"They weren't that discreet when he was around. He was assumed to be of low intelligence because he was doing a physical job. These were people with a narrow world view and an ancestral attitude to serfs. Unfortunately I can't recall anything of what I found out."

"You went there?"

"I did. I went there twice. The first time I remember. It came back to me when I saw a picture of the castle in a book. On that occasion I didn't get inside. The second was undercover and it's gone. Memory wiped clean."

"So what did Jeremy tell you of the guests at the shoot? The men notionally shooting grouse?"

"A mix of nationalities and personality types but broadly speaking power players, no need to be liked, no need to chat. The Gulf and north of there, a Saudi, couple of oligarchs, past or current, a solitary straight-up Yank, though not that straight I imagine, a Philipino and a little group of Aztecs or Incas. Theo and the guys who were working with him on the technical side, he thought were from somewhere in the Caucasus. Bright guy, Jeremy. He thought they might be looking for the next thing after oil. His guess of course. Those that weren't into regime toppling. They paid off the hired help with full pay half way through the season, he thought before they got down to the real business."

"And you never found out what that was?"

"I found out that they've taken care to erase it from my memory."

"How?"

"My guess is I became a guinea pig for a drug they were experimenting with. Quite successfully in my case."

"And how did you reach that conclusion?"

"I'll come back to that. First I have a question or two for you.

What can you tell me about your – er – disciples? Followers of the prophet Hector? I don't know what they call themselves."

"The Enlightened. I'm happy to say they came up with that themselves."

"If I were you I'd be wary of what they come up with themselves."

"Why is that?"

"He whose name we fear to speak may have got at them. I was staying in the hotel where they held their conference. Where I have reason to think some people working for him were also staying. Just before the conference I overheard something. A conversation between men not afraid to speak his name. One of them said 'You might be about to witness an experiment in Celtic Exceptionalism.'"

Ewan reacts to this by a deepened state of listening. He stands up, walks across to the window, comes back, reaches for the decanter and tops up both their glasses. "That might explain a lot. You think he's got at them?"

"I think he's got into their heads and now he's writing their script."

"Why would he do that?"

"To show the paying guests how to manipulate people into thinking they have a grievance and then finding common cause."

"The Passively Enlightened."

"They took their title from a desire to associate themselves with the Scottish Enlightenment of the eighteenth century, I imagine. They seemed like perfectly decent people with a strong interest in history. Perhaps a tendency to the romantic view. In the aftermath of the independence referendum they were looking to get some affirmation of an eventual victory. A sign from the gods you might say. That was when they first heard about Hector. Whom you had previously discovered."

"There is a little evidence. Oral mostly."

"This part of the Highlands has everything going for it but a name. Loch Ness has the monster, the south west has Burns.

Hector rather fell to earth. A creative solution to the problems of a remote economy."

"I'm with you in spirit. He clearly has potential. Not too clear on the epiphany though."

"I was talking about the prophecies of the Brahan Seer, with one of our tenant farmers. How much power they would have had among the less sceptical. Duncan said that his granny used to talk of someone like that in these parts. Seventh son of a seventh son. I asked him if she mentioned a name. He said Hector."

"Of Farr?"

"He needed grounding. He became something to talk about in the dark days. Gaby got behind it pretty quickly. She did the art work. Someone must have overheard us and word got around. I was contacted by a local amateur historian who got very excited about Hector. He did some research and found there was someone who more or less filled the bill in Farr. He convinced himself."

"That must have been a felicitous reassurance."

"He found something in the oral tradition. In Gaelic of course. Really I was only the enabler."

"Or the godfather. Was that man with you on the occasion of my timely rescue by you? For which I owe you a belated thanks. There was a man in the room, rather fiercely spoken and fierce to look at who was conversant with the original."

"That's him." The urban seagull of Adam's recollection satisfactorily identified.

"Hector gradually took on a life of his own. I never quite understood that. Perhaps I do now."

"When I returned to the conscious world I found a card in my wallet. No contact details, just the company title, Synchronised Solutions. On the reverse it said Off-Centre of Excellence. It could be read as a reference to their location or to the nature of their solutions. Probably both."

"From what you overheard he is into mind games. I wonder who his targets are."

"I have the impression that he would be too dispassionate to have targets of his own. It seems likely that he is selling his solutions to people with their own agenda."

"Has it occurred to you that you are the exception?"

"I don't follow."

"You were his target. Probably still are." It's true. He has absorbed without personalising. "Where were you when you realised that someone had been practising mind games on you?"

"It was some time before I began to come to that conclusion. To start with I had no idea who I was, so no concept of normal."

"Where were you, then, when you recovered consciousness?"

"In bed. In a first floor front-facing room at the Achindarnoch House Hotel. Where the conference was about to take place."

"So why didn't you seek help from the hotel?"

"I didn't know who I was or what I was doing there."

"All the more reason. I would have marched down to reception and demanded to know who I was. They would have it in the register in your own writing."

"I don't believe you would have done that. Not if there was a dead girl in bed with you."

"Aaaah . . ." Ewan has perceptibly stiffened. "Perhaps it's my turn to be afraid of you."

"A girl in a green dress."

"The Romanian girl?"

"I would have thought so."

"That does change things. How did you – er – dispose of her?"

"I didn't. Someone took her away. Theo's people I'd guess."

"OK. Now we're singing from the same sheet. You can count on my help."

Back in his room at the hotel Adam takes from his pocket the scrap of paper put there by the man in the crowd and calls the number. "Can't talk now," says the voice on the other end. "I'll call you back." Not the words a man without a mobile wants to hear. He goes down to the reception desk. "I made a call just now from the phone in my room," he says. "They're calling me back. Would that go to a central switchboard?"

"All outside calls come to the desk. We have no facilities for incoming direct dialling."

"So, if I was to be at one of your outside tables rather than my room . . ."

"Someone will come and find you sir."

"That is more than kind."

The outside tables are sparsely populated yet the buzz of the morning's events is still in the air. When the girl once again in red trousers comes to take his order he settles for lentil soup and something called a buttery rowie with a pot of tea. Ewan's single malts as well as his informed in-fill are still at work in his head and he craves comfort food and low-key distraction. When the Fieldings arrive and join him he is absurdly happy to see them.

"Any wolf sightings today?" he asks Holly.

"I would think it was a sensitive wolf," she says. "A wolf that avoids crowds."

"I'm sure you're right. What did you think of the performance?"

"I liked it. Mummy says Hector was a ham actor. She's seen him in Eastenders. I didn't think he was bad enough to be shot."

"It's lucky it wasn't a real bullet." He turns to Brian Fielding. "Have you heard anything about the man who shot him?"

"The police are questioning him. To be specific, the policeman who came to see the wolf and I imagine a colleague of his. Ah, here he is now."

The police car draws up and the two Glasgow guys get out. The car drives off. "They had to give a statement," Brian explains. "They were standing next to him when he fired. Who would have thought a May holiday break in the Highlands had so much to offer?" He calls to the men to come and join them.

"My father," Holly tells them, "wants to ask you about the assassin. I told him it was probably *sub judice*."

"Is that right? Well no one told us."

The girl in the red tartan trousers comes to the table and as the newcomers are deciding between craft beers she tells Adam that the call he expected has come through. At the desk he tells them he will take the call in his room. The voice is English and curt. "Look, I'm not happy with land lines."

"I understand. Only I don't have a phone at the moment."

"OK. Meet me down on the bank below the hotel. Where the rowing boat is moored. Half an hour."

Back outside they are still listening to the story of the mystery gun man. Everyone is laughing. The men are telling it in a mix of Highland and foreign accents peppered with misunderstandings.

"I'm so sorry," Adam says. "Can you fill me in?"

"To cut a long story short," says the straight man of the pair, "a Bulgarian lorry driver. Guy gave him a hundred quid. He was happy to play his part. They told him he was to be an actor and the shooting was in the script. Not a happy guy when we jumped him."

"I'll bet. Any clues to the guy who set him up?"

"That's what Jim's onto now," says a man at the next table. "Hopes to get it tied up before they send in someone from Glasgow."

The girl in the red trousers brings his lunch and he devours it with the appetite that has stayed with him. The baked item has the taste and texture of a round croissant. "I got the chef to heat it up for you," signalling that she is aware of his edgy behaviours. She comes back with a fresh pot of tea and with all that under his belt he excuses himself and walks round the building and along the bank of the loch towards the moored rowing boat. The man is already there standing under a weeping willow.

"I'll be brief," he says. "When we're done here walk on along the loch side. I don't want you on my heels and I don't want anyone seeing us together. I'm taking a big enough risk as it is."

The crowd at the tables has dispersed but he is in no mood for conversation. He needs to keep moving as he turns over what he has just heard. He goes for a walk, several walks, changing direction to stay close to the hotel while staying on the move, oblivious to the landscape, He has to unload this, share it with someone. There is only one candidate. From his room he calls Ewan. Gaby answers. Ewan is out with an estate employee organising the thinning of trees and won't be back for two or three hours. They agree that Adam will go there in the morning. But by evening the hotel is abuzz with a fresh piece of news. A man's body has been found floating in the loch.

Chapter Twenty-One

The Highlands and Islands Major Investigation Team arrive by chopper. There's been a road traffic incident involving a lorry taking sheep to market and a camper van whose driver has little or no English. The guests are corralled in the residents' lounge.

"Now we get to guess which of us is the guilty party," says Holly.

"She's a Marple fan," her mother explains.

"I think they may decide to take us one by one," Adam suggests.

"That's true. Though I expect they'll make an exception for families. Interrogating Abby on her own might be counter-productive."

"That's enough Holly."

"I expect they will." There is no doubt in his mind that he will flash up as the prime suspect among the guests, an outsider and on his own. No advance booking, no proof of identity beyond the card. He had explained to the girl on reception that he had left a bag behind at his last stop. They weren't going to turn away a man of evident stature who could turn on such a self-deprecating smile.

When asked to account for his movements he will have to come up with a cover story for the phone call he so publicly expected and received. If the man found floating in the loch is who he assumes him to be his phone will have the evidence but none of the explanation. But if the man he is working for is behind the killing as surely he must be then he will have taken his phone. He was, Adam reminds himself, also seen to leave the company and walk round the side of the hotel and towards the loch. But after all this is landscape and in landscape to go for a walk is culturally, environmentally and socially sound. But his back story is full of holes and he is presently functioning under a false identity. Flight is not an option. This time he'd be caught.

Ewan could vouch for him but only as a man going by the name of Adam Maxwell, and not without summoning from the shadows the man whose name it seems blasphemous as well as incautious to utter. In Greek perhaps the vocative of God and in many languages a short form for Theodore, gift of God or Theophilus, beloved of God, the small, slight, pleasantly featured face in the crowd, the man who conjures up hi-tech interventions for the benefit of the community. The man who, if his name comes up, a Highland police force will surely place on the side of the angels.

The girl in the varying tartan trousers whose name he now learns is Eilidh brings tea, coffee and biscuits for the guests to serve themselves and there is an agreeable hum of complicity in moving events with no more than a token expression of grief for the dead man which seems to confirm that he is not local. The hotel staff will know.

The door of the residents' lounge opens with a flourish and four people come in. The hotel manager thanks the guests for their patience which they will be asked to exercise for a little longer and introduces DI McCracken who in turn introduces DS Singleton and DS Swan. DS Swan is female if it is not a gross breach of gender-neutrality to notice that. His degenerate assumption is that he will fare better with her. DI McCracken asks if any of the hotel guests has a departure scheduled for before ten o'clock tomorrow morning. No one has. He might have been thus inclined but no need to bring that up. That is just as well, says McCracken, as they would now be obliged to change their plans. Adam's plan to share the afternoon's revelations with Ewan which would surely have advanced a resolution will now have to be put on hold.

The straight man of the Glasgow double act goes off with

DS Singleton, his friend with DS Swan. Is there a race memory of gang wars in the decision to deal with the Glasgow guys first?

DS Singleton returns alone and carries off one of the recently arrived East Midlands Munro-bagging sisterhood. Of course, they won't mix the questioned with the still to be questioned. DS Swan returns flushed with laughter and leaves with the second climber. They'll keep him till last and that will confirm him as the man most likely. Two more guests go off. The staff are being questioned elsewhere. Then it is the turn of the Fieldings. He is now alone with the DI who starts a conversation that Adam takes as a courtesy to fill in the waiting time. As the time passes and the questions become more direct he realises that this is it, his moment in the spotlight.

He is writing an article on the Highlands for a magazine, his story for the Fieldings. Which magazine that will be has yet to be decided. He is a freelance who prefers not to work to commission. He will sell his story to the highest bidder. Not the most felicitous of self-parodies, but he can live with a charge of arrogance.

Where had he spent the time after he watched the filming? McCracken understood that while he had gone there with the Fieldings he had not returned with them. Why with Ewan Cameron-Gunn of course. For a chat over a single malt or two at the stately pad. If this is name-dropping, which it is, it doesn't work. The Highlands are a democracy and he probably knew that already.

"Then you drove back?"

Nice try, DI. "I did not. My car was here at the hotel. Ewan asked one of the men on the estate to bring me back."

"And then?"

"I had some lunch. Soup. And one of those delicious rolls that tastes like croissant. At one of the outside tables."

"During which you were called to take a phone call I believe."

"That is correct."

"I'll need to see your phone."

"I don't have a phone at the moment. I used the extension in my bedroom."

"May I ask why you don't have a phone? You must see that that is unusual."

"Oh I'm not phone phobic. I lost it."

"And where was that?"

"If I knew that I would have been able to find it." Bit of bad judgement there. Probably just confirming his arrogant bastard status.

"Roughly. Give or take fifty miles?"

"I can't even fine it down that closely I'm afraid. I've been travelling the highways and byways for several days now. No cause to use it."

"For your magazine article."

"That's right."

"You didn't even use it as a camera?"

"Once a magazine has signalled interest I'll contact a local professional photographer. Point of principle."

So now, Adam thinks, we'll be moving on to the overnight stops. Mitch Carruthers knows too much about his dual identity to be a character reference. And his previous hotel history is a car crash waiting to happen. But for the moment at least McCracken seems to be done with him. He gets to his feet and yawns. "I needn't keep you any longer but of course you'll be on hand if I have more questions. Thank you for your time."

As he leaves the room the others return. "Are we allowed to go outside now?" Brian Fielding asks the room

"It's chilly, Brian," his wife says.

"We're not allowed anyway," Holly says.

"What authority do you have for that?"

"Common sense. They can watch the doors but they can't watch the outside."

For the Munro baggers this is the first experience of Holly.

They are teachers, they know children and obviously Holly is a rarity. Out of the conversation now Adam considers his options. If he can get out of a locked cottage he can get out of a hotel where civilised behaviour is assumed. It is only at this point that he sees how far his secret history has taken him along the road less travelled. The hotel guests are not prime suspects, only people to be ticked off the list before they go on their separate ways. "Does anyone know anything about the victim?" he asks to bring himself back into the real world. Slip of the tongue there. From the reaction it's clear that he may be the only person making an assumption of homicide rather than death by misadventure.

"I don't think there was any suggestion of foul play," says Brian Fielding. Except perhaps from your daughter, Adam thinks, whose lead I was only too happy to follow. The others seem to share his point of view. "Unless you know something we don't know," he says, and, turning to the others, "Charles is a journalist." It seems that accounts for a tendency to hype. "On the other hand would they have held us here if they hadn't clearly excluded his death being due to natural causes? It did seem an over-reaction."

When the girl now known to him as Eilidh comes into the room with the news that the hotel is laying on a light buffet for everyone there is general rejoicing and they head for the dining room. Drinks will be brought from the bar as required, the bar itself is out of bounds, but there are no takers. They are talked out. Adam has a last chance to suss out his assumption that the dead man is his informant and his death, retribution for that. He asks Eilidh when she comes to clear the plates if she knows who he is.

She says that no one so far has recognised him. The hotel manager who seems to be owner rather than manager was asked to view the body when it was first discovered. "And he knows everybody," she says. "He wasn't from around here." That settled, the obligation for retrospective sympathy finally removed, the company decides that it's time for bed.

In his room Adam tests the window. It opens and the drop to the grassy bank below has the start of the gradient in its favour but it's the guilty guy's way out, and he is innocent. Shifty maybe but innocent. And more to the point he needs the car. He closes the window and sits in the armchair to focus on his innocence and to consider the reach of his plausibility. And when Ewan calls the way is clear. He cleans his teeth, combs his hair, puts on the cashmere sweater and the parka, puts his suit jacket and heathery accoutrements in his bag and descends to the front door. Where he tells the girl on reception that he has just had a call from Ewan to tell him that his mother is seriously ill and has just been taken into hospital. If he can now settle his bill he must head south immediately.

DS Swan, sitting over coffee and his laptop in the reception area gives Adam his blessing and good wishes for a speedy recovery for his mother. She will clear it with the DI.

Peace of mind restored he drives to Dunchattan House where there is a ground floor light showing and where Ewan himself comes to the door. In the now familiar drawing room Ewan throws two logs onto the fire and pours two more single malts from the decanter and Adam, sinking into the fireside armchair, for the first time in as long as he can remember, feels safe. Almost.

Chapter Twenty-Two

The man found floating in the loch, Ewan says, had no phone, no clues to his identity. He heard this from his ghillie who helped fish him out. No one knows who he is.

"Except me," says Adam. His words hang in the air, ungrounded. This power to frighten, it's unearthly, and because it's not his to own, fascinating. This is how some people live. "I spoke to him this afternoon. Not long after I left you." Actions, now, behind the words. He watches it play out. Ewan had been disposed to like him. How easily that can change. This visit to the dark side is a learning experience.

"He was in the crowd at the filming." Something like complicity brings Ewan into the picture. "He slipped a note into my pocket with his mobile number. The sheet it was torn from was headed Synchronised Solutions."

"And?"

"I met him. He was at that hotel where the conference was held. He was one of the men I overheard talking about sabotaging your disciples. Hector's disciples. And before that he had pulled a stunt on me."

"A stunt?"

"Played with my mental state. Pretended to point a gun at me and laughed when I fell on my face. It was just a couple of hours after I'd recovered consciousness."

"In bed. With a dead girl."

"If you can imagine how that feels. When you don't know who you are or how you got there. When you don't know if you killed her."

"Not at the top of your game I imagine."

The vibe from the other side of the fire is interesting. "Prep school bully," says Ewan. Of course, his own experiences will out-gross those of a grammar school boy. "So, you met the guy."

"It was pretty rushed but he filled me in. He'd been a schoolboy computer whizz, done time for hacking, had a job with a games company when he was approached and offered a crazy sum to join a new company start-up. The dosh came with a secrecy clause and the obligation to live in. His girlfriend had just kicked him out and a castle in Scotland sounded cool. He was flown in on a private plane with a bunch of assorted eggheads and a Ukrainian chef. They were picked up at Inverness. At the castle they were shown around by a girl he described as 'like a real Comptessa, an English Comptessa' who was to be the meeter and greeter. The castle was at the head of a glen with no other habitation in sight.

"The household staff were local and straight. He already knew he would be mixing it with illegals on the hard and soft tech sides. They were kept apart from the guests who were there to shoot grouse. Ostensibly. His job was to create cyber solutions to problems the guests came up with. In some cases where they needed fundamental know-how he was brought in as a tutor. They had a psychologist, a behaviourist, and some scary people on the pharma side."

"And the guests, the guns, what were they like?"

"Power players with no need to chat. Unbribable, he thought, speaking from his own background, so with money behind them. Different nationalities, institutions or in one case at least a regime. Generally speaking, the unbribable."

"So their ambitions may have lain beyond industrial sabotage?"

"Way beyond. Ultimately way beyond what the guy imagined he'd signed up to. And beyond my ability to articulate cyber terminology until I can get hold of something that can access Google and Wikipedia."

"I'd lend you a tablet if I could say off the top of my head that my conscience was entirely clear. I can't."

"Understood. Search headings are still fizzing in my head. Neuropolitics, predictive analytics, prescriptive analytics, necropolitics. To come back to earth or closer to earth, Hector's disciples became the subject of an experiment. Theo's own pet project. That's why they were at the Achindarnoch House Hotel."

"Go on."

"Finding himself in Scotland and knowing nothing about the culture beyond Braveheart and recurring independence headlines he wondered whether people of such strong conviction and sense of separateness would be more or less malleable than rebels without a cause or with a Rust Belt outlook. I'm paraphrasing, the guy's English was passable but not that idiomatic.

"He said Theo became hooked on what he called a Historic Antipathy. Kneejerk Anglophobia though everyone said some of their best friends were English. He replayed newscasts of the Tartan Army. He thought that something had been implanted in the race memory dating back more years than he could fathom, two or three hundred years.

"If he could manipulate them into going beyond their own limits or acting out of their thought-through sphere that would be a model for clients with regime change on their minds. It was Theo's idea to set them thinking their cause was so just it had to be silenced. Hence the hotel bomb. It was supposed to induce corporate paranoia. As was the gunshot aimed to silence Hector. The gun originally had a real bullet. Our guy was charged with setting up the shooter. He changed the bullet for a wax one and skewed the sights. Unfortunately the Bulgarian lorry driver had an astigmatism that made it a dead shot. Which might have produced the Trump Effect. But that seemed not to happen."

"Ah," says Ewan, "I can help there. Those people he thought he was brainwashing were not natural disciples, more like natural anarchists. They were becoming disenchanted with Hector. The lady in the cape asked what he had had to say about the role of women. It seemed the role of women hadn't crossed his mind. And on the environment he was remarkably unspecific for a man who lived, one would think, at its mercy. There were contrasting views on the environment. Some thought that oil production should continue in Scotland until the alternatives were sufficiently reliable to replace it, others wanted to blow up rigs. One man thought that the proliferation of wind farms meant that England would be stealing Scotland's wind. Hector had failed to foresee that. There was an outbreak of rampant individualism which even I could have predicted. And the guy you spoke to . . . what was it that convinced him to turn King's Evidence, which, one way or another, he would find himself to have done?"

"First and last, the drug component. He began to react when he saw what it could do. He was repelled by that."

"He was that squeamish?"

"His mother had a problem."

"And where exactly did the drugs come into it?"

"A lab somewhere in the Czech Republic with an offshoot in Vienna was working on something they hoped would erase part of the memory without overt effects on a person's perceived functioning. This was to be the big money-spinner. You can see how useful it would be. In the conversation I overheard in the conference hotel I thought I picked up something about Marco Polo. In fact it would have been Narco Polo, their term for the politics of narcotics but also the experimental use of narcotics to influence politics. Through memory loss I imagine."

"And you were their guinea pig."

"A fortuitous guinea pig. I had, I'm told, talked myself onto the list of prospective shooters from whom they chose their clients. I became increasingly unconvincing. I asked the wrong questions. The magic potion still had some way to go but they thought they could wipe my memory and get me out of their hair while seeing how it worked.

"They'd brought in a few girls to replace some of the household staff, chosen for their looks, the guy thought. They decided to try out the drug on one of them to see if there was a different female reaction."

"The Romanian girl. Your surprise package."

"She was a totally innocent and a totally valid human being."

"Of course. I'm sorry."

"And he'd begun to fall for her. He didn't know they'd tried the drug on her. He didn't know they'd brought her to the hotel. Someone else got that job. She had suffered an extreme reaction. Mine was closer to what they had been working towards. But still . . . The solution was to plant her beside me. If I came round I'd be blamed and my story would have no credibility. Sadly for them my curiosity is as strong as my survival instinct. And puzzling things out is my day job."

"It's making horrible sense. Your assumption, then, is that the guy in the loch was your informant."

"A safe assumption I'd say."

"And that was retribution. Discouragement and retribution."

"Rather a clumsy retribution. But they would have been banking on no one knowing him and no one much caring."

"He was on the point of bailing out but hadn't actually done that I take it."

"Contacting me was his insurance. If the whole thing came apart I could speak up for him."

"So now you, if they know that, are a prime target. There is a limit to how much I can protect you."

"Don't worry. I'm not planning to hang on here."

"So what next?"

"Chateau Theo is not far from here I take it?"

"Twenty-five miles east. Fifteen as the crow flies."

"And the Achindarnoch House Hotel? You'll understand I had no sense of distance when you brought me here."

"Twenty miles south."

"With you as my insurance I've decided to head back there. Drawing them into the open seems the way to go while staying demonstrably always in company. I'll sleep in the car until it's a decent hour for a guest to arrive. I imagine you're of the same mind as I am on the next step to take. Police inappropriate."

"Totally inappropriate."

"I'd like to call an editor I know. Old friend. He'll hear me out long enough to grasp that I'm serious. He'll know who to call. I may need to go into detail. Knowing that, can I use your phone?"

"Best not use the landline. Use my mobile. You'll stay here tonight?"

"I think not. If they know anything they will know that I'm cocooned with the other guests back in that hotel by the loch. Under lock and key till the breakfast bell. Luckily my mother took ill and I'm driving south."

"A fiction I trust."

"My dearly beloved mother died two years ago. She and my equally beloved father died in an avalanche on an anniversary ski trip to the Dolomites."

Ewan is clearly weighing this for probability. "You're an orphan," he says.

"I am. No one to come looking for me."

"So you haven't remembered a wife?"

"So far, I have not."

"Right then my friend." He brings up the route south on his phone and hands it to Adam. "I'll turn in now. Just leave the phone on the table when you've made your call. May the god of hacks be with you."

"Thank you. I'm in your debt. Incidentally, are you the wolf man?"

"Not guilty. Don't know who is. My guess would be Theo. I'd say he comes from wolf country."

"Right. One other thing?"

"Yes?"

"If you have cause to contact me at the Achindarnoch House Hotel they'll know me as Charles Merchant. That's the name on my card."

Chapter Twenty-Three

The sky is lightening as Adam finds himself awake and on the back seat of an unfamiliar car. He sits up and the facade of the Achindarnoch House Hotel fills the windscreen. Recognition, the act of rediscovery, undervalued until it has been lost and found.

The air is fresh but the morning mild as he checks that his muscles and joints are equal to whatever a new day has in store. He turns slowly through every one of the three hundred and sixty degrees, beginning and ending with the mountain and the waterfall whose sound fluctuates between a rush and a tinkle, a heavy tinkle for there is nothing tentative about this waterfall, just sometimes there hasn't been much rain. All these words in his head as he climbs the stile over the fence from the car park to stand by the pool where he had an earlier outbreak of internal verbosity, plant names and the colour spectrum, he recalls. The drug still at work? No, the day job kicking in. He puts names to the plants round the pool and reprises their defining tones of brown and green in sharp contrast to the artifice of Charlotte's pink hair. Charlotte. She has not been in his thoughts except in those moments when his credit card reminded him of the similarity of their names. He is Charles, he must not relax into being Adam. When Charles is expected, Charles must show up.

On autopilot he follows the instruction of the fingerpost and starts to ascend the track as it winds round the mountain. He should use the time to run over what he now recalls discovering about Theo before they made contact. Father a Ukrainian coal merchant of Georgian descent, mother a Lebanese dancer. When the coal merchant sold his mining interests and moved the family to an estate in the Caucasus young Theo was dispatched to be educated in Greece, France and England. Multi-lingual and rootless with an outsider's eye and ear for human frailty he made himself useful to a succession of power players, acquiring along the way expertise in various fields and his first billion. Of his own apparently inept relationship with him he remembers nothing.

When you know who you are the world is a beautiful place, though perhaps slightly lacking in edge. Though danger, he reminds himself, is still in his portfolio. Reaching the bend where the path starts to curve round the mountain, he recalls his promise to Ewan that he will stay in the company of others until the cavalry arrives. He stops to look down on the start of the glen with the loch and the plantation and hears the sound of footsteps coming up the path behind him. No time to react, he will meet his fate with dignity. He turns slowly and sees Charlotte coming up the track, a Charlotte with scissored light brown hair, ecru cargo pants and a fleece in one of those shades you can pass off as taupe. Different look, same attitude. "Charles Merchant," she says. "Still in the charcoal suit pants."

"Charlotte Kaufmann, fresh from a total make-over, but still knows how to make a man feel boring. What news?"

"I wouldn't know where to start. You?"

"Likewise. But I can start with a correction. I'm Adam Maxwell."

"Are you indeed?" She arrives at his level and looks him over. "It suits you. Have you reached your limit or are we going on?"

"Let's go on. And perhaps you can start to fill me in. As you've already spotted I haven't been close enough to civilisation to find a change of clothes."

"Whereas I have been to Vienna."

"Vienna. Why Vienna? Ah. I remember."

"I was tailed all the way to London. I shook him off. It turns out I'm rather good at that."

Adam stops walking. "You were tailed from here? Why?"

"Long story."

"Look, if this is going to be more than a travelogue I'd rather hear it back in civilisation. The backdrop is distracting." He can't see the plantation without seeing the wolves.

"OK. It's quite episodic. Couple of centuries, a war or two, cast of thousands." They descend in silence, their thoughts along with some strange bird calls and the sound of the waterfall quite enough to contend with.

"Actually I'm rather hungry," Adam says. "Have you eaten?"

"Not yet."

"You're staying here I take it?"

"That's right. Same room. How about you?"

"I haven't checked in yet. I spent the night in my car."

"The end of another long story."

"Not quite the end. Close to it I hope." At the pool by the waterfall they pause again before they climb the fence. "Shall we meet in the breakfast room in, let's say, twenty minutes? I'll get my things from the car and check in."

"Fine." She starts off towards the hotel and Adam scans for watchers before he follows her.

"I'm Charles Merchant now," he tells her as he catches up and sees the reassessment start up in her posture, slowing the turn of her head. "That's how they know me here. It's the name on my card."

"Good morning sir," says the girl at reception. "How may I help you?"

"I'd like a single room if you have one. One night, perhaps more."

"Certainly. Have you stayed with us before?"

"That's the thing, I was here last week and I left in a bit of a rush. I believe I still owe you for my room. The name is Merchant. Charles Merchant."

"Your name is not familiar, sir. Let me check. No, we have no record. Which room was it, do you remember?"

"Room Twelve."

"Ah. Then you're with Synchronised Solutions. We have that booking, certainly."

"When was that booking made?"

"It's an ongoing booking. Two rooms, eleven and twelve. Both still in their name."

"These would be front-facing rooms, am I right? Then if you have a room facing the garden at the back I would be happy with that. For a change, you understand." He tags on a smile which she returns.

"Of course."

He signs the register in the slightly slanted script he chose for Charles Merchant, adds a flourish, then picks up the key and climbs the familiar staircase feeling a familiar panic start to build until somebody's very friendly spaniel lollops up against him and accompanies him to the door of his new room.

In room twenty-three he hangs up the suit jacket, puts his shaving things in the en suite, washes his hands, cleans his teeth and goes along the less familiar corridor, this with a selection of botanical prints on its walls and the same golden carpet dropping to its ethnic variant in what he now knows to be the Buchanan tartan.

Over yoghurt and prunes, kippers and toast he suggests that Charlotte should tell her story first. There is no way of knowing whether the occupants of rooms eleven and twelve are among the company. Her story begins with that scrappy padded envelope she carried around sticking half out of her bag. It had a plot of its own apparently, a plot he hasn't much time for right now. It is only when the Mitteleuropean names and locations develop a narcotic slant that he starts to listen and the wolf of the Carpathians lifts its head and sends out a cry that is answered by the wolf of the Highlands.

"Did you have time in Vienna to take in the sights?" he says to cover his reaction and to turn this back into a travelogue and slow his pulse. "The Spanish Riding School? The Stephanskirche?"

She arrests her fork and meets his eye. She knows there's something up. "The Hofburg and the Leopold Museum," she says. "Also the Zentralfriedhof. My great-aunt is there."

"Your new friends in Vienna, will you stay in touch?"

"Certainly. In fact they have asked if I might do some more work for them."

"More work? You already did some?" This is confusing and disturbing. What sort of work and why is she even considering it. He'd imagined her hanging around for a bit. And right now this is a massive distraction from the main event.

"Not for them. Something I did turned out to be incidentally useful to them."

"So?"

"I'm thinking about it. I should know soon if I have an apartment there to call my own. That would make me independent."

"Indeed. A professional relationship then?"

"They were very grateful. They paid for my flight home."

"Did they indeed?"

"I paid them back."

"Ah. You're in funds then."

"I sold some emeralds." Now the whole room is listening.

"Have you finished? Shall we go?"

Out in the lobby he is finding himself too unsettled to function. Things he thought he had a grasp of are shifting, probabilities and possibilities are dissolving, certainties are totally fucked up and his need for the tools of his trade are off the scale. "You know the village better than I do I expect. Is there somewhere I could buy a phone?"

"Probably. I don't know for sure. You could borrow mine."

"Thank you but I need my own. I have an urgent call to make. Last night I phoned an editor I know to tell him gist of the story."

"The story you haven't told me yet?"

"I'll tell you on the way. He was to phone a friend in a high place to get things moving. I need to know how quickly that might be. So if you'd like a walk?"

"As your bodyguard?"

"Something like that."

"Cool."

Skipping the detail he has brought her more or less up to speed by the time they reach the village where on the High Street next to the funeral parlour and opposite a tea shop cum confectioner called The Fairy Dell they find a shop that sells phones.

Out on the pavement with a cheap fully charged phone more precious than an ingot in his hand he calls Andrew. Charlotte steps away to answer a call on her own phone, so the shot when it comes passes between them and cracks the window of the funeral parlour.

More or less simultaneously a car parked nearby starts up and she is pulled into the back seat as it speeds away.

Chapter Twenty-Four

Prone on the massive lap of a total stranger with car chase sound effects and a trace of Sauvage, Charlotte says, "And who the hell are you?"

"Pete," says a voice from the front. "Gorilla in the back seat is Garry."

"Hi."

"We're friends," says Pete. "Don't sit up."

Charlotte works the heel of her left foot back into its shoe and sits up. Garry makes room for her on the back seat and she has a rear view of the driver who by process of elimination is Pete. He has longish fairish hair over a rather preppy collar. "I don't have any friends," she says.

"Friends of friends then," says Pete. "In Vienna."

"In Vienna I was always treated with the utmost courtesy."

"Gross lapse then. Sorry about that. It's for your own good."

"You sound like my mother's boyfriend."

"Your mother is still alive?" He sounds surprised.

"Long gone. Also fortunately the boyfriend. You've been checking on me."

"Checking's not my bag. I hear you haven't left much of a trail. Close to zilch."

"That's good, is it?"

"It can be."

They are out of the village and on a country road, speed normalising. "You have some explaining to do, and perhaps you can prioritise where you're taking me."

"Away. We had to get you way from that guy, the guy you were talking to."

"By shooting him?"

"Garry's a former Quick Draw champion of the West Midlands. Diversionary tactics. No blood spilt."

"And what is Adam supposed to have done that makes him such a danger."

"Adam?"

"The man you've just saved me from. Adam Maxwell."

"He may have been passing himself off as Adam Maxwell but his name is Charles Merchant."

"I really think you need to look again at your sources."

"This comes from the top."

"Then the top's been got at, or it's getting at you."

"Is there someone who can back you up on that?" The car is slowing. Whoever Pete is his foot gets it, but for a second opinion there's only Adam.

"Look, how away do we have to get? We need to talk."

"OK, let's try it your way." Pete slams on the brakes and reverses to the lay-by they have just passed.

On the pavement outside the funeral parlour the funeral director, the butcher and a lady with a dog have joined Adam to review what has just happened and to check the damage to the window pane. Its status is cracked, not smashed. A restrained gunshot? Is that possible?

"Did you see what happened?" the funeral director asks.

"I didn't," says the lady, "but it came from over there." She points across the road.

"The car?"

"No, the shot. The car was parked here."

"Do you have any enemies?" Adam asks the funeral director. He is an innocent passer-by with a pleasant personality.

"Plenty, but they're dead and buried. And with witnesses." Everybody laughs.

"Did you see anyone?" the butcher asks Adam. They all look at him.

"Alas, like this lady I did not."

"Boys," says the lady. "It'll be boys."

"I didn't see any boy. I saw a young lady," the butcher tells Adam. "I thought she was with you."

"She was standing here when I came out of that shop. I had just bought a new phone so I wasn't paying much attention but I'm pretty sure I didn't know her."

"Well they'll have to stump up for my window pane," says the funeral director. "Or their parents will. Did you see any boys?"

It is agreed that no boys were seen and the butcher and the funeral director go back to their businesses.

"There was a girl here, wasn't there?" says the lady with the dog. "She was on her phone. I wonder where she went."

"Perhaps she was a fairy," says Adam pointing across the road to The Fairy Dell. "Fairies vanish."

"Don't get me started on that place. The cakes are great but to sit down you have to go along with her nonsense. It'll be boys. Hamish goes rigid when he sees boys. He thinks they're letting off fireworks."

Adam pats the dog which he thinks is some kind of Scottie. "I'm with Hamish on that." And with friendly relations concluded Hamish is led away and Adam calls Andrew again.

"Was that a gunshot I heard?"

"Some sort of gun was fired. Nobody hurt."

"Where the hell are you?"

"Still in the Highlands. Village High Street, don't know its name."

"Last year Lebanon, this year Brigadoon. Still living dangerously."

"I need you to listen."

"All ears."

"Did you speak to your scary contact, friend in high places?"

"I did. Friend of a friend, my guy's not that scary. He's aware of your mystery man with a penchant for the dark arts. He turns out to be quite a philanthropist."

"Go on."

"He has brought fibre optics to his local community at his own expense and he's helpful with heavy lifting when it's needed. He has the toys."

"There now."

"You're doubtful?"

"That's his front you're describing. I would have thought he might have aroused interest. Some background checks. How high is the guy in high places, your friend's friend?"

"Very. Philip gets a kick out of knowing him."

"Only if he's not a total boy scout there might be more than he could make in a couple of lifetimes persuading him to stick with the story."

"The clincher for Philip's friend was the wolves. No one with that much to hide would draw attention to himself by illegal rewilding."

"That sounds more like an opinion than a fact. Opinions are Theo's thing. He creates them."

"That sounds like admiration."

"His set-up is admirable. Also lethal. But the gun shot you heard was to divert attention from a very smooth kidnap that would not have been his doing. If he was going to kidnap anyone that would have been me."

"Who was kidnapped?"

"Someone I'd just told the whole story to."

"In the village High Street?"

"If you can shelve your picture postcard prejudice . . . When did you speak to your all-knowing friend?"

"Last night just after you called me."

"Someone reacting to something bundled her into the back of a car. I'm thinking to discredit me and what I'd just told her."

"Her?"

"This is serious."

"*Mea culpa*. I'm listening."

"Ah. Ben."

The rain has started. He needs somewhere out of it to think. The bar where he went when he first found his way to the village, where he first met Charlotte, is on this side of the street just a few doors away. There may be a few morning drinkers but no one will bother him. They didn't last time.

Ben, he thinks as he zips his jacket and heads in that direction, another of the London press corps tempted north by the notion of Celtic Supremacy. But press were barred while he, stripped of identity, was accepted as some sort of benign southern interloper. And another thing, Ben addressed him as Charles and so presumably knew of his planned undercover visit to the dark side. Ben might spark the return of that still hazy memory.

But coming the other way are two men who seem slightly familiar. Nothing about them but that and the scarcity of people in this part of the world who might fit that slot. Muting his reaction he crosses the road and with a guileless glance around spots The Fairy Dell and strolls towards it. The tables are empty and there is no one at the counter but the door opening triggers a blast of music he recognizes as the Dance of the Sugar Plum Fairy from The Nutcracker, two concepts hard to mingle, and in the background something like a parrot squawks. He takes a seat at the table furthest from the window on a chair that seems to be woven from some craft shop stuff, raffia or rushes. From behind a curtain comes a gauzy lilac-haired lady in a tutu or some longer version of that his vocabulary doesn't extend to. There are wings attached to the back of her costume which flutter slightly as she approaches.

"Aha! A stranger!" She twinkles at Adam as she lays a menu in front of him. "We don't see many of these, do we Merlin?" She appears to be addressing what indeed is a parrot in an ornate cage. The parrot shifts from one foot to the other by way of response or perhaps from terminal resignation. Outside the window the two men arrive and hover.

"If this is the Fairy Dell," Adam tells the lady, "you must

be the Fairy Queen." He picks up the menu and hands it back throwing in a smile to cement this as polite rather than dismissive. "I'd really just like some tea," he tells her

"Hibiscus, chamomile, mint or orange blossom?"

"Just normal tea. The sort that is often called Builders Tea although I have no idea why builders should be singled out for what is presumably a pejorative intent when it is the tea that more or less everyone drinks."

Out on the pavement the men have turned their backs. One of them takes out his phone.

"With lemon or milk?"

"Milk."

"And of course you must choose from our wonderful selection of gateaux, pastries and tea bread."

The men are facing the window again so he follows The Fairy Queen to the counter where he fills a good three minutes deliberating before he settles for a fruit scone and, if time is to be a factor, a millefeuille.

His tea arrives and he has just taken a knife to the fruit scone when his phone buzzes. It's Andrew. Before he can speak the Fairy Queen swoops down and seizes the phone from his grasp. She stands over him, shaking her finger and generally hyping up non-verbal displeasure.

"This is a No Phone Establishment. People come here to converse, to talk about the beauty of the countryside. So we don't allow people with their phones to spoil that."

"However that may be there is no one else here to upset."

His phone is still in her hand and Andrew's voice, signals impatience. "Adam, are you there, man?" The Queen of the Fairies looks at the phone with disapproval and a first hint of indecision. Andrew's voice grows louder. There must be a precedent, Adam thinks, recognising his all-consuming interest in other people's reactions and its ability to interrupt whatever else is going on. She lays the phone on the counter and turns back to him.

"I'm here," she says, "so I ask you to respect my policy."

Out on the pavement the men seem poised to enter. He slices and butters the scone, pours the tea into a cup decorated with woodland creatures and has just raised it to his lips when a car draws up and the men disappear. He puts down his cup and sees Charlotte get out accompanied by two unfamiliar men who show no impulse to restrain her. They stand on the pavement looking up and down the street, then Charlotte turns and sees him and they all come in. The Sugar Plum Fairy starts up, the parrot squawks, they react to all that and side-step the Fairy Queen to take the other three seats at Adam's table. Garry's chair creaks and sways. He stands up and up-ends the chair. "Hi, I'm Garry," he says, "I can fix this."

"Can you really. They've been a worry. I'm Audrey."

"The load-bearing struts are mis-aligned."

"This is Adam," lately abducted Charlotte tells the two men.

"Hi Adam. Pete."

"Hi Pete. Give me a minute, will you?" And he scoops his phone off the counter and goes outside. There's no one around. "Sorry man. Logistics."

At the table Pete is eyeing the scone. "Go ahead," Charlotte tells him. "Adam won't mind."

"I don't suppose you have any tools here, Audrey."

"I have a workshop out the back. This was my father's place."

"Let's have a look then."

Pete offers Garry a half scone as they pass but Audrey passes it back. "Garry can choose whatever he likes. On the house."

When Adam returns he passes his phone to Charlotte. "Andrew wants to speak to you. Don't go outside. We've had company."

Charlotte takes the phone to another table and Adam pushes the plate with the scone towards Pete. "You're spooks then, you and Garry?" But Charlotte passes his phone back as her own phone buzzes.

"With you in a sec," he tells Pete whose phone is now also clamouring for attention. "It's Martin in Vienna," he tells Charlotte. "He wants to speak to you."

"Ask him to wait," Charlotte says. She now has Herr Strauss on the line.

"I'd like to talk to him," Adam tells Pete. "And Andrew would like to talk to you."

Garry and Audrey return with a drill and some pieces of wood.

"Uh-uh," says Audrey. "Phones."

Chapter Twenty-Five

Something that will have a name in Neuro-Speak is playing in Adam's head as he and Charlotte reach the mountain end of the high street. Something like déjà vu which he doesn't experience and totally discounts. And now the tarmac's running out. This brief essay into urbanisation gives way to wilderness and his metropolitan persona loses its cool as, not so long ago, it lost its memory.

"We've done this before," he tells Charlotte.

"We have. Right here is where you got scary."

"I'm sorry. Was I really scary?"

"For some reason, no. You should have been but you weren't."

"Any idea why not?"

"You were interesting. I was curious. I tend to be curious."

"For me it's a habit and a day job. No respite."

"For me it's basic. I'm curious to know if you've discovered a wife and two children. A mortgage. Golf club membership?"

"I was curious about that too. I thought not, but that seemed intuitive. It was a hunch."

"And?"

"None of those."

"Siblings? Parents? Pets?"

He owes her the truth. "My mother is happily married for the third time. Somewhere south of Sydney. No sibling."

"Your father?"

"Still doing time I believe. Tax evasion."

"How did that affect you?"

"Gave me a comfortable childhood. No end of background checks taking out a credit card, though."

They have passed through the gates of the hotel grounds when Charlotte stops walking. "This is where it hit me. I knew I'd been here before. Sensed it rather than knew it. To know things you need people to tell you."

"Do you?"

"There's that bird call again. It freaks me out. What is it?"

"Sounds like a peacock."

"Let's look for it."

This is crazy, Adam thinks as they step off the path. Biggest story of his life unfolding and they're chasing bloody peacocks. It was Charlotte's idea to walk back to the hotel and he had no problem turning down a lift from her abductors who Andrew's mate in MI5 says are kosher. He needs space from the info overload to process it. And now that the guys who take the serious stuff out of one's hands have done that he is currently *de trop*, but why is she calling the shots? One peacock doesn't make a birdbrain. She's a bit of an alternative alpha, intriguingly so. And there's this intel thing going on in Vienna.

"So," he says, disentangling himself from a gorse bush, "you have a talent for the secret world and no living relatives. Anything else?"

"I live in a squat in Belgravia. Had enough of that though, no one washed up. Anyway I have an apartment in Vienna."

"You have? Since when?"

"You mean when did I hear about it?"

"I expect I do."

"An hour or so ago. I was taking the call when they grabbed me. I called back."

"That's quite a male brain you were hiding under the pink rinse."

"Male? Why male?"

"Out of pure bloody chauvinism. You're into precision. You don't let things pass."

"Only when I choose to. Surely that's female."

When an actual peacock struts out from behind a bush and fans its tail he is astonished. That was pure guesswork.

"Definitely male," Charlotte says.

"Definitely. That thing with birds, that reversal where it's the male who lays on the glamour, that's fascinating."

"Reversal?" says Charlotte

There are guests in the foyer, a group of Americans checking in and two men with bags waiting to check out. Charlotte heads upstairs and Adam goes back outside to await the call from Andrew. Only then does the message from his eyes reach his brain. These men waiting to check in were familiar.

The Americans are making a meal of it, telling the receptionist about their Scottish links. Why does the ancestry thing go so viral in this part of the world? The soil was thin, the winters fierce, the landlords brutal and there were mouths to feed. You can see why they went. But down the line when you trace your roots to a place of such heart-rending beauty you have to go there and see what they left. And these good people are delaying a departure he has to stop. The skill set he doesn't have, the ability to land a plausible punch, to aim it with conviction is not in his CV. They'd grab *him* and apologise to the men. As the Americans drift towards the staircase he flips through options, the citizen's arrest procedure, probably archaic, and simply telling the manager who would surely demur. This needs muscle. He'll call Ewan. And then a second receptionist comes out from behind the counter and he beckons her over. She comes.

"Look, there's something I need you to help me with. It's urgent or I wouldn't bother you. Those two men checking out . . . they're wanted on a terrorist charge. Can you delay them while I call the police?"

"I'll call the manager."

"By the time you've called him they'll be gone. Trust me. It's major. Of national importance. You'll be a heroine, hero, whatever." He lobs in a smile.

"I'll try."

Outside he phones Ewan who has an ear for urgency and

knows who to call, then he hovers, pacing the gravel, until the wail of a police siren – a sound he has never thought of as calming – hits its high note and the car arrives, scattering gravel and disgorging two men in uniform who barge through the hotel doors. Adam sits down at a rustic table and takes a call from Ewan.

"I called H&I HQ. They know the whole story. They said they'd call the local guys."

"And they're here."

"Meanwhile your own story seems to be playing out on another level. People that were described to me as the big game hunters are moving in on our local wildlife enthusiast."

"I don't know that big game hunters are good with wolves."

"We'll know soon. "

"Watching and listening. Thanks man."

Charlotte comes out. "They're locking down the building. I just made it out. What's happening?"

"Why don't you take a seat while we find out."

It's barely half an hour before a helicopter lands on the lawn and the former occupants of room eleven are uplifted and spirited away, leaving a beautiful space with no context and, in Adam, a lingering unease. This is too tidy. Whether it is tidiness itself he rejects or that he finds it premature he can't say.

To Charlotte he says, "Stuff to do. Dinner later?"

"Cool. Sold the emeralds but I might break out Saskia's pearls."

When Adam knocks on Charlotte's door she is taking a call from Sean.

"Don't go. Sit down somewhere . . . No, not you, Sean. Yes, I am taking care. You too I hope . . . No, not Vienna, back in Scotland . . . Oh, just run-of-the-mill stuff. I saw a peacock and a helicopter landed on the lawn. No, they're not native to the Highlands, someone brought it from somewhere, maybe India, there's a lot of stuff here from India. Look I might not be back for a bit. Don't worry, the bad guys have gone . . . no, not killed, maybe neutered . . . No, they don't do that in Scotland, I was speaking figuratively. Bye for now Sean."

In the foyer the second receptionist is at the desk. "You were brilliant," Adam tells her. "When I write this up you'll be featured. Can I ask what you did?"

"I said there had been a complaint. From a guest. A woman guest. They asked to speak to the manager. I guess they thought that would put them in the clear. It turned out there was once some such complaint and he's paranoid about it."

"It's very effective," says Charlotte. "I've used that one myself."

In the dining room they are shown to a table for two by the window. On the table are spring flowers in a slightly faulty hand-thrown vase and around them a number of people in knitwear are talking. None of this accommodates unease.

"This feels strange," says Charlotte.

"It feels wrong. I wonder why."

"There's no crisis. You're not on the run. We need a crisis."

"I have an impending crisis. Not one I can share. I've been commissioned to follow this all the way for an exclusive, Andrew's doing, with spin-offs already in negotiation. I can buy a new shirt."

"All the way? To the castle of your nemesis on the other side of the mountains?"

"And as far beyond as he takes us, probably to your part of Europe."

"Then you'll need a couple of shirts. That one's on overtime."

"I had the hotel laundry wash it."

"It looks good with the jacket. I've never seen you like that."

"Whereas you have a wholly unfamiliar Chanel jacket over something the colour of your eyes. What would you call that colour?"

"Blue."

"Petrol blue, Ice Blue? Steel blue?"

"You're scaring me. In another incarnation you were in the rag trade."

"Once upon a time on a local paper I had to do the women's page. I got hooked on colour names, started making them up."

"Are you ready to order?" A waitress is hovering. Adam smiles apologetically.

"What do you recommend."

They have just ordered when two men come into the dining room, one in a kilt whom Charlotte recognizes as the hotel manager, the other a stranger, an unobtrusively distinguished stranger whom Adam recognises as from the top of the deniable food chain. The manager scans the diners and they come across.

"Miss Kaufmann, I don't know if you remember me?"

"I certainly do."

"This gentleman would like a word with Mr Maxwell. Perhaps in my office?"

"Here is perfect. Thank you." The manager leaves and the stranger pulls up a chair from another table

"Apologies for this, you'll understand the urgency, I'm Miles Goodrich."

"Adam. And this is Charlotte."

"We have a team now approaching the estate where you were a recent guest," he tells Adam. "You are uniquely qualified to give me an idea of the set-up as you experienced it. Obviously we'll need a full debriefing later. This is off the record."

The waitress arrives with their starters. "I'm so sorry," Adam tells her. "Perhaps the kitchen can keep them warm. Mine anyway."

Charlotte takes the cue and stands, pushing back her chair, Miles indicates appreciation of her sensitivity which, however, is overtaken by the need for her to stay. She sits down. "There will be nothing you don't know I imagine and I hear your story is also crucial."

"I should tell you my recall does not stretch to my time at the castle. That bit is missing."

"In itself interesting. To our apothecaries and alchemists especially interesting. Unexplained memory loss, I wonder..."

"I didn't actually lose it. It was stolen."

"Of course. Weaponised, targeted, tailored memory loss. You will find yourself a rare and unusually articulate guinea pig. How much did you forget?"

"Everything. I didn't know who I was."

"Although your personality and your vocabulary were intact," says Charlotte.

Miles is silent, making notes. He stands and puts back his chair.

Adam says "I *can* tell you what I found out before and after the event."

"Perfect," he says, then takes a call. "All of them? Lock stock and barrel? And they've released everything? OK. Keep me posted. Perhaps the Highland Wildlife Park would help with that."

"Developments," he says. "I must go. I'll fill you in later. You're not thinking of going anywhere right now I hope? Excellent. Otherwise we might have had to insist. Feedback will be needed as well as both your stories. Inevitably there will be leaks, but I'm sure I can rely on you ... Perfect."

Tentatively the waitress returns with their starters.

"What's that on the lawn? says Charlotte.

"A musk ox? That or a buffalo."

"Was the buffalo ever indigenous?"

"I don't know that authenticity mattered much to him. He was after the reaction."

"Those wild boar, though, they had ancestors here."

In the lounge the hotel guests have gathered round the TV screen.

"There are reports of wild animal sightings over a considerable stretch of the Northern Highlands," the news reader is saying. "Lynx, wild boar and musk ox have been mentioned. It is thought that they have been released by a controversial landlord of a shooting estate who was known to be interested in rewilding, although some of the species he is interested in have no context in Scotland. Experts from the Highland Wildlife Park are on the scene and are arranging temporary accommodation for the animals. It is believed that no animals likely to cause harm to people are involved, however the public are warned not to approach any unusual animal but to phone this number. Reports of a zebra swimming across a loch have been discounted."

Adam turns to Charlotte seated beside him in the corner of a sofa. "What are your plans?" he says. "If any." To his own ear that was over-stressed.

"I haven't made any."

"No flight booked yet?"

"I'm hanging around for a bit. Does it matter?"

"Very much." She shares his unease. He considers mentioning this but it would sound like a qualification.

Charlotte turns away. "I don't iron shirts," she says.

"Understood."

When Ewan arrives with the girl with the long legs – forget her legs, remember her name, albeit an ill-conceived short form of the mellifluous Gabriella – he has news. Not in a hurry to share it though, raised eyebrows, extended pause. Oh, OK. He introduces Charlotte.

None of the estate's foreign residents was there when the team arrived, although one was picked up trying to hitch-hike near John o' Groats. It seems he had no sense of direction.

"Word got around and the old staff moved back in and took charge," he tells them. "On the dining room table there were papers. A card propped up on a whisky tumbler said To Whom It May Concern. It was a document handing over the estate to the community. A lawyer has checked it and it seems all the paper work has been done."

"And Theo?" says Adam.

"A helicopter took off. It was intercepted. He wasn't on it. So it was probably a blind."

The hotel guests have drifted off when Miles comes back.

"Lost him," he says. "Got some of the others, though."

"In the world of ultimate accountability," Adam wonders, "how does handing your estate to the community stack up?"

"It may be a first. Can I have a word?"

When Adam returns he is alone – Miles had a driver waiting to take him to the castle – and in the lounge Ewan is yawning. He puts a hand on Gaby's nearer knee. It's a signal, Adam thinks, something he's taught her, as she gets to her feet and Ewan follows suit. Interesting, the ways of his fellow men.

"I wonder," Adam says, "if Hector foresaw any of this."

He did say something, Ewan offers. "When the land calls it lies open to all who may answer."

He brushes Charlotte's cheek with a kiss and lands a matey hand on Adam's shoulder. "Catch up tomorrow."

"Well?" says Charlotte when they've gone.

"My neighbours from room eleven, they've been talking."

"And?"

"Theo sees me as a work in progress. A project close to his heart and not yet completed. He believes my memory of my time at the castle will return. I'm a walking case study as well as a witness."

"So he'd like to have a word with you before he shoots you."

"Only the first, they say."

"Do you believe that?"

"I'd like to."

"Then no peace of mind just yet?"

"I don't know if this is new or if it was always there but peace of mind holds little attraction for me."

"It's just another form of boredom."

They are in the foyer heading for the stairs when a flustered hotel manager in kilt and pyjama top appears waving a package which he hands to Charlotte.

"My apologies, Miss Kaufmann. Graham MacMillan gave me this to pass on to you. He has just heard you are here. Papers from your deceased relative's estate that slipped his mind. She wanted them to be passed on to you."

"With luck another crisis," says Adam to Charlotte as she takes the package. "Aren't you going to open it?"

"Not now," she says. "I think we'll sleep on it."

Acknowledgements

First I would like to acknowledge the role of my late mother who, long before the arrival of the internet, kept tabs on our ancestors, who include seventeenth and eighteenth-century ministers with parishes in remote parts of the Highlands and, among thousands of outwardly mobile Scots, a brother and sister who took the road less travelled, to Habsburg Vienna and Bohemia. None are models for characters in this book but their own stories are fascinating enough to have pointed me in their directions.

Similarly I want to thank Harry Reid who, when editor of The Herald, unwittingly sent me on a travel writing trip to New Zealand which would end in my losing my memory during the return journey. Transient Global Amnesia was the diagnosis, and having had the privilege of experiencing that it was a small step to imagining the extreme episode that dictates the plot of this novel. Since my hope was to capture something of Richard Hannay's out-of-touch predicament in John Buchan's forever brilliant *The Thirty-Nine Steps*, that trip was fortunate.

Of the many books on the Habsburgs Martyn Rady's *The Habsburgs: The Rise and Fall of a World Power* is exceptional in its reach and readability. And for Cold War Vienna *MI6: Life and Death in the British Secret Service* by Gordon Corera is as gripping as it is informative. To one whose working life was spent among manual typewriters, cuttings files and phone boxes, Google and Wikipedia are a daily miracle.

My deepest gratitude goes to Vagabond Voices and Allan Cameron for his singular decision to bin improbability rather than the manuscript.

A sight-impaired octogenarian turns out typos on an industrial scale, and arthritic fingers create exotic computer disasters. Without the unravelling and resetting skills of my son Dorian and his quite extraordinary patience this novel would not have reached fruition. Love and thanks to him and to other family members who spotted blips that had slipped through the net.